Far from Home

Also by Anne DeGrace

TREADING WATER

Far from Home

a novel

Anne DeGrace

AVON

An Imprint of HarperCollinsPublishers

This book is a work of fiction. The characters, incidents, and dialogue are drawn from the author's imagination and are not to be construed as real. Any resemblance to actual events or persons, living or dead, is entirely coincidental.

A previous edition of this book was published in 2007 by McArthur & Company, Canada, under the title *Wind Tails*.

HarperCollins books may be purchased for educational, business, or sales promotional use. For information please write: Special Markets Department, HarperCollins Publishers, 10 East 53rd Street, New York, NY 10022.

ISBN 978-0-06-172880-8

09 10 11 12 13 WBC/RRD 10 9 8 7 6 5 4 3 2

For my mother, Peggy DeGrace: my first storyteller

Far from Home

Tailwind

The north wind doth blow,
And we shall have snow,
And what will the robin do then, poor thing?
— Mother Goose

It's the first day of the third week. Jo never thought she'd get used to starting work at 6 a.m., but the truth is, she's starting to like it. Even college classes, when she last attended, didn't require rising so early, and then mornings included the bustle of her mother heading off to work at the clinic, her father's newspaper rattle at the kitchen table, the morning banter—on the good days—between them. It's September: she should be at home, just starting second year, perhaps sharing an apartment with other students. Every Sunday, dinner with her parents, a load of laundry churning away in the basement while they eat. She pushes away the small pang she feels for that domestic scene.

Instead, Jo turns her attention to the earthy smell of coffee as it begins to percolate in the big countertop urn. When it's done, she'll pour herself a cup and hope for enough time to savour it before the first customer comes in. The early fall sunlight begins to slant across the worn linoleum as the sun crests the tops of the pines across the highway. There is birdsong, and the relative, temporary peace. Temporary, because the first customer can pull in to the gravel lot at any time; relative, because there is outward peace, and then there is inward peace.

As the coffee perks, Jo ties her straight red hair into a ponytail; nothing like a long hair in the soup to send a customer squawking and Cass scolding. There are four tables on either side of the door, two in the middle of the diner. As the sun glances off their surfaces, Jo can see the remains of coffee rings, small scatterings of salt and sugar, evidence of sloppy clean-up, and so she begins wiping the plastic covers. Cass would have something to say if she came in and saw a less-than-clean table, not that it's likely. When Jo hauled herself up from her cot in the back room of the trailer a half-hour ago, Cass's snores suggested an extended lie-in, something Jo has come to expect. Twice, so far, Cass has spent the whole day in the trailer, ankles propped on the coffee table, reclining in a nest of pillows and crocheted afghans, watching soaps on the one channel available to this part of British Columbia.

Jo leans across the swivel stools to wipe the Arborite counter that runs along the back of the room. At one end is the cash register—behind it, the coffee urn, dishes, cutlery, cooler—and cut into the wall behind them, a window with a ledge on which to set the orders. A set of swinging doors to one side blocks the kitchen view from the restaurant.

Surfaces clean, there isn't much to do; she's got the grill heating, everything's ready to go. Sitting on the corner stool, jeans sticking to a peeling edge of duct tape, Jo scans her surroundings, now becoming familiar. On each table, salt and pepper shakers in the shape of jumping trout, or chickens, or, on the table nearest the door, skunks embracing; plastic flowers in a tomato paste can covered with wallpaper; a cylindrical sugar dispenser, the sun through the glass casting a glow across the table's surface. On the washroom door, a sign that reads *Abandon all hope, ye who enter here.* On the wall, the plaster Jesus hands beside the Coke cooler angle upwards towards last year's 1976 classic car calendar. Above that, a chalkboard proclaims the soup of the day—yesterday's rubbed out, today's still unwritten. The glass display case holds three pies of varying degrees of wholeness labelled carefully: Apple, Rhubarb, Lemon Marrang. *Real Lard Crust* reads a fourth sign, folded to stand like a little pup tent.

There is the whoosh of a car passing on the two-lane highway: an early riser, not stopping. Jo pulls the lever on the bottom of the urn, watching the level of coffee in the glass tube adjust downwards as the liquid swirls into the cup. Cream, two sugars. This is her time.

"Biker Baby Born with Gang Tattoo" reads the tabloid headline on the newspaper left by a customer. It's ridiculous, of course. It should make her laugh, but instead, Jo feels the push of tears. It's just the suggestion, she knows. Maybe it's just the word "baby." She wonders how long it will affect her in this way. She folds the paper and shoves it with the others on the corner of the counter, leans back against the wall, and closes her eyes.

***

Seven months earlier, Jo is sitting in a dark living room waiting for her mother to come home. It's better in the dark: the shadows in the room match the sinking feeling that roots her to the couch. She tries not to think of the associations she holds with this piece of furniture; she feels as if she could drown beneath the floral fabric. Death by upholstery. She watches the last shimmer of sky wither to black. She doesn't know how she will answer the questions.

The subtleties of the dark intrigue her as she waits, looking out: how the gradations of bark on the maple meld, as the light fades, into flat black. *Contrast is relative*, she thinks, then: *Everything is relative.* Black to blacker. Before, and after.

She hears the click of the door; inhales sharply. The cold air curves around the entrance and strikes Jo before the sound of her mother unzipping her winter boots reaches her ears.

"Jo? Why are you sitting here in the dark?"

Light floods the living room, and the maple tree outside disappears altogether. There is nothing but this room, this couch, her mother, the new hardness of her belly.

"I need to tell you something."

Jo's mother stands in the yellow pool of light in her camelhair coat.

***

Eamon is thirty-two, but he looks younger. It's the long black hair, curling around under his ears. Even with the laugh lines, his blue eyes look young, playful. But it's the accent that really gets her, making her think of a children's fairy tale: a leprechaun, a pot of gold. And it's true: there is a sparkly quality to him when he walks into a room, bright points of light dancing around his words as he speaks.

When her mother introduces him, she explains that he is distantly related, by marriage: "Your cousin James's half-brother. Uncle Arnie was married a long time ago, before he met Patsy." Jo isn't altogether sure of the lineage—her mother had five sisters—but sees that this tall, friendly man has been welcomed by her mother as family.

"He's going to stay while he looks for a job. Maybe even at the college, Jo. You two could take the bus together."

Eamon twinkles at Jo, who imagines him teaching her first-year journalism class, imagines going for a beer with him afterwards, the easy conversation between them, the envy of the other girls in the class. Later, "Does Dad mind about Eamon staying with us?" she asks her mother. Jo's father is away on business.

"He's family. It's just for a short time," her mother replies.

But Eamon stays through September. Jo's father comes in from work each day, heads for the den with a rum and Coke and the *Calgary Herald*, emerges for dinner. Over pork chops and mashed potatoes, Eamon charms them with stories from Ireland, where he'd returned with his mother when he was "just a young lad."

"I'll make you all a real Irish stew," he tells them, "to thank you for your wonderful generosity." The stew never materializes, but Jo's father's bottle of Jameson's diminishes.

"How goes the job hunt?" Jo's father asks. It's a friendly inquiry. Eamon's shown a real interest in the woodworking shop in the basement, asking questions about joinery and wood finishes, exclaiming over the craftsmanship in one or another of his host's projects. Like Jo, like her mother, Eamon's blue-eyed gaze appears to make Jo's father glow. There's no question, Jo's father is sure, that Eamon will find employment soon enough. Perhaps there may even be a position for such a promising young man once the new franchises have been set up, and Jo's father can concentrate again on the home office. He has some pull, there. Meanwhile, Eamon's presence in their house is a pleasure.

"Ah, it's a hard world out there," Eamon replies now, shaking his black curls. "Can I give you a hand with the dishes, Mrs. P?" and Jo's mother smiles and flutters and lets him help her carry out the plates, normally Jo's job.

Eamon has been living in the spare room for almost three months when Jo comes home through the swirling flakes of the first big snow from a late class to find a note from her mother: *Helping late at the clinic. Bert's flight cancelled, so just you two for dinner. Leftover M&C in fridge.*

Jo is just placing the casserole dish in the oven when Eamon leans his tall frame in the kitchen doorway.

"Are you making tea, then?" he asks. He means dinner, but Jo is used to his figures of speech.

"Mum's working late at physio," she tells him, tucking her hands in the back pocket of her jeans. When she sees Eamon looking at her breasts, she crosses her arms. "Probably all the snow. Back injuries, twisted ankles." She doesn't know where to look, feels herself colour.

"It's just you and me, then," says Eamon, pushing himself off the doorframe and striding into the kitchen. "Shall we have a little party?" He's taken the whisky from the cupboard, two glasses. "Fancy a drink before we eat?"

It feels just dangerous enough to be exciting. Jo looks at the snow through the kitchen window, feels the warm houseglow envelop them both. She is just eighteen. Sure, she's had a few beers at parties, cheap wine: Labatt's 50; Calona red. The Jameson's is her father's domain. The first taste, when the whisky hits her throat, makes her cough. Eamon puts a friendly arm around her. "Easy, girl. Small sips, let it warm your mouth, then slide down your throat, slowly—like this." Jo watches his lips where they touch the glass, close over the amber liquid, thin as he swallows, then smile, dimples forming in his cheeks. The next sip doesn't burn, just warms, and she wonders if it's possible that the liquid is flowing directly into her veins, warming every part of her. She can feel it in her fingertips, her toes, even *down there*, melting through her body like warm honey.

They sit on the sofa, the only light coming from the kitchen, where the macaroni and cheese slowly dries out in the oven. He asks her about her classes, how they're going. If she's serious about journalism. His face is earnest: he asks her about her opinions on current events. What about the election in Quebec? Will this René Lévesque character push for separation? He listens to her words, considers her replies, leans forward to ask another question, touches her shoulder, meets her eyes. She could drown in that much blue. Her body feels like liquid, itself. She has never felt so—*noticed*.

"Do you have a boyfriend, then?" he asks her, holding her with his eyes as he refills her glass, not spilling any. She shakes her head. "No? A pretty, smart girl like you?"

She doesn't know what to say. She doesn't have to say anything. He takes her glass and sets it on the coffee table with exaggerated care. His fingers, where they touch her chin, are electric; she can feel the current. Her own lips, when they meet his, are numb from the whisky, but his tongue in her mouth is a living thing. This is not the kiss of a boy, not the sloppy groping party-bedroom kisses: this is the real thing.

They make love on the couch. She marvels at the extraordinary act in these ordinary surroundings, thinks she will never be able to sit on this couch again without steamy thoughts betraying her. She grips the piped edge of the upholstery.

Later, they will scrub the bloodstain with baking soda and then flip the cushion over. By the time her mother returns, wondering at the amount of snow, busses not running, and the taxis so busy it's a miracle she got home at all, they have already scraped the blackened casserole contents into the garbage, washed their glasses, and are sitting at opposite ends of the living room, lights blazing. Jo has a textbook in front of her, but she has been reading the same paragraph for a half-hour. She realizes how lucky they were: her mother could have walked in at any moment. She hopes the toothpaste masks the scent of the alcohol. She is absolutely sober, but the living room, now, looks completely different to her. Or maybe it's Jo that's different.

"Mrs. P!" Eamon looks up from his book and smiles winningly. "Back, are you? We were about to send out one of those Saint Bernard dogs after you. Here: let me get you a glass of whisky. Just the thing after your ordeal."

Jo winces, but Eamon's on his feet. Her mother thrills at the attention and tells Jo there's a fresh bottle of Coke in the cupboard. "We'll have a little party!" she gushes.

"And do you mind if I have a wee taste myself, Mrs. P?" asks Eamon, tucking the bottle back in the cupboard before she can see how little is left. He has already poured himself a glass.

Over the next three weeks Eamon and Jo find several more occasions to get together. Jo cuts classes, coming home midday when she knows her parents will be working, to find Eamon lying on the couch, exhausted after a morning of reading yesterday's Help Wanted section. Her father has offered him use of the Smith Corona in the den to type résumés or cover letters, but she has yet to see him use it. She doesn't care: he is there when she comes in, sitting up, letting the paper fall, like he has been waiting for her all morning. In the light of day they descend to the basement where they test the springs of the old couch her father keeps in the workshop for mid-project napping on Sunday afternoons.

The subterfuge, exciting at first, begins to wear on Jo. She longs to be seen with him, walking beside his Irish good looks, holding his hand. Her parents like him; surely they'd be pleased. But when she asks, he strokes her hair. "I just want you all to myself, darlin'," he tells her, before changing the subject.

Jo's father has begun to notice a fishy smell in the workshop, and wonders if the foundation might be leaking. He and Eamon spend a boozy evening down there trying to find the source of the odour, pouring beer after beer while moving furniture and wood to inspect the concrete. Later, they can be heard singing Irish drinking songs while Jo sits in her upstairs bedroom, sulky because he's not with her, but also guilty and strangely excited, full of her own womanhood. It's the smell of sex that has her father so bewildered. Later, she comes down to the living room to find her mother watching *Rowan & Martin's Laugh-In*, a show her mother has always maintained is stupid. The volume is louder than usual. "Look that up in your Funk & Wagnall's," says Goldie Hawn. From the basement comes a burst of laughter as if timed for the punchline.

It's only first year, she tells herself when she misses a deadline for a paper. She's really just killing time anyway, keeping her parents happy by taking courses at the college while she figures out what to do next. But she's missed too many classes, now; things are slipping. She's stopped seeing her friends, stopped going out in the evenings or having anyone over. Her mother doesn't appear to have noticed.

Eamon comes into Jo's room one evening. There's an exam tomorrow; it's the last stretch before Christmas break. She's sitting on her bed cross-legged, books spread out in front of her. He leans in the doorway, hands in pockets, and watches until she looks up. She feels the little heart rush that's still there, and still surprises her. That he wants her is sufficient for her to melt like wax. She read enough Harlequin Romances in her pre-teen years. It bothers her that the clichés come so easily to mind, and yet she is all of them.

"Darlin'," he says, and she feels herself puddle. He curls his frame onto the floor beside the bed. When she weaves her fingers into his hair, he tilts his head back and smiles at her, eyes closed. Then he rolls down her sock, gently eases it from her foot, and with his tongue begins stroking each toe.

With some effort she pulls her foot away. "Let's move out," she says. He's looking at her, tongue still outstretched like a cat, playful smile on his face. "I'll quit school, get a job. We could both get jobs, get an apartment downtown."

He pulls her foot back and begins stroking the arch with his thumb. It tickles, and she laughs. "Where's Mum and Dad?"

"Your delightful parents are both out. At the *same place*. Some Christmas party, for your father's office. We are *all alone*." His tongue slides up her ankle, practised hands at her belt buckle.

***

In the doorway, Jo's mother stands in her camel-hair coat.

"Tell me what?"

She sets her handbag down on the chair and begins undoing buttons. Jo is grateful they are alone: Eamon has taken to going out in the evenings lately, saying he's "making contacts" around job prospects, mostly at the bar. Her father is away again, and Jo wishes he was home, an ally perhaps, she's not sure, but in any case another full week until he returns seems too long to wait. Still, she can feel her heart speed up, a thudding in her chest. Does she really want to do this now?

"No, don't tell me," her mother says, one hand palm out, face turned away. "I know all about it."

For Jo, the air in the room quickens. "You do?"

Her mother disappears around the corner, and Jo can hear the tinkle of hangers in the closet. She has been holding her breath; she exhales slowly, calming herself, but when her mother returns, arms crossed, Jo looks at her, feels her breath catch again. *How could she know?*

Then: "Joan Quentin came into the clinic today." Jo looks blank. "The *registrar*."

What is her mother talking about? How could the registrar know about her and Eamon?

"You failed the whole semester, Jo. Not one pass. What on earth have you been *doing*?"

In the hallway, the clock ticks in time with the thudding of Jo's heart, her head; she wonders if it's a sign of a coming migraine. Everything feels out of whack lately, sick in the mornings, headaches at night.

"Well, what do you have to say for yourself?"

"I—"

"Don't say another word."

"You wanted to know what I had to say for myself!"

But Jo says this to her mother's back. She can hear her in the kitchen, the familiar squeak in the hinge of the cupboard door.

"Where in God's name does all the liquor go in this house?"

Jo has been feeling sick for days, but the next morning is the worst. She gets herself on the bus, thinking she'll see if she can get an appointment with the dean, arrange some rewrites, try to salvage the semester. Eamon has promised to "help" her, but she doesn't know what that means. She needs time to think. She needs to get away. Will he come with her?

"Ah, Jo, girl, It's not a good time for me, now that I'm just on the verge of a good job." The Irish lilt is not so sweet, now.

She'll try again with her mother. Tonight, after she's had a chance to talk to the dean. She'll tell her mother she's been given a second chance at the college before she breaks the news. Her mother will say, as she often does about matters concerning Jo: "Now, you let me break this to your father when he gets back, and then we'll talk about it." She imagines them all sitting down together, Jo and Eamon holding hands on the couch, facing her parents as two people in love, imagines her father's dismay, her mother's disappointment, but together they will come to a pragmatic solution, ways to help the two young lovers to get set up in a place of their own . . .

The bus lurches, and Jo's breakfast spills from her stomach onto the floor, vomit running in small rivers down the furrowed slip-resistant mat along the bus's length. She is off at the next stop and running, boots slipping on the packed snow, back the twelve blocks to her house, her home, her own room where she will pull the covers over her head and pray for oblivion. The cold wind bites at the tears on her cheeks.

When she opens the door to her room, they are there, her mother and Eamon, an impossible amount of flesh exposed in the flat white winter light.

***

Standing at the edge of the Calgary General Hospital parking lot two weeks ago, Jo gazes out at the white light of the day around her, its hard edge of unreality. She is glad she remembered to bring clothes to wear afterwards. She had to fold her now-loose belly into the blue jeans she had bought at the Sally Ann at four months. Her body doesn't feel like her own: it's weirdly empty, utterly changed, someone else's. Everything is brighter than it should be. In the heat, waves rising from the pavement create small mirages around the feet of parking lot pedestrians.

To anyone passing through the busy parking lot, she is easy to miss; there is a transparent quality to her. Just a young woman in jeans and a t-shirt, straight red hair, a duffel bag at her feet. A person waiting for a ride, maybe, a taxi, or a bus.

A station wagon pulls over to where Jo is standing and disgorges a family: mother, father, a boy about ten, a teenaged girl a little younger than Jo. The girl, dark-haired, round face, looks at Jo, then looks away as soon as their eyes meet: similar species, different breed. The mother holds a box of chocolates, the kind with soft centres. The father, juggling a potted plant and an armload of magazines and newspapers, drops a *Maclean's* magazine at Jo's feet. Prime Minister Trudeau looks at her from the cover, his chin resting on her sneaker. She makes no move to pick it up.

"Excuse me," says the man as he reaches. Reuniting the magazine with the others, he gives her a look, a glance of concern, but his family is already halfway to the hospital's front doors.

Jo gathers herself and hoists the duffel bag, crosses the road, and extends her arm, thumb up, against the whoosh of traffic. Her first ride is a chattering young pharmaceutical salesman with thick glasses and bad breath, who seems unperturbed by her monosyllabic replies. "Good luck!" he calls cheerily when he drops her off by a gas station, rolling hills rising to forest and then mountain. In the front seat of the next car that stops, a Volkswagen Beetle, Jo barely has room for her feet amid the flotsam of books and clothes and empty bottles. "Sorry," says the man with the long hair and sideburns, but he makes no move to clear any of it away. After a while he stops trying to talk to Jo. Her feet wedged into the only spaces she can find, the next two hours pass in silent discomfort before the Beetle pulls over. "Heading up here," he says, pointing to a dirt road, looking grateful to be relieved of this disturbingly unresponsive passenger. "You'll probably get another ride soon." But when she stands at the shoulder in the settling dust, the road stretches empty in both directions.

She walks for a little over an hour. Dusk begins setting in, making Jo think of a large, dark bird, the settling of wings.

When the truck slows, she runs to catch up, one hand tender at the base of her belly. Behind her are the long months: first with a high school friend in Lethbridge, sleeping on a couch amid the detritus of the first-time teenage apartment-dweller, the first landing place after flight. Later, the basement apartment she could barely afford on welfare, seeping water, the frequent stab of aloneness despite kind neighbours. Behind her is the roll and sway of new life, the pain of labour, the release of birth, and so many tears she feels scraped raw from the inside out.

As she jogs a bit to catch up to the truck, her insides feel fragile, loose porcelain rattling in a cardboard box. The driver, waiting, leans across the broad front seat and opens the door. His grin, set in a round face, is friendly.

"Goin'?" he says.

She gets in, musters a few words. "The last ride told me there's a diner up the hill a ways."

"Yep. Quite a ways. 'Sclosed, though." Like some other language. "Goin'?" he asks again.

"Just drop me off there," Jo tells him. "I'm meeting somebody."

"Hmph," he grunts, and Jo gets the impression he knows she's lying.

"Archie," he says, looking in his mirrors before pulling back out. He looks at Jo, and she looks ahead, feeling his eyes on her, wondering how long he can keep his eyes from the road without running into the ditch. "Veronica" she says finally, because he said Archie, and it was the first name she can think of.

There's a pause, and then he laughs. "Pretty smart. I'd of pegged you for a Betty, though."

Jo, caught, smiles back in spite of herself. She doesn't offer her real name, and the driver doesn't ask.

"Some people don't like to talk," he says. "Some like to talk a blue streak. Looks to me like you're the first kind."

"Uh huh," says Jo.

They drive in silence for several minutes, Archie transferring the toothpick from one side of his mouth to the other, Jo looking out at the gathering dark. She feels him appraising her, although he's looking at the road. She doesn't care what he thinks. The trees that flank the road appear to be moving closer.

"Who you meeting at Cass's diner?"

"I told you. A friend."

"I told you, it's closed."

"My friend will wait for me."

"Cass don't like people hanging around the parking lot."

Jo doesn't know what to say, so she doesn't say anything.

The cab seems impossibly high up off the pavement moving beneath them. Moths swirl in the headlights. She thinks she can hear the soft thump of small bodies against the front grill over the engine noise, but of course that's ridiculous.

"Might be you're looking for a job?" Archie eyes Jo sideways.

"Might be."

"Got an idea," Archie says, and starts to reach forward in the general direction of Jo's knee. Has she misjudged him? She grabs the big chrome door handle, thinking: can't be going more than thirty on this hill, maybe I can drop and roll; scanning the door pocket for something sharp, something besides B.C. highway maps and magazines. But he reaches for the CB, the receiver lost in his hand like a ball in a catcher's mitt. She sits, trying to slow her breathing, surprised at the rush of adrenalin.

"Cass," he says. "Cass, I got someone here."

Great, thinks Jo. There's two of them.

"Yep," he's saying, "cute little thing." The truck revs on the downshift and she doesn't hear what he says. Then the CB's back in its cradle and he's grinning at her. "You'll like Cass," he says. "She's a real sweetheart."

Jo looks at him then, for the first time, really, and there's a softness there that makes her want to cry. She looks out the window, determined to keep herself together.

"You never did tell me where you were goin', didja?"

It's not a question Jo can answer. Since she put out her thumb this morning, *where* wasn't something she had considered. She was just going.

It takes less than ten more minutes to reach the diner at the summit, a little coffee shop with dark windows. Between two

Coca-Cola signs, dimly illuminated in the light cast by the lamp standard, a third sign reads: Cass's Roadside Café. There's a broad gravel parking lot that could hold several cars, with a long pullout big enough for a couple of trucks. Archie pulls into the middle of the empty lot while Jo sits, one hand on the door handle, unsure of what to do. A light comes on in a trailer she didn't see before, tucked in the trees behind the diner. The woman who trundles out wears a housecoat and unbuckled Kodiak boots.

She hauls open the cab door, looks at Jo appraisingly, and clucks at her. "Well, come on, girl, let's get you settled. I got a bed in the back room; we can make it up in a jiffy. Lord knows I could use a little help around here. Cup of hot chocolate? Sure, you would. I've got some instant in the cupboard, pretty sure."

***

That was the first night. Now, Jo returns abruptly to the present—cold coffee in hand, swivel stool beneath her—with the metallic protest of the hinges on the trailer door. Surprise, she thinks; Cass is up. You never can tell. Jo can smell the hot grill, suddenly, and jumps from her perch on the stool. Lost in thought, she has let the grill overheat, with the day's first customer still nowhere in sight. She's turning down the gas as she hears Cass's foot on the back doorstep, winces as she hears Cass's whisky voice, but there's humour, there, too.

"Jesus, girl, you'd think you were trying for Hell's Kitchen in here." Cass pauses, head cocked. She's wearing lipstick the colour of spawning salmon, Jo sees now, even if it's not quite six-thirty in the morning.

"Come to think on it," says Cass, "I do believe I hear the Devil himself this minute coming on down the highway."

Jo's ready to apologize, but Cass is already through the swinging kitchen doors. Turning, Jo can hear the downshift of gears, and at Cass's Roadside Café, the day begins.

Cass

I sure never had any arrangements with Archie to leave runaways and whathaveyou on my doorstep. Archie wasn't even scheduled for a haul 'til next week, so when the radio in the corner started sputtering that night I jumped right out of my chair where I'd fallen asleep watching late night TV. Archie's picked up people before he thought shouldn't be out thumbing rides—too young, or messed up, or whatever—and there's been more than a couple landed here for a meal. I feed them and they pay what they can or I put them to work, and I don't pry into their stories. Okay, I pry a little.

Funny how a little kindness makes you want to cry. I've been there myself. So that first night—Archie kept going, said he'd see me on the flip, had a deadline—I give the girl some hot chocolate from the mix in the cupboard, even make it with milk thinking she could use a little something healthy, and when I hand it to her I can see her bottom lip shake a little like it does before you cry, so I turn around and start banging dishes around. Like I said, I've been there. I hate crying, and I hate it when people cry. Crying is not something you should have to do in public.

So when I think she's had time to pull it back together I turn around and tell her she can have the back room in the trailer, the one that's usually the dumping ground for stuff I don't know what to do with, where I keep a single bed against surprise guests. Hand her an armful of bedding and a pillow like I'm saying this ain't no hotel and you ain't no charity case, just so she doesn't feel like one.

Well, that girl's got a story, no doubt about it. You can see it, just about eating her up. Been there myself, you get stuck inside whatever it is that's eating you, and you can't see past about two inches in front of your nose because of all the stuff whirling around inside like a pack of dogs in a cage. When that happens there's no getting out of it but by your own choosing.

But then, everyone who comes through this place has a story. Everyone's going somewhere. Everyone's coming from somewhere. Cass's Roadside Café is a stop on the way, that's all. Sometimes, *sometimes* I get a repeat customer, someone who remembers the slice of pie on the way through, decides another on the return trip is a good idea. And I do get some regulars, Bob, mostly, on duty or off. And Archie, but Archie doesn't come for the pie, although if you asked him, he'd say he comes for the sweet stuff and wink at you. It's a good arrangement, works for both of us. Sometimes I think that's all life is, a series of arrangements. That, and whatever drives into the parking lot. I like the chance of that. The luck of the draw. Toss of the dice.

People who come through here all come from somewhere. One day they get up and think to themselves: I've had enough of this, or: I can't wait to get to that. They turn to their wife or husband or whatever and say: I'm leaving, or they call their lover and say: I'm on my way. Or they just say to whoever is closest: let's go.

And some people just like the road.

Bottom line is, though, I can use some help around here. For one thing, I hate getting up early mornings. I could use an early riser, someone to open up. But next morning there she is in a nest of blankets and sheets, all the stuff that had been piled on the cot shoved onto the floor. I wake her up and tell her where she can find a towel and some soap and shampoo, and to come to the diner when she's done. Takes her an hour before she finally makes her way across the parking lot and then I take one look at her and say: work starts tomorrow. She might be cleaner than she was, but you can tell she's bone weary. Send her back to bed with a cinnamon bun fresh from the oven and one of those newspapers somebody left behind with a front-page story about aliens, and tell her to take all the time she needs. And she needs it, you can tell.

There's this moment when I think she's going to cry again. Just a moment, her standing there wearing the same clothes as before but a little colour in her face, those pale eyes looking at me. She has the newspaper pressed to her chest with one hand and the bun on the plate I've just given her, the sun was slanting through the window and lighting up her hair still wet from the shower. You can see she's a pretty girl, and no dummy, either, and I don't know, I feel like—like she's my kid, for a minute, however weird that sounds since I don't have a kid and I didn't ever want one, at least, not one of my own. There was Donnie, but that's another thing. Happier on my own: grew up with a whack of sisters in a house that was never quiet, never one damn thing that was just mine. I never wanted a kid or a dog or a cat or a husband. In any order.

"—Go!" I tell her, waving my hand, looking away. "Get lost and let me get to work. And fix up that room of yours, make yourself a little space. Go on."

But I say the last bit to the back of her, because she's out the door and striding across the parking lot on the longest, skinniest legs I think I've seen, red hair flapping behind her and her mouth around that cinnamon bun like there's no tomorrow.

Jo

I put away the cinnamon bun, which is delicious, and then, like it's obviously the next thing to do, I put away my clothes. What there is of them. Plaid flannel shirt, green. It always makes me feel warm, and happy, though I can't say why, exactly. I'm wearing my jeans, but there's a pair of cords I brought, a couple of t-shirts, sweaters. Mum always said I dressed like a lumberjack. Man, if she could see me now, in the back of this trailer in the middle of nowhere. Lumberjack Central, that's what this is.

Once I've hung my clothes in the small banged-together plywood closet and thrown my underwear and stuff in the drawer in the bottom, I sit on the single bed and look at the room. The whole room is tiny, and stacked up one side right up to the casement window are boxes; this is a storage room for Cass's stuff, obviously. "Just throw this stuff wherever," Cass had said, referring to the pile of papers and things on the cot, so that's what I did. On the top of the pile I put on the floor last night, a photo album. I feel a little guilty, looking, but Cass didn't seem to care about privacy, leaving me to clear some space for myself.

Inside the front cover is a brown folder with Cass's birth certificate, title of ownership for this place, and a few other odds and ends. They're the sort of things you'd think would be kept in a proper file, but this seems to be Cass's style, and after my mother's insistence on order, it's comforting, if you want to know the truth. Cass was born in Vancouver, British Columbia, January 12, 1930. The title for this place is dated June 17, 1958. There's not much else in the folder except a photograph. Little girl, maybe three years old. Red hair like mine.

The photograph album is the kind with black paper and picture corners, and I spend some time looking at the black-and-white photographs of people I don't know. Cass is there, I can tell it's her, still chubby, and not more than ten or eleven. She has that same smile that takes up her whole face. She's with four other girls who could only be her sisters. I wonder at that: what it would be like to have sisters or brothers. Someone to take your side.

The baby was a girl. I didn't get to hold her.

I hope that, in her new family, she has sisters.

Windswept

And blow ye winds, heigh-ho!
A-roving we will go.
— *Folk song*

The pavement is heating up: Pink can feel it radiating, warming his right side. It's good to be out this early, even if there isn't a whole lot of traffic. The way the sunlight lines the pines as it rises over the curve of mountain, the smell of earth and leaves, birds going crazy in the treetops. He can hear the call of a song sparrow, answered by another more distant, perhaps a mate or a lover-to-be, a heartbeat later.

A car approaches, a pale green Pontiac coming over the rise like a sea creature. The man in the driver's seat is middle-aged, jowly, and reminds Pink of Stan, not because of the car—Stan has been driving the same red pickup as long as Pink can remember—but because of the plaid shirt and something about the way the driver grips the steering wheel with both hands, mouth firmly set. In the pickup, if Nora was there, she'd be all soft in the seat, where Stan was a hard, straight line at the wheel. As a boy, Pink always sat behind Nora, as if siding with her maternal, comfortable sponginess by virtue of proximity. But there were the times with Stan, in the woods, in the workshop. The patience when he showed the boy how to do something new, the shared pride of accomplishment. He can feel, even now, the weight of that hand on his shoulder, the warmth of it. *Good job, son,* it said. *I'm proud of you.* The warmth might last a day or a week, sometimes months. At other times, *he means well*, Nora would say.

As the Pontiac passes Pink's outstretched thumb, the driver gives him a look: another hippie, it says. Get your hair cut. Get a job.

Leaning now against his pack at the side of the road, Pink sits in the peace of the moment and remembers another time: a massive oak tree, sunlight, like today, streaming through its branches, while beneath it two small boys play with plastic soldiers. Eight-year-old Elvis—as Pink was known until recently—particularly likes making the sounds of explosions. Elvis's friend Kevin likes to be the captain, barking orders. Before them is the battlefield: ambushes, hoards attacking from behind roots. Blood and gore everywhere. Lots of sound effects.

Then, one afternoon Stan finds them at their game. Hauls Elvis up and tells him it's about time he grew up. Says he'll show the boys how to shoot after lunch. Elvis tries avoidance: he takes his *Classics Illustrated* comic book under the back step and stays there for half the afternoon, reading *Oliver Twist* by flashlight. When he hears the crunch of boots he looks out from his cave and sees two pairs of shoes, Stan's work boots and Kevin's running shoes. There is no getting away from this. The sound of gunshots and tin cans being hit—and Stan going off at him over the cans that are missed—permeate the neighbourhood.

Later on Kevin gets a B-B gun for Christmas. It's all anyone talks about in the neighbourhood, Kevin's B-B gun. Elvis hears Stan tell Nora that maybe they should get Elvis one for his birthday. "First thing, they cost an arm and a leg," Nora tells him, "and second thing, somebody's bound to lose an eye."

The day Stan and Kevin's father, Lloyd, decide to take the boys deer hunting, the rifle is oiled and gleaming by the back door when Elvis comes down to breakfast. Despite his apprehension, Elvis feels the heady power there. It looks formidable, imposing, all metal and woodgrain. No-nonsense. Not a plaything.

"Can I have eggs?" asks Elvis, who always has oatmeal with brown sugar for breakfast. He wants to ask for coffee, too, but doesn't quite know how.

In the woods, the boys flank the men, quiet in the seriousness of the event. Dawn has just broken, and the early fall air paints their breath white, makes boots crackle on dry grass. There is a quickening in the air at the outset of the adventure that subsides as the sun traverses the sky towards midday, the excitement settling into an irritable resignation at the absence of game that both boys can feel. Now, Elvis and Kevin just want to go home. Elvis thinks of his comic book, of the character's forced apprenticeship to the coffin-maker, and feels an affinity for Oliver Twist.

The wild turkey has a bewildered look about it; perhaps it is already injured in some way, because it doesn't take off in a rush of feathers when they accidentally flush it from some low brush, the edge of stealth on the part of the hunters long since dissipated. It's Elvis who spots it first, the sound out of his mouth before he has a chance to think better of it. "Here you go, son," says Stan proudly, down on one knee to help him sight the rifle. Elvis catches Stan's glance at Lloyd, knows this to be a contest.

Elvis fires, and misses. The turkey finds its wings, and is gone.

The missed shot sends Stan and Lloyd into a must-kill frenzy; the boys, Elvis knows with eight-year-old perspicacity, are just excuses. "Gotta make sure these boys don't go home empty-handed," Stan and Lloyd say to each other, ploughing across fields, through stands of trees, the boys stumbling behind with burrs in their pants, snot-nosed and cold and just wanting it to be over. Elvis catches Kevin's eye and receives a small grimace in return. After a while, Elvis is determined that one of them will kill something, just so they can go home.

As it turns out, it is Elvis. Stan sees the doe, and Lloyd has to admit Stan saw it first and so Elvis should get to shoot it, but Elvis can tell Lloyd wishes it were his son Kevin. The deer just stands there, and part of Elvis is thinking *run*, and part of him just wants to kill it and make Stan proud. At the moment Elvis sights the deer through the scope, he really does want to kill it, the feeling drug-rushing through him, powerful. Intoxicating. He's come a long way from playing with plastic soldiers; this gun is real. The feeling that has enveloped his whole body comes to a knife-sharp point, pulsing where his finger meets the trigger.

It takes three shots to get the deer to stay down, Stan taking the gun from Elvis when it is clear the boy will not shoot again. Elvis can see her thrashing, trying to get up, falling. The men beckon the boys closer, shouting, urging the final shot to finish her, and Elvis sees the look of terror in her eyes. Stan pushes the gun at Elvis, shoots a look at Lloyd; Elvis throws an agonized look over his shoulder at Kevin, but there's no help there.

"Between the eyes, boy," Stan hisses, and there is blood on the dry autumn grass and on the soft dun hide of the doe; there is the thrash of legs that seem impossibly delicate; there is the limpid brown of the eye as it rolls. From a place Elvis did not know existed comes a sob.

It is Lloyd who grabs the gun from Elvis, finishes her off with a shot to the head. Elvis can't make his hands do anything. He's trying not to throw up. When he does, heaving into a patch of brush, Stan, to Elvis's embarrassment, begins to laugh.

"Buck fever," says Lloyd to Stan knowingly, humour in his voice.

"Come on now, son. It'll be easier next time," Stan says, but Elvis, feeling humiliated by the laughter, pushes away the proffered hand. It's all too horrible: the doe, the vomit, the laughter. There will be no next time. The ground swims in front of him, and his ears roar; he thinks he will be sick again. Behind him, Elvis can feel Kevin standing, arms at his sides, watching.

Later, Lloyd cleans the doe, hanging it in the shed by the Ford he's restoring. Elvis sees the dark stain in the earth floor below the slack, hanging head, the milky white of the dead eyes. The meat is divided between the families, brown paper–wrapped packages in odd shapes in the old freezer. When Elvis looks inside, his chest feels funny, so after a while he doesn't look.

***

A crow calls, and Pink comes back to the moment, the highway stretched before him. The Volkswagen van appears on the road like sunshine: yellow, carefree, friendly-looking. The girl, filling bowls with granola and applesauce in the back, smiles at Pink under a soft moustache, raises her heavy eyebrows and gestures at the empty bowl. "You?" Thérèse asks, and he hears a French accent. Her breasts swing under a peasant blouse as she moves. Stefan, driving, turns and smiles, eyes friendly beneath a leather hat, feathers in the rawhide band. They look tanned; there is the smell of earth, sweat, and patchouli.

After a while they pull over at a rest stop. Thérèse stretches out in the morning sun while Stefan brews coffee on a camp stove. Pink's pack is in the van, and he ambles over to pull out some packets of sugar he keeps in a pocket and waves them, his small offering, but Stefan shakes his head. "*Miel*," he says, pointing to a jar. As they drink their coffee, Stefan lounges beside Thérèse, lying on her back on the grass, her legs under her long skirt crossed at the ankles. Pink watches them, thinking of the ease with which they live together, picking up work through the summer: cherries, peaches, apples. He thinks about companionship, the warmth of a body in the night. He envies Stefan's hand on Thérèse's thigh. Abruptly, he rises and walks to the creek.

He's taking off his socks to cool his feet in the water when he hears the van start up. "Hey!" he yells, running after it. He grips the door handle, feels the panel door slide as he runs alongside, bare feet on sharp rocks. With his other fist he hammers against the side of the van and manages to get one foot up to jump inside, his face wrenched with fury.

"No way, man!"

Stefan looks over his shoulder, and, as if surprised to see Pink still hanging on, accelerates. Thérèse shouts, her voice panicked. *"Oublie ça—donne le lui, Stefan!"*

With that his pack hits him full in the face, knocking him backwards out of the van and onto the shoulder where he rolls, grating his face against the gravel. He clutches his pack while the van speeds away, and lies there for a full minute before rising awkwardly. He had pulled his jacket from the top of the backpack when he looked for the sugar. It was still in the van, now vanishing over the curve of highway. Most of his money in the lining.

He goes back to the creek, and there spends some time bathing his cut feet in the icy water before letting them dry in the sunlight, propped against a rock, all the while willing his heart to slow. Anger, at being ripped off, but resignation, too: bad stuff happens. What goes around comes around. He thinks of that John Lennon song, about Karma. He thinks of Stan and Nora, of all the times he's taken off, taken with him a part of somebody.

After a cold night in a picnic shelter Pink wakes early, thinking of coffee. The wind's blowing west, so he plants himself accordingly on the highway shoulder, feeling the sun warm the pavement, his right side. But there is no traffic, so he begins walking. When he turns at the sound and sees the massive truck that comes over the rise it looks almost prehistoric in the morning light. Pink is grateful when the rig pulls to a stop fifty feet down the road.

The guy in the cab smiles in a friendly way and says: "Goin'?"

"Yes," says Pink, and although he hasn't answered the question about where he's going, the driver waits while he hauls himself into the cab.

"There's a diner a ways up," says the driver. "Cass makes a mean breakfast, missed it last time I was through. You can go on from there or stop along with me, makes no difference."

6:25 a.m.
Two eggs over easy

Cass stands at the screen door in the slant of morning sun wearing stretch pants and tennis shoes. On each pudgy finger is a ring; to Jo, looking through the kitchen window into the restaurant, Cass looks like a costume jewellery store. When Cass makes pie dough, as she did last week, she takes every ring off and lines each one up on the side of the green Arborite counter in the kitchen.

"Don't you have anyone wondering where you are?" Cass had asked the day she taught Jo how to make pies. "She must've blown in from *somewhere*," she heard Cass say to Bob the Mountie later, when he stopped in for pie and coffee.

Now, Archie's truck pulls into the lot, chrome glinting in the sunlight, and Jo smiles to herself. It's like a dog whistle: Cass hears it first, and then, there it is. But what she hears next isn't Archie's voice, so she peers from between the swinging kitchen doors so she can better see the front door, to see who spoke.

He's slight of build and ponytailed, with eyes like a Husky. There's an accent. American. Then Jo hears Cass's voice, raspy like the gravel in the parking lot.

"I only got regular eggs. Nothing fancy. Scrambled, over easy, or sunnyside up," says Cass.

"Over easy, man."

He stands a few feet inside the restaurant, dust motes swirling around him in the morning sunlight. He's wearing a multicoloured t-shirt and jeans. His sandy hair is long, reaching his shoulders. His face looks soft, almost feminine. Jo watches Cass take him in, sees her little eyes narrow.

"Can you pay?"

He takes a few bills from his pocket: two green one-dollar bills, a brown two, crumpled around a handful of small change. Cass nods, and he sits down at the counter.

"Jo?"

He doesn't look up as Jo pushes through the swinging doors. He's looking at the pine trees across the road, at the way the tops blow in the wind. She fills a cup and sets it down in front of him.

"Eggs'll be a few minutes."

Cracking eggs the way Cass has shown her, Jo peers through the little window where the orders get set when they're ready. As Cass ambles over to wait at the doorframe, Jo watches the customer scan his surroundings. With her hands doing what they've become used to doing—eggs in pan, salt, pepper, toast in toaster—she follows his eyes as they take in the room.

The screen door bangs. "How's my Mama Cass?" says Archie, and then he nods towards the kitchen. "And how'sa girl making out?"

"Good enough."

Archie settles on the stool beside Pink, the vinyl seat disappearing beneath him. Resting both elbows on the countertop, he lights a cigarette, holding it between his thumb and forefinger. When he exhales, he speaks to Cass, ignoring Pink, who's reading the words on the side of his mug: *Where are we going, and why am I in this handbasket?*

"Picked this guy up back a ways," he tells her. "Get this: hippie says he won't go against the wind."

"Says what?"

"Against the *wind*. Like, now it's blowing southeast and I'm heading northwest. I told him I'm going northwest 'til I get on the TransCanada, but noooooo," his thumb jerks at Pink while he rolls his eyes, "says he's gotta stop here."

"Well, that's one way to get a customer," Cass laughs. Pink doesn't speak, but smiles to himself and sips his coffee, glancing once again at the treetops on the ridge.

Archie nods at Cass, the tilt of his head indicating the trailer. "Got some breakfast for me at home?" he asks, winking. Cass looks at Pink, tilts her own head in his direction, a question. Archie shrugs his shoulders: he's okay, the gesture says. Cass appears satisfied.

"Jo! Look after things for a bit, hey?"

When Jo brings him his eggs, she takes a good look at him. He is nothing like Eamon in his manner; none of the cocky self-assurance there. She refills his half-empty cup, watches as he wraps his fingers around it. When he offers his name there is a softness, perhaps even a shyness.

"Do you really only travel with the wind?" she asks him, overcoming her own. She studies his face while he speaks. Slightly overlapping teeth. Mole above one eyebrow. Those eyes.

"A good traveller has no fixed plans, and is not intent upon arriving." He waits a beat. "Lao-tzu. Actually, the rules aren't quite that strict. I just can't travel against the wind. But the wind tells me where to go."

"Whose rules?"

He smiles, but continues eating.

"The wind told you to come here?"

"Well, I'm here, right?" When he looks at Jo she feels the colour rise. To mask her blush, she busies herself writing today's soup on the board. Vegetable beef. Cass made it yesterday afternoon.

"And you like it? Just travelling with the wind?" she says over her shoulder.

Pink appears to consider this. "Most times," he says finally. "Stuff happens, sometimes. Good stuff, bad stuff. It's all part of the journey." The last statement sounds to Jo as if it's something he's said many times before.

Pink nods towards the trailer. "That your mother?"

She laughs, shaking her head. "I don't have a mother." It's the first time she's said it: I don't have a mother. She's not going to consider what that means, the import of having said it. "I suppose I sort of blew here, too." She likes the way that sounds: carefree, a leaf in the wind. It sounds a whole lot better than lost.

"Well, man, that's cool," he says, and there's that American twang again.

"Where are you from?"

"Ah. Now *that's* a story." He grins, and Jo waits. There's work to be done, but Cass will be gone for an hour at least. She pours herself a cup of coffee and leans against the counter behind her, trying her best to look carefree.

Pink looks around the café as if taking inventory for a second time, his eyes eventually coming back to Jo, who is looking into her cup. He watches Jo watch the small whirlpool of her stirred coffee while he eats his eggs.

"Why's your name Pink?" Jo asks at last.

Pink smiles slightly, mouth turning upwards just at the corners. "My parents called me Elvis. Mum loved 'Heartbreak Hotel,' apparently. The song came out in January and I was born in May. Anyway, I figured I'd update."

Jo looks at Pink blankly. "Floyd," he says.

"Never heard of him."

"You know. *Ummagumma*?"

Jo shakes her head. Is he speaking another language?

"Pink Floyd. It's a band. How about *Dark Side of the Moon*?"

"Oh. Okay, yeah. Right." The song "Money" had been all over the radio the summer Jo turned fourteen.

Pink smiles almost apologetically. "I thought, you know, keep the music theme . . ." He shrugs his shoulders, and goes back to his coffee. At the window, a fly tries to push through the speckled glass.

"So . . . what's this thing with the wind?" asks Jo. She settles herself on the stool on her side of the counter, resting an elbow on the Arborite, blowing on her coffee, which is no longer hot. The fly buzzes; sunlight warms the room as it slants across the floor.

"I just—have this thing about the wind, I guess. From my earliest memory. It's always kind of—been with me. So after a while, I decided to let it guide me."

Jo opens her mouth, a question forming, but Pink stops her with a finger on her forearm; tanned brown hand, a little dirty, against pale, freckled skin. She thinks of Eamon, and wants to pull away. But she holds still for a heartbeat, two, before refilling both their cups.

"The first time I remember really hearing the wind I was maybe six. I was in my bed, and it had to be pretty late. I remember lying there, listening to the noises of the house, the way an old house will pop and creak. Sometimes I could hear the crack of the embers in the woodstove in the kitchen. There was a small hole in the stovepipe of that stove that Dad never got around to patching, and I liked to watch the sparks fly by on their way up to the outside. Anyway, the quiet in the house meant my folks were asleep. Only I was awake, my ears straining at every sound, lying still like any movement might set off some chain of events, wake up the monster under the bed, I don't know. It's funny how you can remember some things so clearly like that, isn't it?"

Jo nods, remembering lying in bed listening to her parents argue. What was it about? How old would she have been? She can remember the feel of the sheets under her fingers, can see, in her mind's eye, the light poking under her closed bedroom door.

"And then I heard the wind. It came in through the space where the window was cracked open for the fresh air Mom always said I needed. And it was spring, so it was cool. It came through and it whispered around my ears, you know? And I heard—it sounds corny, but I swear—I heard it call me by name."

"Pink?"

"Elvis."

Jo thinks about the wind calling Elvis.

"Anyway, I was like a sleepwalker, you know, only I was awake. I remember looking down at my blue flannel cowboy pyjamas—I loved those pyjamas—and seeing how the wind was tugging at them. So I walked across my floor, all lit up by the moon, and I opened the door to my bedroom and looked outside. You could feel the house—breathing."

Jo realizes she is holding her breath, and she lets it out.

"The wind told me to go outside, so I did. I walked outside and looked back at the house, the siding all kind of washed in moonlight. I couldn't see the houses below because we lived on a ridge, with a dirt lane that curved down and around before it met the road, so it felt like you were alone up there, especially if you were only six. Anyway, all around the house were these tall pines, spindly things with branches mostly at the top, and they were swaying like dancers, like they were waltzing, and that's when I heard the music. I really remember thinking I heard music."

"Music?"

"Probably it was the creaking of the trees and the hiss of the wind, but sometimes I think it was more like that Pied Piper story, you know? Anyway, I looked away from the house and there was our car, a 1960 Chevy station wagon. It had a front grille like a set of teeth and wings like eyebrows over the taillights at the back. My folks had just got it, and they were really proud of it. I always had to wipe my feet before I got in, my hands had to be clean, and I sure wasn't allowed to play in it. Here I was all excited, like they were, about this shiny new thing and I couldn't understand why they got to play with it and I didn't.

"It was like the wind led me right to the Chev and I touched the handle and pushed my thumb in to unlatch the door. And then I was inside, and I started playing with the pedals, you know? And before I knew it I had my foot jammed down hard on the clutch and the car started rolling and I couldn't see where it was going because I was too short and since I didn't know what the pedals did I didn't think to take my foot off the clutch at all. And then all at once I'm bumping down the road and over the bank and the car doesn't roll, you know, it just keeps going until it stops in a grove of trees, and I can hear the crunch of metal and I can't hear the wind anymore, not at all. Just the sound of me breathing and the car making a sort of settling sound, the way the house was."

Pink pauses. "I don't know why I'm telling you all this."

"Go on."

The plate is empty, and so is Pink's cup. Jo fills it for the third time. He wraps his hands around the cup and looks into it as if seeing something quite different.

"I wasn't hurt because I was all tucked down under the dash anyway, and I guess the car wasn't going very fast, really. I couldn't get the door open because of the brush on all sides. And I was scared of what Mom and Dad would say, so I didn't want to go home. So I just—curled up on the seat.

"I guess I was sound asleep when the fire started. The neighbours thought I had died in it, too, along with my parents, until someone noticed the car was gone, and then noticed the tire marks going down the drive and over the bank. That was the first time with the wind." He stands up, wiping his mouth on the napkin, draining his coffee.

"Wait," says Jo. "Is that really true?"

"I think so, yeah," he said. "Things shift in your memory. Sometimes I think your mind puts things together later, to make a good story."

Jo raises her eyebrows. Pink shrugs again.

"But your parents really did die in a fire?"

"Sometimes I tell people I was raised by wolves. Sometimes I say it was the wind." He grins. "Actually, it was my Aunt Nora and Uncle Stan near Pullman, Washington."

The screen door bangs. Cass comes in with Archie, looking flushed. Archie sits down beside Pink, swivelling back and forth on the stool a few times as if settling in. "Got summa that apple?" he asks.

Cass looks at Jo, who is still looking at Pink.

"Better go," Pink says, standing up.

He holds up a hand, a wave that becomes a peace sign. Long fingers. Jo's own fingers twitch, but her hands stay by her side.

She watches his back as he turns and walks out, screen door banging behind him, colours like a garden against the parking lot. She watches as he steps out on the highway. The first car going east, a blue Valiant with dice hanging from the rearview mirror, slows. Before getting in, he turns and waves again, the wave this time turning into a thumbs-up. Before she can return the wave, he is gone.

"American kid," said Archie conversationally. "Just another of them kids on the road, I guess. Like that song, what was it? Gone to look for America. Lots of 'em on the highway, like they got no idea where to find it. Or what country to find it in." He laughs at that with a kind of snort. Jo is still looking out the window at the empty highway. "Forgot to leave a tip, I see."

"Forgot to pay, too," says Cass. "Jo, where's your head?"

Cass

Well, I've seen that look before, that's for damn sure. If you'd asked me in the first place I'd say that girl had boy trouble. Now here she is looking off after that hippie as he heads out the door like she'd follow him anywhere. They never learn. Me, I learned. Don't ever give your heart away. Find a mutual arrangement that works; it's the best you can hope for. And don't get in too deep.

Got to wonder about Jo. She can't be more than eighteen or nineteen and she's not giving anything away, but like I said before, that girl's got a story. Got parents somewhere, probably wondering where she is. Look at her: good teeth, healthy complexion, freckles and all, good shoes, even. Someone took care of that girl. Not all kids get taken care of, I should know. But kids these days, they only think of themselves, not about who might be pining after them.

My own mother had ambitions, always figured she was a damn sight better than the place she landed. She named me after Cassandra, a Trojan princess who could tell the future, thanks to this guy Apollo. I read up on this stuff, even though my mother did give me a sketchy version early on. The story goes that Apollo figured he'd get lucky in return for this great gift he gave her, of being able to see things that hadn't happened yet, but when she told him to take a hike he put a curse on her so that nobody'd believe her. Typical, men thinking mostly about their dicks and pissed off when they don't get to put them where they want to. Gotta wonder why she never saw that coming.

Anyway, Mum gave me her version when I was fifteen or so, and I liked the part about Cassandra having the foresight to give some horny bastard the cold shoulder, although it ticks me off if I can't get anyone to listen to a bit of advice when it counts.

The name makes sense, though, when you realize that before I was born Mum was an aspiring actress. She was almost four months pregnant when she married my father. He'd told her he was a producer when she met him in a bar on Hastings Street. She bought it, but then, Dad was a salesman. As for her choice of names for her girls, she stuck with the Greek theme all the way through, like it was her nod to classical theatre or something. She gave the next four babies Greek names, too: Acantha, Phoebe, Eleanor, Tess. I can see her, walrus-sized, sitting on the purple couch ticking off possibilities in the baby-name book, turning the pages with the fire-engine-red nail of her index finger.

Acantha, who came eleven months after me, means thorny, because her entrance into the world—she was a breech birth—"hurt like hell." She named Phoebe—*bright one*—in an uncharacteristic moment of optimism. Tess means fourth-born. Eleanor, the last one, means Mercy.

My father was a Fuller Brush Man, keeping us well stocked in that department if nothing else. We had the top two floors of an old house downtown, the five of us crammed into the two rooms in the attic, with Mum—and Dad, when he was home—sharing the second floor room beside the bathroom. The five of us flushing the toilet over the course of any given night must have made life on the road seem pretty good to Dad.

On the rare occasions Dad was actually home, we were close. He'd pick me up when he still could—I was a chubby child, still do carry an extra pound or two—saying: "How's my Cassie today? Didja catch any fish?" which never made sense, living where we did.

I inherited this place from Dad when he died in '59, which made Mum spitting mad. Turns out he had something going with the woman who owned the place, and who, having died the year before of some kind of cancer, left it to him. No real surprise, said Mum, but *still*. She grilled me, thought I knew something about the affair, but I didn't, and after a while she just stopped speaking to me. I couldn't say why he'd done it. I don't know, maybe he thought I'd finally catch a fish out here.

It was boarded up when I got to it, once the legal stuff had settled out, taxes paid up and all mine, free and clear. Acantha couldn't believe I didn't turn around and sell it. When I called it Cass's Roadside Café, she laughed at me. "*Café!* It's a side-of-the-road diner, Cass," she said. "Face it." But she hung around that first summer. We drank a lot of wine while we fixed up the place. We laughed a lot. We talked a lot, too, more than we ever talked growing up together, even squashed into that room we shared. But she knew herself: "Cass," she'd tell me, "don't count on me. I could be gone tomorrow."

Then one day, she was. She'd roll back in from time to time, and she'd never tell me what she'd been doing no matter how many bottles of wine we killed. By then the place was earning me a living, and I liked it. Boyfriends would come and go, hanging around for a while, but I never wanted them to stay, not if it meant sharing the place. I'd have shared it with Cantha, though, if she'd wanted, but she's a cold wind, that girl, always blowing in a different direction.

The day she showed up with a baby I hadn't seen her for two years. At first, I didn't believe the girl was hers. "She's called Donalda, after Dad."

"What?"

"Dad. Donald."

Mum always called him That Man. Of course I knew his name was Don, but I never actually put the name together with my father, who was just Dad. Seemed like a dumb name for a girl, but it told me that Canth missed him too, which wasn't such a surprise when I thought about it, her relationship with Mum being what it was. Just the same, I couldn't remember Canth and Dad spending any time together, not that any of us did all that much. "Wanna hold her?" she asked. The baby in the blanket was scrawny and pale and ugly, with a brush of red hair across her head. I was instantly in love.

I started taking Donalda—I called her Donnie—more and more. Cantha moved into town, and it was easier for me to have the girl in the restaurant than Cantha ever could in the places she worked, mostly in one bar or another. When Cantha was on night shift Donnie slept over in a nest of blankets on the couch. In the morning I'd sit her on the kitchen floor in the diner with a drawerful of spoons and ladles, and she'd take them all out and put them all in again, over and over. She never banged them on the floor like most kids would. That kid was always quiet; when she made any noise at all, you knew to pay attention.

The first time Cantha really didn't show up, instead of just being late, I'd had Donnie—who'd just had her fourth birthday—for almost a week. The girl was a sweetheart and no trouble, but I was pissed off. So I guess I let Canth know how I felt in no uncertain terms when she finally did turn up, when I tried to find out what the hell was going on, where she'd been. I guess I was really yelling, that's how mad I was.

"What the fuck do you care," Cantha screamed back. She looked like hell and way too thin, and she scared me. "Come here, baby," she said from a crouch, skinny fingers beckoning, and when Donnie ran to her I wanted to take it all back. Leave her, I wanted to say. I don't mind. I'm sorry. But she was out the door, Donnie on her hip, and into a pickup. I couldn't see the man driving, except for a handlebar moustache and a ballcap.

It's been years, and no sign of Cantha or Donnie. Not that I didn't try to find out where they'd gone. Bottom line, said Bob when I asked him, is that she's the guardian. Unless I can prove she's not being a good mother, that there's some kind of abuse or neglect, I haven't got much to say where the law is concerned, and I sure haven't got any way to find that out. "You ever report them missing?" he asked me, but by then it had been years already, and I never figured they were actually missing, just didn't want to be found, at least by me. Well, Cantha didn't anyway. When I think of that little girl sitting on the kitchen floor with a bunch of spoons and bowls spread around her, pretending to cook like her Aunt Cass, it breaks my heart. Now, Donnie would be about the same age as Jo. Red hair, too, but Donnie's was curly where Jo's is straight, so curly she'd cry when I tried to comb it after the bath. There I go now, feeling sentimental just remembering it.

Learned my lesson, I guess. I'm not going to be tied down, not me, and I know not to give too much away. Not my heart, anyhow. Might do Jo some good to learn that, but I suppose she'll find out for herself. Just the same, I'll try to give her a bit of advice—or my name isn't Cassandra.

Ha ha.

Jo

The morning's barely started and yet the day feels full. Cass is in the kitchen making soup and I'm filling the salt and peppers and waiting for the next customer.

Pink has left me thinking. Thinking about what it's like to go where the wind takes you, the freedom in that. When I was pregnant, I felt the pull of life from inside me through my feet. I could imagine the reach of roots into the ground, binding us. Afterwards, I was a hollow tree, walking around in just my bark, root system fragile, a tentative grip on earth, hardly anything. Won't think of home, won't think of what I've lost, not my mother, not the baby. What should be a line of daughters is broken in two places, and here I am, filling Heinz bottles from the giant jug with the plain label that says: *Regular Catsup, one gallon*. I feel as blank as this label.

When I was small I had a best friend whose name was Genevieve. She was the youngest in her family, with a much older sister and brother. So she was a late child, and I was an only child. Genevieve was five when her father died of a heart attack at the breakfast table, leaving no insurance. Her mother had to take a secretarial job, and my mother, who didn't start working until I was in high school, began looking after Genevieve. For a short time, we were like sisters.

Genevieve's mother would drop her at our house on her way to work. I would still be in my pyjamas in front of my cornflakes, our Airedale sitting at my feet looking for a handout, and Genevieve would be already dressed in her kilt skirt and matching leotards, her fine blonde hair in twin barrettes. As my mother dressed me, "Your mother must get up early to get you all dressed and ready," she said to Genevieve.

"Oh, I dress myself," said my friend, and my mother raised her eyebrows at me while I shot a look at Genevieve. I liked my mother's no-nonsense fingers at the buttons of my blouse; I liked the way she pulled up my tights and gave me a little pat on the behind as if to say: everything is in place, now, just as it should be.

By the spring of that year it was clear that something was not right with Genevieve. She was losing weight; she bruised easily. There were visits to the doctor, and then there were stays in the hospital. I heard my mother talking on the phone about a bone marrow transplant.

"What's a—" I looked for the word "—bone marrow?"

"It carries blood and oxygen. It's something you need to have working well in order to be healthy."

"And Genevieve's isn't?"

"No darling, not right now."

In kindergarten, we all made pictures to put up in her hospital room. I made a painting of a teepee, bright suns on the outside like the one in the corner of the picture.

At Christmas, Genevieve got an Easy-Bake Oven. We'd seen the commercials on television, during the breaks between *Razzle Dazzle* and *Beany and Cecil*. We talked about the things we could make with an Easy-Bake Oven, imagined wedding cakes with pink and white icing. For Christmas, I received a paint set. It was a good set, with lots of colours and three sizes of brushes, but it wasn't an Easy-Bake Oven.

"How come Santa brought Genevieve an Easy-Bake Oven, but not me?" I asked my mother.

"Oh, darling . . ." she said. Genevieve was back in the hospital. If she wasn't going to be able to play with it, I thought I should be able to.

In January, just before my birthday, my mother sat beside me on my bed. My room was yellow, like the sun I painted in my picture for Genevieve, and I remember looking at the walls that always made me feel happy when I'd wake up in the morning.

"Genevieve has gone to Heaven," my mother told me. Later, I overheard her talking about the funeral. When I asked about it, "a funeral is no place for a child," she said.

"I want to say goodbye to Genevieve."

"She's gone, honey. You wouldn't see her anyway. She's already buried in the cemetery, beside her father. It's just a service."

Later, I came home from school to find Genevieve's Easy-Bake Oven on the kitchen counter. It looked smaller than I thought it would. The spoons were small and plastic, and the round cake pans were barely the size of my palm.

"Genevieve's mother wanted you to have this," my mother told me.

"Did Genevieve want to give it to me?"

"Of course, dear. That's what she would have wanted."

I opened the first package of cake mix. In it were tiny oval things I thought might be some kind of nuts, but as I pushed one with my finger, it curled up.

"Oh!" said my mother. "Weevils!" and she swept the bowl away and tossed the powder in the garbage. "It's too old," she explained. "It's past its shelf life. When that happens, sometimes things get bugs growing in them."

"Like Genevieve in the ground?" I asked. I was curious. It's what kids at school were saying.

My mother gave me a look. "Let's open this package and see if it still looks good," she said.

I poured the powder into the bowl and used the tiny cup to measure out the water. I watched through the window as the heat from the sixty-watt bulb made the mixture in the pan rise. When I took it out, I touched the top with my finger, watched the tiny indent spring back to life. Then I cut a wedge.

"Here, Genevieve." I held it out to the air. After a while, I set it down on the counter. I thought that maybe she would only come if I went away, that maybe now that she was in heaven, she didn't want to be seen. I thought that for a long time, and would sometimes speak to her when I was playing in the backyard, in case she was out of sight, listening. I don't remember when I stopped doing that. I know I never said goodbye.

Shortly after my mother sat with me on my bed and told me about Genevieve, I heard her talking to one of her friends, the phone pressed to her ear as she looked out the kitchen window, unaware of me standing in the doorway. "I can't imagine what it would be like to lose a child," she said.

Well, now she's lost me. I never told her about the baby. I never said anything about what I saw. I went back later that night, when I knew Eamon would be at the bar, Dad still away on business, Mum at her bridge club, and packed up what I could. I called from Lethbridge and told Mum I decided to drop out of school, since I was failing anyway.

"What will your father say?" she said, but the alarm in her voice sounded false. As for Dad, he'd had less and less to say anyway, since Mum started working, and, I suppose, since I stopped being a little girl. And he was away more and more.

Dad.

He would bounce me on his knee when I was small. I must

have been about four; it seems to be my earliest memory. *This is the way the gentlemen go, gentlemen go, gentlemen go . . . Gallop! Gallop! Gallop!* I would squeal as I was bounced around, but the best part was the way the farmers went on their pretend horses, *hobbledy-hoy* all over the place, me slipping and laughing, Dad catching me and then tickling me under my armpits. Mum would tell Dad to stop: he'd get me all excited, and then who would have to deal with me? I never knew what that meant.

Once I asked Dad if I was adopted. I was sitting with him on the front porch and he was playing with my hair, whispering "carrots" in my ear, like in *Anne of Green Gables*, my favourite book that year. Neither he nor my mother had red hair.

"Adopted?" he laughed. "Why would you think that, my little plumber?"

Dad called me Josephine the Plumber, a joke I never understood until I found out she was a character in television ads for cleanser, white overalls, hair in a kerchief, red-painted fingernail wagging. When I protested—I must have been twelve or so by then—he laughed. "Plumbing is a noble profession," he told me. "Whatever you decide to do in life, make sure you have one good, saleable skill. Learn to cut hair. Or type. Then you'll never be without work."

Of course, Dad thought I'd go to college, on to university, become a journalist, a teacher. But as for a good, saleable skill, I guess waitressing fits the bill. If Dad knew where I was, if he knew what had happened, what would he think? What does he think now?

I'm sure Mum never thought she wouldn't hear from me again, her voice coming through the payphone receiver like she was on the other side of the country. She never thought I wouldn't come crawling home when I'd had enough of low-paying, dead-end jobs and Kraft Dinner. She was angry with me for taking off. She was angry that I didn't want to tell her where I was. She was angry when I asked to speak to Dad, and told me he was away on business. I told her I was between places.

"Well, you're an adult, I suppose. You'll do what you do."

"Yes, that's right. And you're supposed to be an adult, too."

"What's that supposed to mean?" She sounded annoyed, and not nearly as worried about me as I wanted her to be. She's my mother, after all.

"It means you'll do what you do."

I'm thinking about all of this, the ketchup container suspended in midair, when I hear a car pull into the parking lot.

Behind me, Cass stops humming whatever is in her head from the radio. "Jo? Soup's done. There's just sandwich stuff now. I'm heading into town." I hear the back door slam at precisely the same moment as the car door opens.

I think about Cass's box, her photographs, the people in her life, the stories she's accumulated. Then there's Pink and his story. Will I see him again, I wonder? Or is that just the end of that story: an intro, nothing more. We cross paths with people all the time, never sure how a chance meeting may alter the paths we travel ourselves.

I have the coffee pot in hand as the old woman steps out onto the parking lot gravel.

Second wind

The sharper the blast,
The sooner 'tis past
— Proverb

"Folks are too polite," Eunice always says. "They don't ever say what they're thinking, and they pussyfoot around, talking to everyone else but the person who really needs to know. That's the worst thing in the world, thinking someone thinks one way of you, then finding out later they think something else altogether. Burns me up. People need to tell the truth."

Eunice knows a thing or two about truth. Raising three boys on her own during the Depression, her husband gallivanting around who knows where, truth was all you had some days. She'll tell you her boys grew up knowing what's what.

"I had to be strong, that's all there was to it," she'll say, wagging her finger, keeping you in your chair. "I had to speak my mind; there was no time for pussyfooting around a subject."

What she won't speak of is her husband, Edmund, who left not long after Bobby was born. Not anymore, she won't. She won't tell you about how they met, him sneaking under the tent flap when the Chautauqua came through town, only to come up right beside her where she sat watching the acrobatics. She won't tell you about how he made her laugh, right from that moment, how his clowning charmed her, made her see everything in a sort of twinkling light. How, when Bobby came seven years after Charlie and that made three boys, he laughed and told her now he had a juggling act. That he'd have to run away and join the circus, and take his three bouncing boys with him. She won't tell you about how, when he did leave, he didn't take the boys, but he did take the elephant girl, the two of them packing up a half-day before the travelling circus pulled up stakes.

The neighbours watched as Eunice's boys grew up and began to find ways to stay away from home: Stuart got on at the mill when he was barely fourteen, most of his wages coming home to add to the money Eunice made bookkeeping for the gravel company. Charlie never told Eunice that basketball kept him out after school most days; she thought he had a job delivering papers, and Stuart gave him a little money to bring home to prove it. Eunice didn't approve of sports—anything fun being a waste of time—nor would she ever subscribe to a newspaper, a waste of money, and a bunch of liars anyway. But Bobby had no luck finding work and, quietest of the Currie boys, was unable to lie to his mother. "You telling the truth, boy?" she'd ask, his chin viced between her thumb and forefinger. Paralyzed by fear, he could do nothing to cross her.

But then Bobby fell in love with Sylvia.

"I remember the time he invited that little snippet Sylvia Bruneau over for dinner," Eunice will tell you, with so much acid in her voice you won't know where to look. "I never liked for any of my boys to be smitten with a girl. Makes them lose their heads." Of course, whatever Eunice thought about men in general, those boys were all she had.

This particular day Eunice tells Bobby as he heads for school: "You can eat that leftover beef stew for supper. Stuart's working late, and so is Charlie, extra route or something. I have a Ladies Auxiliary meeting at the church." But when Bobby opens the door late in the afternoon, Sylvia's small hand in his, the smell of roast chicken strikes him right in the face. Has he got the day wrong? There is nowhere to go; Eunice has heard the door and here she is, heels sharp against the hallway linoleum, tea towel in hand, ready to tell her boy to go wash up. But who is that she sees, hanging back in the shadows?

"Ma, I'd like it if Sylvie could stay for chicken," Bobby musters.

Eunice looks over Sylvia, her white ankle socks and her pink cardigan. Sylvia extends her hand.

"So pleased to meet you, Mrs. Currie," and Eunice thinks: well, she's respectful, anyway. So she says yes, she supposes there's enough for one more and turns back to the kitchen, thinking she'll ream her boy out later for being inconsiderate, bringing a guest home without warning. She doesn't like surprises. Bobby looks nervous, she thinks, but then, he's probably ga-ga over this silly girl; Eunice will have a few words with Bobby about that, that's for sure. She pulls the chicken out on the rack for a final baste, thinking as she does that she can't remember when any of her boys brought someone home. It's when she realizes that she wasn't supposed to *be* home that the fat misses the bird and hits the hot oven door, spitting. The pain on her wrist is knife-hot.

Bobby and Sylvia sit in the living room, side by side on the couch.

"I'm sorry," he whispers. "I didn't know." In his mind he can see the evening play out the way he had hoped it would; his palm tingles when he imagines his hand cupping her breast through her soft cardigan.

"I want to go home," says Sylvia, but he puts his hand on her arm. "No, please," he says. "It's better if you stay." Maybe, he thinks desperately, it will be all right. "Maybe you could offer to help in the kitchen?" Knowing, as he said it, that it was like sending the maiden into the dragon's den. "I'm sorry," he says again.

She feels the tremble in his touch, leans forward to kiss him on the cheek.

That's when the tea towel comes down, *crack!* across the back of the couch.

"You're just like your mother!" Eunice hisses as Sylvia recoils, eyes wide. Bobby has his hands in the air, palms out, as if to ward off the tidal wave that is his mother, but there is no stopping Eunice. "Carrying on the way she does with that gypsy with the knife cart every time he comes through town. That Eyetalian fellow walks through the streets ringing that bell pulling that wagon, looking like he hasn't bathed in a week. Everyone knows what's going on except that dingbat of a father of yours, but no surprise since he's got less than half a brain upstairs. So don't you come in here with your ways and your wiles and go after my Bobby!"

Eunice says the last words to empty air. There is the shudder of the front door, followed by the slam of Bobby's bedroom door. He refuses to come out for dinner. Serves him right, she thinks, as she eats roast chicken alone, fork stabbing at its flesh. She's not hungry anymore, but she eats every scrap on her plate, stabbing, chewing, swallowing. She leaves Bobby's plate on the table; he can have his dinner cold for breakfast.

The boys grow up and move east. Stuart works the docks in Halifax Harbour; Charlie opens a corner grocery store in Moose Lake, and Bobby winds up a drunk somewhere in Toronto.

They are as far away as they can get. Every year or two she'll get a postcard, a few stark lines. Sometimes she'll get mention of Bobby, Charlie down to Toronto for a weekend. *Bobby says hello* is the closest she's got to news of her youngest.

"Heard from your boys, Eunice?" asks Blanche Fowler in the hardware store.

"Mail's slow," she answers. "Don't know what's with Canada Post, used to be next-day delivery, now it costs three times as much and takes a coon's age to get across town," Eunice says. "Don't know why we pay taxes if we can't even get a decent postal service."

The house is empty without the boys. She hates the sounds it makes as it settles, hates the tick of the clock. She hates the sound of her own heels on the hard linoleum. Against her better judgment, she gets a phone. That's what she tells the man behind the desk when she orders its installation. Against my better judgment. She doesn't say: perhaps Stu will call. Or Charlie, or Bobby.

The phone is black. It has a presence, and she likes that, just as she likes the heft of the receiver in her hand. Eunice gets a party line; it's cheaper.

"Long-short-short is your ring," the man behind the desk tells her. "You'll hear the phone ring for others on the line. That won't bother you, Mrs. Currie?" She is about to demand to know how he knows her name, and then she remembers she wrote it down on the papers in front of him.

"We'll see," she says.

When the phone rings the first time, echoing around the walls of the hallway, it's not her ring, but she picks it up anyway, her hand pressed against the mouthpiece. She recognizes the voices at once. It's Mary Popoff talking to Blanche Fowler.

". . . Eunice Currie in Henderson's Hardware yesterday. What she was wearing? God only knows what century she thinks she's living in," says Blanche.

Somebody guffaws.

"Not that she's trying to impress anyone. Oh, I felt sorry for her when that husband of hers left, but she's made damn sure nobody else would ever come sniffing around, didn't she? And she was still a pretty thing back then. But now . . . well, you know how she is. At cards the other day we were talking about what she said to Brenda Spencer, and you know, everyone at the table had a story just like that."

"Hard to imagine her ever married, least long enough to produce those three. Does anyone even remember that husband of hers? No wonder those boys lit out like they did. But then, none of those Curries were worth a lead penny. What gets me is how stuck up she is, that mouth going off at the church bazaar committee meetings, like she knows everything. If she makes that thing she calls an upside-down cake again, I'll throw up."

Eunice hears Blanche giggle. "Well, that's what it looks like, anyway—something the dog threw up. My kids won't go near that place, say she's a witch. No, it's not nice, but she's earned it, hasn't she?"

There's a pause, and Eunice holds her breath.

"We'll just have to go on being nice to her, Mary, that's all. That's what Reverend Johns says, and we've all got to be on that committee."

"Well, try not to sit beside her, that's my advice."

Eunice goes to the next meeting. She plans to confront them, and she takes along her cane in case she needs to use it. She's not above defending herself. But when she gets there, the Reverend is addressing the ladies, and Eunice has always liked him. And as usual, Sally Symonds, Mitzi Brunfeld, and the others are polite, even respectful, and she thinks that maybe she misheard, somehow, that maybe it's just Blanche and Mary, going on the way two women do, sometimes . . . Until Blanche asks her if she was going to make her upside-down cakes again this year, and Eunice sees the knowing smiles bloom, and she feels the momentary softness turn granite. But when she turns to speak, the pain in her side makes it hard to think straight. It's a good thing she has a doctor's appointment in—yes, in a half-hour, and, feeling shaky, she asks the Reverend if he might be kind enough to drive her there.

"Three months," says Dr. Pinkham after all the tests are through. "At the most."

She hadn't felt all that bad before, but as soon as she hears, Eunice begins to feel terrible. She is unable to catch her breath; the least thing tires her out. The pain in her side is a gnawing animal. There are nights she wakes up and wishes it would just eat her and get it over with.

"Hospital," Dr. Pinkham insists. "They'll monitor the pain."

"There's something I have to do first," she tells him.

The receiver feels even heavier in her hand than when she had picked it up to hear Blanche and Mary. She knows now, without a doubt, that her boys will never call her, and if it makes her sad, the feeling is eclipsed by the sense of righteousness as she calls the first number.

"I'm dying," she tells each person. "I haven't got long to live. Doc Pinkham says a few weeks left, that's all. I want you to come and see me." She gives them each an appointment.

They come, one by one. They bring flowers and candy, and tell Eunice what an inspiration she's been, how proud she must be to have raised such fine young men, how much the community will miss her. Eunice accepts it all from her deathbed, the scent of lilies fighting one another across the room. She pats her patchwork quilt and whispers to sit close, smiles as if she loves them as sons and daughters. "Give me a kiss on the cheek, dear," she tells them. "Come closer, so I can tell you something."

Eunice watches while they shift and squirm. She watches them arrange their faces into expressions of sympathy and caring. And when their faces are an inch from her own, she tells them exactly what she thinks.

Your husband hates you, she confides. Your friends laugh at you; your boss doesn't trust you; your kids are embarrassed by you. Personal things: things everyone knows but nobody has the guts to say out loud. Who *had* to get married; what stalwart, respected citizen was caught shoplifting ladies underwear. She tells Muriel Brooks how everyone thinks she is so boring they'll drive right past the Overwaitea rather than risk meeting her in the soup aisle and have to stop and talk. She tells Gloria Bruneau how, when her husband Frank fell in the vat at the winery, everyone might have *said* it was an accident, but that everyone *knew* it was because of the Eyetalian, and that she's going to have his death on her conscience 'til the day she dies.

When the last appointment is over, Eunice begins to laugh. She gets up, opens the window, and tosses the lilies into the yard. Then she leans on the window frame, feels the sun on her face, and realizes that in one day she has purged a lifetime of resentment. She doesn't blame a soul for anything, not anymore.

The telephone rings, three short. She doesn't pick it up.

It occurs to Eunice that she still might die, especially when she throws out the medicines from the nightstand. But she doesn't. As the days go by, the house takes on a glow, and it's not just the open curtains, the fresh air. Even as it settles, as old houses do, there's a musical quality to the creaks and pops, Eunice's personal percussion band. Twice, she catches herself whistling.

And yet there is the matter of carrying on, medical miracle or not, in a town where she has told every individual exactly what she thinks. In the end, she realizes there is nothing left to do but leave. The thought itself is liberating. But something is missing; something keeps Eunice from turning the latch for the last time. Something left unresolved, but she can't quite put her finger on it.

Eunice's bags are packed when Sylvia Bruneau knocks on her door. Eunice, carrying the last bag to set it with the others, is pretty sure she hasn't seen Sylvia since that day she ran her off, and now Sylvia's forty if she's a day. Mousey little thing, thinks Eunice when she opens the door. But the venom is gone. Eunice hadn't even asked her to come when she assigned her appointments, that's how little she thought of Sylvia, but now the day comes back to her and she steps back with a small intake of breath, thinking: *Bobby.*

Sylvia looks at Eunice's bags and says, brown eyes wide: "Mrs. Currie! Are you going away?"

Eunice remembers then that she is supposed to be dead. "Just a little trip," she says.

Sylvia sits down on the wooden chair Eunice keeps by the door. Eunice sets the suitcase she is holding down and watches while Sylvia leans over and runs her hands across the top of Eunice's old green suitcase, fingers brushing the frayed canvas surface. She does this for a long minute, as if she is stroking a cat. Finally, she speaks, her voice soft.

"I kept waiting for you to invite me to visit, like you did the others. Yesterday I was coming down McPherson and there was Muriel coming around the corner from your house, looking all flushed the way she gets when she's excited or upset, you know the way her cheeks get blotchy. She told me what you'd said to her. And then when I got home there was a call from the hospital; the doctor said Mama'd had a heart attack. Even though her heart was always strong as anything. The doctor said she'll make a full recovery, Mrs. Currie, in case you're worried about her. Although I don't imagine you are. When I went to see her, she just turned her head away. Her own daughter. What would make her do that? Did she come to see you, Mrs. Currie? What did you tell her?"

Eunice doesn't answer. Her heart is beating in such a way that it crosses her mind to note the irony in having a heart attack now, after not dying of cancer. The words in her head, *would serve me right*, come unbidden. With a stab, she recognizes their ring of truth, and closes her eyes for a moment.

When she opens them, she sees that Sylvia is watching her with interest. Or is that concern Eunice sees there? After a few moments Eunice sits down on the bigger of the two suitcases. Their eyes meet, and Eunice notices for the first time how large Sylvia's eyes are, and how brown. She can see the pretty thing Sylvia must have been when she was sixteen, could see, she thinks, what Bobby might have seen.

"You know, I didn't stop seeing Bobby the day you ran me off. I'll bet you didn't know that, did you? Even if you thought you knew everything. We kept on, in secret, for two more years. There were a lot of things your sons never told you. And yet they couldn't cross you, not any of them. They could only tiptoe around, like they were walking on glass. Like thin ice. One wrong step, and they'd be under. And you'd hold them there, thrashing. They all knew that.

"After my father's funeral I begged Bobby to take me away somewhere. I wanted to run away worse than I ever had. I felt that if I didn't run, then I'd never get away. I remember we were out behind the reservoir, lying in the leaves, me weeping into Bobby's sweater and him promising me that, yes, we would go, he'd pick me up before dawn, he'd have everything arranged. Then he looked at the darkening sky and knew he was late for dinner and that you'd have his hide, like you always did, and it was suddenly as if you were standing there, looking at us where we lay in our winter clothes in the November leaves. I could feel his heart speed up in his chest, heard his breath catch, and I sat right up and looked down the road in the twilight, that's how sure I was you were marching up to whack us with a tea towel. Or a shovel. And then Bobby was up and brushing himself off, and then me, and telling me he had to run, and then he did: just lit out through the woods, down the path that came out behind his house—your house.

"Even then I thought he'd come, and I was packed, just like you are now, Mrs. Currie, and ready to go. But the early morning dark got lighter and the crows started up and when I heard Mama rustling in her bedroom I quietly set the suitcase in my closet and went to put the kettle on for her tea. I lit the gas and touched the corner of the flame to the note I had written, watched it burn until the last word reached my fingers and I dropped it. 'Smells like smoke,' was all Mama said when she came into the kitchen.

"What was it like for you, Mrs. Currie, to get up that morning and read Bobby's note?"

"There wasn't any note," Eunice tells her. "I never knew why

Bobby left." She places her hand on her heart. "I worried myself sick. Got a postcard two weeks later, then it was a year before I heard from him again, then two. No return address, not ever."

Eunice looks at Sylvia, imagines her four streets away, pining for Bobby, while in her empty house Eunice pined in her own way. They are quiet together, two women almost forty years apart in age, oddly mirrored in the pose they both take: feet together, hands in lap, eyes looking past the room around them. Shadows form in the corners of the room. It is peaceful there in the darkness.

"You still living in that little apartment above Henderson's?" Eunice asks her finally. Her voice sounds sharp to her ears, and she thinks: I don't know how not to sound sharp.

"Yes."

"I'm thinking it would be good to have someone staying here while I'm away," Eunice begins. "You know, I've just this minute realized I've done nothing to close up the house: the gas is still on, food still in the fridge. I expect I'll be gone a good while. You could stay here, save yourself some rent."

Sylvia looks at Eunice like she's crazy.

"Please," whispers Eunice, and the word hangs in the air. She can't remember when she last said *please*. Then: "Bobby might call." The words are out of her mouth before she knew she would say them.

Eunice has four hundred miles behind her when she makes the call to the lawyer to transfer the title. He doesn't try to talk her out of it; it's just one more strange action on the part of Eunice Currie in a series of strange actions. He's just there to follow instructions, after all. Afterwards, she pulls the Morris into a rest stop and allows herself to imagine him arriving at her door, imagine Sylvia's doe eyes taking him in, a lawyer on the front step with a briefcase full of surprises. She can imagine it perfectly, but she can't imagine the moment when Bobby does call.

When she pulls back out, there's a young man on the other side of the road, a hitchhiker, looking like so many do these days, but Eunice isn't going that way. She's heading towards a place where she can get a bite to eat. She's seen a sign: *Cass's Roadside Café. Last food for 57 miles.* A cup of tea would be just the thing.

She looks at the hitchhiker as she passes, and he grins at her. The wind blows the hair around his face; he looks impossibly young, a whole lifetime ahead of him. Without even realizing she's about to do it, she blows him a kiss. In the rearview mirror, she sees his hand touch his lips, the kiss returned.

9:10 a.m.
Pie a la mode

The old lady emerges from the parking lot dust. She's driving an Austin Morris with a dented hood. Deer, Jo thinks.

"Deer," the lady nods towards the car as she settles herself on the stool at the counter. "Thought my number was up. Ha," she says. "Not the first time. Got a cup of tea?"

When Jo brings the teapot, the old lady pours sugar into her cup straight from the dispenser.

"You can call me Eunice," she says, tapping her bony chest with a bonier hand. Jo hasn't asked to call her anything, and she's not sure how to respond. With Cass in town, she's alone with this crazy lady. "I've decided I want people to call me by my first name. I'll have a piece of pie, too. You only live once, after all. Rhubarb."

When Jo sets the pie in front of her, "Ice cream," Eunice says, as if Jo had forgotten. Then her voice softens, like she's checking herself. "Didn't I say ice cream?" When Jo comes back with a scoop of vanilla on the side she smiles, creases in her skin multiplying while she's licking her lips. She heads for the kitchen, but Eunice's voice follows her.

"Ah. Time was, I'd have said this is no sort of breakfast. Oatmeal. That's all I ever ate. That's what I fed my boys, every day, so they wouldn't grow up expecting fancy pastries and such. So they'd have an appreciation for a good, solid, no-nonsense breakfast. But the rules have changed.

"Now, you'll at least talk to me, won't you, dear? I've been with my own company too long; I need a soul to talk to. Can't swing a cat in this place, it's so small. You can talk to me through this window, here."

When Jo looks at her through the window, Eunice's mouth is full of pie, but her eyes are knife-sharp.

"How old do you think I am?" she asks.

"Ummm . . ." She is more than Jo wants to deal with.

"Guess," says Eunice, ignoring her.

Six, she thinks. "Sixty?" she guesses. To Jo, Eunice looks about a hundred.

"Hah. Shows how much you know. Let me tell you something."

Outside, the wind blows. Jo watches it, thinking about the direction Pink must be travelling. West. What would such a thing be like, travelling with the wind? No direction home, like the song. She imagines a road without beginning or end. No starting point, nothing left behind. If there's a destination, it's too far away to see.

"I've lived a long time on this earth—what did you say your name was?—Jo. I'm eighty-one today. Bet that surprises you, doesn't it? Yup, eighty-one, but I wasn't supposed to live a day past eighty. Know why?"

Jo shakes her head and takes the hard-boiled eggs from the fridge. "I really have to work," she says again.

"I'm supposed to be dead. That's why." Jo looks at her. She's chortling. "Got my second wind, you could say."

Jo waits, but she doesn't say anything else, just digs into the pie. She eats as if she hasn't eaten for days, like rhubarb pie is the best thing she's ever eaten her whole life. When she's finished, "There," she says, and pours another cup of tea from the pot.

"Here's my advice to you, girl," Eunice says, settling on her stool. "Don't look at me like that, now. It's the same advice I give to anyone who'll listen. Ha! You could call it my new mission in life. Now you pay attention, because I'll just say it once. If there's one thing in life you want to avoid, it's regret."

Jo looks down at her cutting board.

"The last time I spoke to any of my boys was . . . let me think, now. Nineteen forty-nine. That's twenty-eight years. A postcard now and then, that's about all, and no return addresses. Bobby, my youngest, would be forty-five, now. The evening he came home, before the morning he left for good, something was up, I could tell. 'Ma,' he said, like he was setting up for something serious. Funny, I can remember everything like it was last night: the colour of the sky through the sheer curtains in the windows, when the sun goes down behind the clouds and turns everything golden for a moment, and then its gone and back to flat, cold grey. I noticed it out of the corner of my eye, and I noticed Bobby's hands and the way they were fidgeting. And I don't think I thought about it, I just *knew*. Stu and Charlie, they'd left a couple of years before, together on the train. They told me they were going to see their cousin, my dead sister's son Julius, about work in the oil patch for a season, and I guess I believed them, didn't know they had no intention of coming back, but then, who wants two more mouths to feed anyway? The ungratefulness of it, after I worked my fingers to the bone raising them. But here was Bobby, the quiet one, and I think I knew what he was going to say and I couldn't hear it. I just couldn't. And him only seventeen years old.

"'What the devil are you doing dripping snow all over the hallway, boy? Did I raise you in a barn? Don't you have any respect for your mother, who works her fingers to the bone for you? You're hopeless, like your brothers.'"

Eunice's voice, mimicking her own of almost three decades earlier, sounds like a nail on a chalkboard.

"That's what came out of my mouth. Now I think about it, that's what I'd been telling my boys for years. 'You're hopeless.' I caught his eye for a moment and I wanted to say something else. Like that he was always such a good boy, and how much I loved him, but the words weren't there. They must have been there once, but I'd been angry so long I'd forgotten how to be anything else. I always said: you have to be tough raising three boys by yourself, or they'll come out soft. You have to be tough in this world, and don't bend, or people will get the better of you. You have to be tough if you don't want to get hurt.

"Bobby was gone the next day. The last one, and I never said a kind thing to him the last chance I had." She shakes her head. "Just told him he was hopeless. Wasn't until things were looking pretty hopeless for me that I figured out what hopeless really was, and it wasn't those boys in the primes of their lives, even if I told them as much every day. And then I started thinking about my own folks. Wouldn't speak to me once I married Eddie. Said he was a good-for-nothing, all charm and no substance, that's what they said. I can still see my mother, hands on her hips, saying: *I didn't raise you to marry some clown. Life's not all fun and games, you know. You have to grow up sometime.* Well, I did, and where did it get me?"

Jo shakes her head, shrugs her shoulders. Eunice looks at her and shakes her own head. "That's what's called a rhetorical question, dear. The answer's in front of you, that's what. 'Course, both my parents died a long time ago. Never did reconcile. You know what I think now? I think it's just easier to forgive than to go on blaming. Takes a chunk out of you, that.

"Nothing like death knocking at your door to make a person

think. Nothing at all like it, really. In fact, I recommend it. You know what I've figured out? That life keeps slapping you in the face with a lesson 'til you learn whatever the lesson is you're supposed to learn. You get a chance, and then, if you miss that one, you'll get another one. That's one thing you can count on. Even old dogs like me get another chance.

"Of course," she says, eyeing Jo over the rim of the cup, "you look too young to have any regrets."

Jo cracks a hard-boiled egg against the side of the bowl and begins peeling. The shell isn't coming off easily; it sticks to the white, pulling off chunks. If she doesn't respond, maybe Eunice will stop talking.

Apparently, she's not going to. "What's your story?" Eunice asks, leaning forward, elbows on the counter.

"Why would I tell you?"

"Ha! That's what I like, a girl with spunk. No reason you should. None at all. Careful, though: you'll be old like me before you know it, one foot in the grave."

The shell is really fighting to stay on the egg; the end result looks like the cat got it; it's a good thing these eggs will be egg salad.

"You have that look about you, though, like there's a story there. Used to be, I never noticed that sort of thing, but now—"

Jo starts mashing the eggs with the back of a fork. Eunice picks up her pie fork and jabs it in Jo's direction. "Right now, you just see a crazy old lady, right? Well, you'd be right, I guess," Eunice cackles for a moment. "But I'm a crazy old lady on the road."

Jo starts on tuna salad, lines up celery, then cuts the stalks lengthwise into long strips, turns the cut stalks around and begins chopping, knife tip never leaving the cutting board. Four cans of tuna, mayonnaise. She glances through the window at Eunice, who's watching her from her perch at the counter. She takes a whole pickle from a jar, begins chopping it to add to the tuna, Cass's recipe.

"You never stop learning, girl. I'm old, and I'm still learning. Even that boy I picked up, drove a few miles. That hitchhiker. He taught me something."

"What boy?"

"With all the colours on his shirt."

"What did he say?"

"Oh, it wasn't what he said. It was what he did."

"Ouch!" It doesn't hurt, but it surprises her. Jo has chopped off the end of her thumbnail with the knife. She's careful to pick the nail up so it doesn't wind up in the celery. "What did he do?"

"Wouldn't you like to know?"

When Jo comes around the counter, Eunice's eyes are actually twinkling. It irritates Jo, so she ignores her and starts rooting around beneath the counter. There's a box of odds and ends, a likely place for a pair of nail clippers that will take the sharp corners off her chopped fingernail. She puts the box on the floor and, squatting, begins taking out the contents, setting them on the floor as she rifles through. She finds needle-nose pliers, a Polaroid cartridge, a large button from a winter coat, an aspirin bottle full of nails, an I.O.U. from someone named Dwayne, a deep-blue glass marble, and a Donovan single with "Atlantis" on the A-side and "To Susan on the Westcoast Waiting" on the B-side. She can sense Eunice peering over the counter. Jo's hands close on the nail clippers, and as she pulls them out the blue marble begins to roll.

"He kissed me, that boy. Here." She points to her tissue-paper cheek.

Jo stands up abruptly, banging her head on the counter. Did Pink really kiss this crazy old bat? The marble rolls past the cash register and, with the odd slope of the floor, turns and begins rolling out into the restaurant, past Eunice where she sits on her stool. She puts out a sneakered foot and stops it.

"Pick that up, would you, dear? After all, I'm almost a hundred. My old bones don't bend so easily."

Jo decides to ignore Eunice's changing story. Eighty? A hundred? Does it matter? She comes around the side of the counter and picks up the marble, placing it in the wrinkled palm.

"We had a pane of stained glass just this colour in the hall window of the house I grew up in," Eunice is smiling, a million creases gathering at the corners of her mouth, and for a moment Jo can see her as a little girl looking through a window pane the colour of the night sky. Eunice holds it up and looks at Jo through the blue, and then tucks it in her pocket.

"Funny, just now it feels like that was yesterday. Like all that time in between didn't happen."

Eunice looks at Jo as if expecting something. Jo can't imagine what that might be. "Pie and tea is a dollar thirty-five," Jo tells her.

"And good advice is priceless."

Jo waits. There's no way she's leaving without paying, not the second customer of the day. She's sure a tip is way too much to hope for. Eunice rummages in her handbag and places two one-dollar bills on the table.

"Keep the change, dear," she says.

Surprised, Jo smiles.

"That's better. You were starting to look like me there for a minute."

There's a pause in which Eunice looks out the window. Jo follows her gaze, watching the trees sway.

"Thing is, I could die tomorrow. I could. I don't look like it, I know, but I could. Meanwhile, there's someone I need to find."

As the Austin Morris peels out of the parking lot, Eunice puts her arm out the rolled-down window, reaching skyward. Jo can't tell if she's waving or just catching the wind in the palm of her hand.

Jo

My grandmother lived with us for a while before she got a place in an old folks' home. She sat in her chair wearing the same brown cardigan every day. She read *Winnie-the-Pooh*, the same page, over and over. She liked to help, and so she would offer to wash the dishes, and later Mum would do them over again to get the stuck-on food off. When our dog, Charlie, wandered into the living room Gran would say "no flies on Charlie!" to no one in particular. To me at fourteen, she was a fixture, like the coffee table, or the standing lamp. Except when my friends came over; then, she was an embarrassment.

There was a time when we would visit her when she still lived in her own apartment, the place all decked out with crocheted doilies, tiny photographs in gilt frames, a brass candy dish that always held Hermits. On the landing was a wavy glass window surrounded by squares of coloured glass—like Eunice's window, I guess—and I would look through them at the garden, imagine a monochromatic world. How different everything looked bathed in green or yellow. Blue was my favourite, the same deep blue as the glass marble Eunice liked. It never once occurred to me to imagine my grandmother's life: daughter, wife, mother, friend. As a child, did she love flowers or horses or the colour red? When she was a young woman, did she tell off-colour jokes with her girlfriends, feeling deliciously wicked as she did? When she kissed her husband, the grandfather I never met, did her heart leap, her breath quicken? When she tucked my mother in when my mother was a small child, did she look at her daughter's sleeping face and feel so touched by its beauty she could weep?

What did she regret?

Of course, this train of thought means thinking about my own mother. And that's where it stops, a black curtain, nothing. I am nineteen years old. I work at Cass's Roadside Café. I am standing here, rag in hand, wiping the counter where an old lady just ate a piece of rhubarb pie as if it might be her last.

Archie

It doesn't suit me to have anyone expecting me any particular time. I have enough schedules to pay attention to, thanks, without that. I suppose that's why Myra and me more or less gave up any expectations early on, even if we stayed married. It's not an arrangement most women would want, their man on the road all the time, showing up whenever. But for me, well, it just suits me, I guess, and Myra's come to some sort of peace with that.

And Cass? Cass is there when I turn up, on my own or, time to time, with someone like Jo, and she takes us all in like we're lost cats or something, and it just damn well feels good. No harm in feeling good.

In between, there's the road.

Don't know where I'd be without the road. Betsy is my home on wheels: she's a 1968 Kenworth, cherry red, sweet as all get out. My name on the door, Archelaus Smith, but Archie's what I go by. Nice chrome, nice lines, but more than that she's my girl: no backtalk, and I treat her nice. Check her brakes, her tires, her lights. Keep her greased up. You gotta respect what you drive, 'cause you're gonna be spending a lot of time together. Coming down a mountain pass some night in the snow, you'll be glad you and your rig are on good terms.

Got a nice little bed to sack out in, everything I need. After a while she's more comfortable than either of my more regular rest stops. And she's just mine, nobody else's. There's something to be said for having a place like that. For one thing, out the window, the view's always new. Mountain, trees, the road ahead. Sometimes elk, bear, 'til I get to the city, then there's all that city stuff, always changing, new buildings going up, old ones coming down, never the exact same thing every time. Used to haul the long routes, now I'm mostly Calgary Vancouver and points in between, sometimes Stateside, but even if I've driven it a hundred times, it's always different. Out my front window in the side-by-side I share with Myra, the view's always the same. Land is flat, for one thing, foothills in the distance on a clear day but otherwise the only thing flatter than Alberta is Saskatchewan. Houses lined up in straight little rows. Myra says she sees it different every time: if it's sunny or cloudy, when the leaves change, the first snowfall. She says it's all that travelling that's spoiled me to see the little things that happen right under your nose.

I got Myra, and I got Cass. In between, I got a lot of road. Cass knows I'm married, so no harm there. Myra's no dummy, either, but she never asks, and I never tell. We all have our arrangements, I guess.

Time was, Myra and I were going to be a team, trucking. She'd give me a little poke in the ribs—had ribs you could poke back then—and tell me she needed to keep an eye on me. And true enough there were some bumps on the road early on, a little cutlery flying, a broken dish or two. But she never did get her ticket and after a while got herself a job babysitting, which is better for those next-door kids than their own mother if you ask my opinion. She's happiest around little kids, Myra is, and a natural with 'em. Saddest thing in the world since she couldn't have none herself. At least, that's what we figure; it's a busy life on the road, hard to find the time for all those tests. I'd have liked a little nipper too, if things had been different, but they aren't, and that's just life.

Here's the thing, though. All sorts of people on the road

these days, a lot of them somebody's kids. I mean, I guess we all are, but it's the young ones that get to me. You see stuff that would break your heart. And I see a kid like Jo, looking lost, and, though she maybe didn't know it, looking for trouble, too, well I guess the part of me that would've liked a kid thinks about how I'd want someone looking out for mine. Just keeping them safe, you know? It's not like I do it all the time, maybe a half-dozen kids the last few years. "Jesus, Archie, I'm not the S.P.C.A.," Cass said to me once, but she doesn't ever say no. Still thinks about that little girl of her sister's. Talk about lost.

Cass. Myra. If those two hens ever met like as not they'd take to each other like ducks to water, but they won't ever meet, and that's not a bad thing either. Don't ever mention one to the other, and that's my rule of the road. It's easier to ignore something that's not right in your face.

You see all kinds of drivers on the road, too. There's guys who stay professional about their driving, stick to the limits, sleep when they got to. There's guys that do the exact opposite, and they're the guys don't last. Then there's guys that kinda come down the middle, like me. You gotta pay attention to your hunches. Can't tell you the number of times I've just had a feeling, better haul off on the gas, then what's over the hump but a Smokey with a cherry on top, sitting there hoping the little bit of brush he's parked behind will cover the evidence so he can reach his ticket quota. Sometimes that Smokey's in a plain wrapper, but you get so's you can see them.

There's good stuff happens on the road: once I passed a guy standing on the shoulder with a sign said: SPEED TRAP AHEAD. I gave him a little wave as I went by, remember thinking that was a strange way of being a Good Samaritan, just standing by the side of the road with a sign, but probably saved me a hundred bucks. Little while later I pass the Smokey, in a little dip off the side and behind a bunch of scrub. Kept my eyes on the road and my foot off the gas, shook my head, thanked my lucky stars 'cause before that I was pushing, no doubt about it. Then come over the rise and there, on the other side, there's a sign propped up in the ditch says: *TIPS, 300 YARDS*. Time enough to stop at the pullout where this other guy sat with a bucket. 'Course I stopped, just like everybody else must've. Gotta tell you, that bucket was full of money. Got on the radio, found out those guys had been out there two hours at least. Laughed all the way to Merrit.

There's drivers know when to push on, drivers know when to stop, like I said. Most times I like to pull over away from the crowd, where I can get some sleep. I've been known to stop at the diner for a meal, shoot the shit with whoever's around, then head on up the highway ten miles and find some lonely siding. Makes sense: refer trucks, to keep cold, they'll run all night, but the motor cutting in and out'll drive you crazy. In the winter, truck's gonna run all night to keep the heat up. Cattle cars are the worst, smell like shit and make a racket. Get a nice quiet spot, park Betsy on a flat, have a drink, conk out. All you can hear are the crickets.

There's guys got their pitstops like me, and there's guys who keep a photo of Shirley or Peggy or whoever on the visor at all times. And there's guys see the road as a mobile cathouse. Me, I tell those lot lizards I don't need their services thanksverymuch, and if they get belligerent I tell them to take a hike, more or less, and I'm not sorry for saying it either. You gotta be able to take no.

One night I was pulled up at a truck stop, a big lot, seven or eight rigs pulled up. I've got a low-bed with a cat on the back, running a little ahead of schedule and feeling pretty good about it. Don't recognize any of the rigs in the lot, but that's okay. You don't always feel like talking. Everyone's in the diner or in their cabs, nobody in the parking lot. I decide to stay put: it's quiet, and anyways there's a mountain pass ahead I know from experience means I'd have to park either slanted up or slanted down, no good place to stop at the top. It's gotta be level or I wake up my face crushed into the back of the seat cause I've rolled with the slope. So, yeah, I decide to have a bite, stay put for a few hours, get forty winks on the flat. The diner's all lit up, one or two guys gulping coffee inside. Overhead there's a million stars. I'm kinda sentimental about stars. I see the Big Dipper, Orion. Cassiopeia, which always makes me think of Cass.

After I wolf a coupla burgers, fries, and a glass of milk (Myra's always after me about the milk) I'm thinking about the Jack Daniels I got in the rig, thinking to listen to what's going on out there on the CB for a while, then hit the sack. But first I have a smoke, look at the stars, and when I pull my head back down there's this lady going truck to truck and of course I know what she's doing. I watch her for a bit but there don't seem to be any takers the first two, and I'm at the end of the row, pretty much. I'd rather she wasn't climbing up onto my cab with me not inside, so I head back a bit ahead of her.

When she gets to my rig I'm just butting out my cigarette, ready to call it a night. She's about forty and looks like something the cat dragged in, dark red nails bitten down, mascara running into the bags under her eyes, little thumb-sized bruises all over her neck and right down into the crack between her boobs where they hang in a blue shirt that says *shake 'em baby.* No thanks, I tell her, but she keeps knocking down the price, first a hundred, then sixty, and before long it's a blowjob for two bucks.

When I told her to take a hike it was with no satisfaction. It felt ugly, you know, dirty and pathetic in more ways than I can tell watching this sorry whore stagger off to the diner, because there was no more prospects after I turned her down.

I watched her through the lit-up window as she slid into a booth seat, only one in the place, tried to see the waitress's face, couldn't see if she felt sorry or just disgusted as she poured the coffee, watched the small change counted out on the counter. She was pathetic, all right, but she coulda been anyone. You just never know what life's gonna throw at you. You never know the story behind the lot lizard in the truck stop selling anything you want for a deuce.

I was tired, I'll tell you, ready for the sack like you wouldn't believe, the JD starting to take effect, but I got out and went over to the truck behind me, a new Bulldog with chrome everywhere and a load of culverts that had to be overweight, probably planning to haul out in the middle of the night to beat the scales. I hammered on the door and there's this big guy, a whole lot bigger than me, pushes the door open. Whadyawant, he asks, and I think maybe this is pretty stupid but I hook my thumb in the direction of truck stop window, light spilling out and the waitress pouring a second cup for the hooker sitting in the booth.

"You even thought about it for ten seconds, you pay up."

"What?"

"You even thought about it, even for one second, that's ten bucks. Ten bucks a second. Takin' up a collection," I jerked my thumb again at the window behind me. "She needs a meal. Hell, needs a doctor. Needs a break, anyway."

He looks at me, looks at her, shakes his head. Hauls out the wallet from his back pocket. Digs in and pulls out a twenty, then digs some more and pulls out a ten. I'm waiting, looking at the bobbing head of the hula girl on the dash. I take the cash and nod, start to walk away. "Wait," he says. "I'm comin'."

Two of us together, we made a good argument. By the time we got to the last rig in the lot, we had two hundred and thirteen dollars. My new buddy went back to his rig, grinning, and I slid into the booth opposite the woman, feeling pretty damn good about the whole affair. We were the only two in the diner, must've been just about closing time. Well, I looked at her, and thought: she may be a two-bit whore, nothing no mother would ever want her daughter to be, but you had to feel sorry for whatever put her there. She's sitting there in that baby blue shirt that says *shake 'em, baby*. And she looks at the pile of bills for a full minute before saying anything, while I wait, looking at her.

"Changed your mind?"

I try to speak soft. "Nah. S'from the boys out there."

She looks at me, looks out at the lot, at the trucks lined up out there, looks at the pile of money. Then she spits on it.

I thought she'd be grateful, you know? Thought she'd be happy. She spit on that money, all smoothed out and in a little pile of twenties, tens, fives, ones, and stood up to leave. I couldn't believe it. Her face all prideful, she stood there for a second looking at nothing while I looked up, mouth hanging open, thinking: what the hell?

When I looked at the table again, the bills were gone. I looked back up to see the back of her, high heels clicking, head in the air as she tucked the bills into the waistband of her miniskirt.

The waitress stood behind the coffee counter, arms crossed,

watching. Then she just shook her head and turned back to filling the ketchup bottles from the big jug. Made me think of my mother, somehow, and Cass and Myra both, all of 'em rolled into one, the way she shook her head like that and turned away. Like something was so obvious, and I was just too dumb to get it.

"She was offering—" I said, but she turned, interrupting.

"I know what she was offering, and I know how low it likely got. But it's service for payment, you know? It's *commerce*. That's how it works."

"Well, she took it, didn't she?"

"Yeah, she did. She took it, but she'll hate you for it. And if she could have, she'd have walked out without it."

Beats me how a whore can look you in the eye and offer her services for two dollars and then spit on you if you offer her two hundred for nothing. Beats me where you draw the line when it comes to what's an insult, what's respect. Or maybe it's just that it's easier to ignore what's not in your face.

The guy in the Bulldog yelled something from his cab when I went by, probably wanting to know what went, so I gave him the thumbs up. I didn't want to talk. Sometimes something happens, you just want to chew on it for a while. The lights in the diner went off. When they did, about a million more stars came out. I had a smoke, watched them for a while, 'til I got dizzy with the number of them all.

Cass

"It's easy to ignore what's not in your face—for a while—but eventually, it's gonna come back and bite you," I told Jo just the other day. "It always does. It's okay, though," I relented, because of the way she was looking at me. "Everybody needs to take a breather now and then. Get their bearings."

We were making apple pies in the afternoon, the quiet time after lunch. Actually, it was still morning for me; been sleeping in, now that I got help. We had quite a rhythm going: chopping, sugaring, cinnamon, let the mixture stand for a bit, and then start making pie dough. I showed her how to fold the rolled-out crust in half, then a quarter, and then put the corner in the pie pan so the fold is the centre, then you just unfold it. Easy as pie, pardon the pun. By the third pie, she was getting pretty good at it.

Although she was pretty quiet at first, Jo's been talking more and more lately. She's like the tame deer I had one summer, out back of the trailer. At first I scared the daylights out of the thing, but after a few weeks she would eat right out of my hand. I can still feel the gentle tongue; see those big, dark eyes. Figure some hunter got her.

Anyways, we're making these pies and Jo says to me: "Do you ever see the future? You know, see something that's going to happen to you, but hasn't happened yet?"

It was an odd question, and I told her so.

"It's just that sometimes I can see little things coming, but the big stuff—it just seems so obvious afterwards."

I wait, but she goes back to the piecrust. It's more than she generally says, and I take that as a good sign, don't try to push her any. As for me, I start thinking about just before Cantha took Donnie away for the last time. Donnie had this dog, a brown mutt she called Smoke and she loved that dog to distraction. Thing is, I'd had this dream that I was running across the highway calling after something I couldn't see, although in my dream I thought it was that dog of hers. It was so clear; it was like I was *there*. In the dream there was some sort of vehicle driving away, and I ran after it but I couldn't catch up.

So two days later there's Donnie sitting on the trailer step, the dog and girl just about the same size. She's counting cars. We'd made up this game that if two blue cars go by it means something good is going to happen, and if three white cars go by it means something bad is going to happen, which is pretty safe because there are a lot more blue cars than there are white cars. I'm in the trailer doing something and she calls out that one blue car has passed, and then after a bit she says "two white, Aunt Cass," and I'm just turning to open the screen door and make sure she's okay when I hear "I mean, blue *and* white," and then I see a blue and white camper pass and right after it there's Smoke taking off after it and some little dog that's barking out the window.

When the truck hits the dog he flips up in a sort of arc and falls back at the side of the road. Then he rolls, like a loose bag of rocks. And Donnie's standing up and yelling "Smoke!" and I snatch her up so she doesn't go running out to him and that's when a white car, coming from the other direction, runs over the dog for the second time and keeps on going.

"I'm real sorry about your dog," the truck driver says after he's pulled over, picked up the dead dog, and walked back with it across the road, blood all over his shirt. "It just ran right under my tires."

I told him to put the dog out back under the tarp by the woodpile, and then to come in. That was how I met Archie.

Thing is, I thought that was the dream, me running out after the dog. It was later; when Cantha came and took Donnie, and I was running across that empty highway calling "Wait!" that I realized when I stopped in the middle of the road, holding my knees and gasping, that I'd been here before.

So I told Jo this story as we were folding and unfolding piecrusts and pricking the tops. All the time looking at her and wondering, because she has that red hair, and because I don't know where she came from. Can't be, though. You'd think I'd know for sure a thing like that. She's quiet for the whole thing—a good listener, that one, which is good, because I'm a good talker, no doubt about it—and then she says: "I'm sorry," and there's something in the way she says it.

"Where did you say you grew up?" I ask her.

"I didn't say," she answers, and I know I won't get anything else out of her.

"Well, sometimes you just don't see a thing coming, that's all," I say after a moment. It is dead quiet, just the two of us with our hands full of flour and the ticking of the clock on the wall, and then there's the hum of Harleys and by the time it's become a roar we're anticipating the hamburger orders clear as day, the sides of fries, coffee refills, that it will be just too busy in a minute to say much of anything.

Jo

I'd like to just leave it all behind. All of it. What's that word? A respite. A chance to forget everything that happened, to pretend I'm just a girl working in a truck stop diner on a mountain pass in the middle of nowhere. No past, just a future, winding ahead like the roads around here. Can't see past the next curve, but it doesn't matter: you can trust that the road is there. Even if the scenery's dull, even if it's just miles and miles of trees, well, you can trust that, too, right? There's a safety in knowing that the forest goes on. Excitement isn't what I want right now. Just knowing the road's there for when I want to step back onto it. Without getting run over by a truck.

It is *not* easy to ignore what's not in your face, whatever Cass says while she's trying to nudge information out of me. It lurks there, in the background, and every so often it comes at me sideways.

I thought I wanted a rest, a chance to figure out which way to go from here. Give me a sink full of dishes, something that doesn't involve thinking. Diner therapy: if Cass could package it, she could retire early and live in style. But I keep thinking about Pink, about the idea of travelling with the wind. No regrets, no secrets, just the road ahead. Who would have predicted that one guy, a couple of fried eggs, and a story would have me thinking this way?

Get yourself together, Jo. Besides, there's a pickup truck slowing, about to pull in. Can hardly see it through the rain that's driving down, a squall out of nowhere. Just can't predict mountain weather, that's what Cass says.

Windwise

Thought is the wind, knowledge the sail, and mankind the vessel.
— August Hare (1792–1834)

The almanac predicts a dry summer, a bad year for forest fires. Buck is sitting at the picnic table at the rest stop as the old grey pickup's engine cools. His ballcap is on the table; he likes the feel of the air on his head, short of hair as it is. He runs a hand across it, one finger truncated at the first knuckle. He has set down the old roadmap with his father's marks all over it and picked up the small paperbound almanac along with his Thermos cup, something to read while he sips his tea. Even if he knows what the weather will be, there is always an odd assortment of articles—astronomy, baseball—that he's not expecting. Behind him, a woodpecker drums a pine, and Buck thinks of the standing dead wood afterwards, how it keeps on giving. A fire isn't always a bad thing. The one that's coming to this spot will be quickly contained, although it will burn right up to the highway, right over the old cabin behind him in the woods, before it's under control.

The first drops of rain surprise him, and then he's surprised to have been surprised. He can never quite fathom how he can miss the obvious. But to not feel the approach of water—well, it's ironic, that's what it is.

Buck's father could feel water. His grandfather could, too, and so by the time Buck's father took up the practice there was a reputation associated with the Waterfield family. Lots of jokes about the name, of course, an old name that once really did reflect the occupation of the bearer, like Cooper, and Ironmonger. And true to the name, Talus Waterfield could look across a piece of land and know where to walk. He'd take a forked branch from a tree—any tree, didn't matter if it was apple or willow or what—and start walking that patch, back and forth, back and forth, until that branch fairly pulled out of his upturned palms. There it would bob its end, and Talus would count the dips. Eighty feet . . . eighty-four, he'd say as the stick made a last small tremor. He never collected his pay—in hay or chickens or whatever in those days—until the well was dug and the water gushing up. He was right every time Buck ever saw him, except the time he went out right after Buck's mother was buried. Talus said the pull of her was greater than the pull of water, and it must have confused him.

The first time Talus put the branch in his son's hand, placing his big hand encouragingly in the small of his boy's back, Buck was eight years old. "My son," Talus told the folks he was witching for, and everyone watched as Buck walked, waiting to feel something. At first, all Buck could feel were the eyes of the farmer and his wife watching him, and it made him nervous but not so nervous as knowing his dad was watching him as he stumbled over the uneven ground, sweat pooling in his palms where they held the ends of the forked stick.

When he tripped, the forked branch spiralled out and landed in the tall grass and stuck there. Buck was afraid to look up from where he sat on his rear on the hard ground in case they were laughing, or worse, that his father would be angry. "That the spot?" Talus asked, and then all at once Buck could feel it, the pull of the water, behind them. At first, he thought his father was tugging on his arm, the pull was so great, but his father was standing a few feet off, hands on his hips, waiting.

After that, Talus took the boy on all of his trips, saying little, but Buck could feel the pride when his father would send him off under the wide eyes of the landowner. "Always use the stick," he told Buck. "Folks are happier when they can see the stick bend. Then they think it's the stick doing the work." Buck has used willow, apple, walnut, maple, forked sticks and straight sticks. He's used a coat hanger, and an old car antenna. He's used a plumb bob as a pendulum, the weight off a fishing lure, a button on a string. He's used nothing at all, but he's found that without some tool, just as his father said, folks are less likely to believe him. And anyway, he's come to like the feel of the branch in his hands, the way the water speaks through the wood, like a radio signal. Music, coming through the wood in his hands.

They logged miles on back roads, exchanging few words. When they reached the location they'd scan the hill, sight the place, exchange a look and head out, Buck pointing like a hunting dog while his father planted the marker. Once, Buck tried to ask his father why he could feel the pull of the water before the stick did.

"Just count your blessings, boy," he said. "Best not to ask too much about them. And best not to talk about them." Buck thought he meant that by talking about the witching he would jinx it in some way.

As Buck got older, he began feeling other things besides water. At first, it was okay. When a lady they were witching for discovered her wedding band missing, Buck saw it, fourth cabbage in the row where she had been weeding. And he knew where to look for their mongrel, Pepper, when he got caught in a snare back of the property.

He knew where a twelve-year-old kid wound up when he went missing from where he was last seen flattening pennies on the railroad tracks. There was family trouble, everyone knew the boy's father beat him, so some thought he'd maybe hopped a train and lit out. Lots of kids took off that young, it was like that in those days, and there were all kinds riding the rails, some shifty characters. Anything could have happened to him. The Mounties called off the search after a week, but Buck could see him, clear as day, snagged in some branches in the river.

When he tried to tell Talus, his father told him to shut up. Using more words than would normally come out of his mouth, he said: "You didn't see anything. You're just imagining things. Forget about it."

But Buck couldn't make it go away. It got worse: one morning he caught the boy's reflection in the shaving mirror when he was walking by, bloated as if he'd been under water a long time. "I gotta tell the cops where to find him," he told Talus, who held him by both shoulders and told him: "You'll do no such thing." Then he sent Buck to his room as if he were a small child rather than seventeen years old, Buck too surprised to disobey. There, alone, he saw the kid in the wallpaper pattern, and in the toss of the blanket where he'd thrown it off that morning. He was afraid to close his eyes, afraid to sleep, but of course, sooner or later, he had to. And then he dreamed.

He did the only thing he could do. He wrote an anonymous letter to the Mounties, put it in the mailbox, and went to the bar. If the regulars were surprised to see him there at first, he became a regular himself quickly enough, and nobody asked his age. Maybe it was the haunted look that made him look older than his years. Whenever he slowed down with the drinking, the boy's face came back: bloated, mouth opening as if to speak. The image continued even after the boy had been found, mourned, buried, his death declared an accident, and Buck wondered at the meaning of that: was there something more he was supposed to do? For the first few weeks he was drunk most hours of the day, and as long as he was drunk enough, he didn't see a thing. When he wasn't, he saw tractor accidents, stillborn babies, undiagnosed illnesses; heard the inner ramblings of the guilty and the plottings of the cruel. Talus came to drag him home a few times, and every time he made his way back, because it was worse at home, sober. Eventually, Talus gave up.

One day Buck awoke to find himself in a boxcar going west, and it seemed like the farther away he got, the less he was bothered, until he didn't need to be stumbling drunk, just a little nip now and then by the campfire to keep things smooth.

At a relief camp near Broad Creek, he got some work on the road crew.

The summer of '31 was a dry summer, just like the one predicted in the almanac for '77, Buck thinks as he folds up the map and screws the cap on the Thermos. As he remembers, he can feel the dust in his mouth, remembers how he scanned for rain, his water sense numbed. When the fire started just east of where they were working, it spread fast. It wasn't long before they were pulled from the road crew to help fight the fire. They had no equipment; nobody showed them what to do. They dug trenches—fire guards—hot, dusty grunt work for two bits an hour, but there was food at the end of the day, and no matter what it was, they were ravenous for it. At night they collapsed, exhausted, in canvas tents that stank of mildew, but for a while after supper the guys would sit around and trade jokes. Buck, like his father, never had much to say. After a while they stopped talking to him altogether.

Lying on his bunk, bone tired, smelling smoke in every pore and waiting for sleep to take him, Buck began to see things: where the fire was crowning, where it leapt the creek, the places it was and the places it was going to be. Places where, if there weren't guys there beating it back; it was going to go wild. Sometimes he could see lightning strikes in places the fire hadn't got to yet. And he could see how big it was going to get. See the homesteads it was going to run over, dead cattle roasting, fish cooking in the streams. He saw a small girl not fast enough to outrun the flames, her parents too stubborn to leave until too late.

The first couple of times Buck told the foreman: wind's shifting, think maybe twenty miles north, that flank's the one to concentrate on. He couldn't keep quiet about what he knew, couldn't just let the fire eat up everything when he could see how they could stop it, get enough men and shovels, enough water on the spot fires. A couple of weeks before it merged with the second fire, then the third, Buck told the foreman what he saw, although he made it sound like guesswork. But when the three fires had indeed become one—the largest in memory—suspicions arose. It wouldn't have been the first time relief guys set new spot fires to keep the work going.

"Why would anyone do that?" Buck asked when the patrol picked him up for questioning. "There's plenty of work already, no need to make more."

Someone had come forward, Buck learned, reported seeing him sneaking out at night. It wasn't true, but it meant a bonus for them, and, his reserved demeanour taken for unfriendliness, he wasn't much liked.

In jail for a year, Buck would walk by another inmate and feel like he'd been doused in something black, tarry. He'd want to go shower but they saw him as a troublemaker and wouldn't let him. He began to feel as if his skin were crawling with vermin, things he couldn't get off, and he started brushing at himself all the time, unaware he was doing it. After two years in a mental hospital, Buck stopped seeing things.

Afterwards Buck got work in construction, working for a cousin of the only guard to befriend him. When he met and married Angela, a gentle, patient woman, he figured the worst was over. He named their boy Talus after his father, even though by then Buck hadn't spoken to him for years. As the boy grew, Buck never said a word to him about the family business. Never talked to him much at all, he's come to realize.

Apple never falls far from the tree, does it, Buck thinks now as he stuffs the map into the glovebox in the truck, feeling the wind pick up, the drops falling harder. He watches as a white Austin drives by, its driver so short as to be hardly visible above the wheel. Deer, he thinks, as he notes the telltale concave of dented hood. *They can take you by surprise, the way they jump out like that.*

Now, Buck's son Tal lives in Vancouver, working the stock market. He's done well for himself; he has an uncanny ability to sense a good investment, and so far as he knows it's a little math, a little savvy, some horse sense and a good hunch. Unlike Buck, for Tal, the gift seems manageable.

Yet when Angela died a few years ago—cancer, just like Buck's mother—Buck never saw it coming. Like a tap, he thought at the time: on and off, off and on, no saying, anymore, how, or when.

Here he is now, Angela gone and Tal married and with a boy of his own. Buck, alone again, settled into cabinetry, working in apple, walnut, maple. He always did love a good wood, the way you can hear the music in it.

When his father's letter found him, Buck knew before he opened it.

"You're here," Talus said from his bed when Buck arrived, like he'd been gone a day or two instead of forty years. "It's time we talked."

Talus, in a flood of words, recounted thoughts and memories, dreams and disappointments. He talked about their gift, without ever naming the thing. He told Buck he hadn't gone out witching in over two years, even though folks from all over still called him on the old phone in the hallway. He showed Buck the topographic maps, marked with Xs, and then names: *Peters. Williston. Nedelec.* The hand was shaky, and Buck recognized the blue ink from the fountain pen Talus always kept. A Waterman, part of the family joke.

The neighbour down the highway, Mrs. Schupmeyer, came in once a day. Buck remembered her, recalled she'd come to the farm as a new bride not long before Buck hit the skids. She'd been on that farm all those years, she told Buck, buried a husband and a son, had a daughter and son-in-law living there now and a mess of grandkids, but still she had time for Talus.

"Oh, I don't mind," she assured him. "If it wasn't for your father . . ."

Buck saw, for the first time, a man with a talent to find the thing people needed most. "It's the root," Talus told him not too long before the morning he didn't get up. "It's what we're made of, water. You remember that."

The morning after his father was buried Buck headed for the

closest farm Talus had marked on the map. He didn't know if he could do it, but he drove out there anyway. When he knew for sure where the water was, he looked at the map, just to see. Talus never even left the house by the time the Thompsons had called him, but the spot he'd marked was the same as the place where Buck was standing.

Buck sits in the cab of the truck listening to the drum of the water outside. He watches the rivers snake down the windshield, but his mind is in the field, in his hands the pull of a forked stick. He puts the truck in gear.

There's a figure on the road looking soaked through. Buck pulls over; nobody should be out in rain like this.

"Oh, man, thanks," says the hitchhiker when he climbs inside after throwing his pack in the back. "Sorry about the water."

Buck looks at the puddles pooling on the seat, and then at the young man who grins at him through dripping hair.

"A little water never hurt anything," Buck says.

He pulls back onto the road and into the liquid grey morning.

10:55 a.m.
Soup of the day

"I suppose we're all looking for something. Water's as good a thing as anything to look for, I reckon." The balding man picks up the water glass from the counter and holds it up, the liquid distorting one sky-blue eye as he looks through it.

Jo has brought him today's soup—vegetable beef—and a roll, and he warms his hands over the steam while his coat, on the chair, creates a small lake on Cass's worn linoleum floor.

"Looks like you found it," Jo says, and he laughs, setting the glass down. Outside, the rain falls in sheets.

"This hitchhiker I picked up earlier said the same thing, when I told him that's what I was doing—looking for water. I told him I could take him about forty miles, and then I was turning off. I had an appointment at the Nedelec farm this morning. Do you know it?"

Jo shakes her head. "I haven't been here very long."

"Well, as it turned out, there's just too much water." He waves towards the wet day. "When the rain stops, I'll go back. Wasn't expecting this downpour out of nowhere like that." Then he laughs again, as if at himself, shaking his head.

"What about the hitchhiker?"

"He didn't seem to mind where I let him off. 'Going with the wind,' he told me."

Jo waits for more, but he's digging into his soup. She looks out at the rain, thinking about how wet Pink must be getting. After a while Cass comes out of the trailer, sticks her head in the back door of the restaurant, and asks Jo if she's okay. "Fine,"

Jo tells her. "If it's quiet, then, I've got a few things to do." Jo knows this means a nap. "Call me if it gets busy."

The guy is looking a little drier when he asks for a warm-up for his coffee. He's gazing at the rain as it drums the gravel in the parking lot.

"Any idea when it's supposed to let up?" Jo asks, for conversation's sake.

"In about twenty minutes," he answers.

"You sound pretty sure."

"Just guessing."

Lunch prep is done, soup's keeping warm on the stove, so Jo starts filling the sugar dispensers along the counter from the big jar. There's one lid she can't budge, so he reaches out a hand, offering to help. There's an index finger missing.

"Woodworker, once," he says when he sees her looking at it.

"Like, tables and chairs?" The sugar dispenser is open, now, and Jo fills it. Together they watch the white grains pour like water.

"Useful things. And, I hoped, beautiful things. I like the way the wood sings, when you find the tone." He sips his coffee. "Once, I made a violin."

It's pouring outside; they are alone in the restaurant, a glowing oasis in the wet grey day. He settles onto the stool like a chicken on a nest and continues.

"I loved building it. The curves, the grain. The way it came to life under my hands. I had a mentor, an old luthier who guided me. It's quite an art."

"So that's what you made? Musical instruments?"

"Just that one. What happened was, as it began to take shape, the music got too loud. I mean, I could imagine all of the people who would play it: I heard scales and fiddle tunes and symphony parts. At first, it was beautiful. But after a while I'd just walk into the workshop—just open the door a crack—and there'd be this—onslaught of sound, all at once."

"In your head?"

He touches his chest with the stump of his finger. "In here. I had to give it up. Stick to furniture. You can have too much of a good thing. Chairs, tables; they say things too, but they're a lot quieter. I made that violin just after my wife died, you understand, herself a musician—played the violin beautifully—and I suppose I was building it for her, in my own way. I think she was trying to tell me something."

"I don't get it."

Buck gazes out at the diminishing rain. "Neither do I, exactly. But after my wife's death, and then my father's, well, it brought a lot of things home, both those deaths. I just needed to make a choice about what to pay attention to. I never realized I had a choice." He swirls the coffee in his cup thoughtfully. *"Then the trees of the wood shall sing for joy, for the Lord has come to judge the earth."*

Jo rolls her eyes. A religious nut. Great. She turns to head for the kitchen, but his voice continues, and it doesn't carry the tone of a sermon. She leans against the back counter and crosses her arms.

"From the Bible. I don't think I have it quite right. But I remember it because of the trees of the wood singing. I like the idea of that. I think of all that clean water, covering the earth, washing away evil, and imagine afterwards whole forests, singing together."

The sky lightens; over the treetops, there is the slightest trace of sun through the clouds.

"But mostly, it makes me think that if you pay attention in the right way, you get the really good stuff. Trees singing. Or the sound of roots growing, or flowers opening. Things people don't normally see or hear."

Through the clouds, the sun breaks, flooding the parking lot with warm light. Jo looks at the clock. Not quite twenty minutes has passed.

"When I was six I had an imaginary friend," Jo offers, surprised to find the memory arise so suddenly. "Her name was Linda, and she had a blue dress. I would meet her at the corner—she was always standing there when I came out to play—and I knew she would always be my friend, no matter what."

"Yes. Well. I guess we all conjure things, one way or another. Friends. Excuses."

"But she was real. Whatever my mother said when she would laugh about it with her friends—like it was the cutest thing that I had this friend that nobody else could see—as far as I was concerned, she was real. I still remember our conversations, although it seems to me that I led the play; that our adventures were made up by me. The thing is she's *still* real to me. I can see her, the way the sun would light up her blonde hair." Jo is looking out at the wash of sunlight across the wet ground. "I always thought, if I had a girl, I would call her Linda."

"To you she was real. That's what matters."

"Yes. She was." When Jo was told, in the labour room, that her baby was a girl, she had to bite her lip to stop from saying the name.

He looks at her thoughtfully. As if, Jo thinks to herself, he knows what's in my head.

"I think that whatever happens to you, whatever you see or feel, it's real enough—that's what matters." Jo, finding herself rambling, shakes her head slightly. "I think the thing to figure out is why. You know, what the point is."

The soup bowl is empty, and now he's draining his coffee, fumbling for money in his pocket. He pauses and studies her, thoughtful.

"What is the point?"

Jo looks across the road at trees swaying in the wind, like some spindly gospel choir. "I don't know. What you were saying, maybe. To learn to hear the trees sing."

He gives her an appraising look. "I'd better be going. Thanks for the soup."

By the time he's opened the door, the puddles are sparkling mirrors; it's almost too bright. From a rent in the clouds beams of sunlight slant downwards. God's Fingers, Jo has heard them called. In the sudden warmth of the sun the wet highway begins to steam, and it is into this that the old truck turns.

Pink

When the wind shifted, the man in the grey truck—a dowser, he said he was—had dropped Pink off at the junction. There is a derelict gas station, pumps gone, but the canopy that covered them is still standing. Pink leans against the support columns and watches the rain come down in sheets.

He hadn't had to ask what a dowser was. When the well dried up for the second summer in a row, Stan said they needed to find a better source on the property. Who knows what's going on under the ground, small seismic upheavals we don't really feel but that shift things in a major way. That's what Stan said: "Stuff going on behind the scenes, son, all the time. We just carry on blind and hope we can adjust."

At the time, Pink thought he was talking about underground water, but as he watches the rain he wonders if maybe Stan wasn't talking more generally. It was about that time Nora's sister Lillian had died of a brain tumour—quite suddenly, although she had been complaining of headaches and dizziness for some time.

"There she was looking after the kids and Walter, volunteering for this and that, being a good wife, mother, *person*, and there was this evil thing growing there all the time," young Elvis heard Nora say to Stan after dinner. Elvis was in the kitchen making a sandwich, something he'd taken to doing an hour after they had finished eating. He just couldn't seem to fill himself up these days. Growth spurt, Nora had said, and as Elvis spread peanut butter, he thought about good growth, and bad growth.

Sandwich made, he stood, leaning against the doorframe,

plate in his hand. Their backs to the kitchen, Stan had his arm around Nora on the couch, an intimacy Elvis seldom saw.

"Eat at the table please, Elvis," Nora said without turning around, her voice a little muffled.

Now, Pink wraps his arms around himself against the damp chill and thinks about Nora's down-to-earth, pragmatic view of life, death, and the necessary logic of eating at the table when you're fourteen years old with a body changing so fast as to be awkward in its new dimensions.

"If you can do something about a situation," Nora would often say, "then do it. If you can't, then live with it, don't gripe, and try to see the good in every situation."

Elvis, plate still in hand and sandwich untouched, listened while Stan reminded Nora: "You always say it, yourself. We all have to go sometime."

"Don't you tell me what I say," said Nora, and she began to cry, great wracking sobs. Elvis, embarrassed, slunk to his room with his sandwich and ate it sitting on his bed. In the morning, when he asked her how she was feeling, she laid her hand on the side of his face, but didn't answer.

The dowser came on a Saturday a couple of weeks after Lillian died. Nora had carried on doing the things she usually did, but seemed, to Elvis, to be just a little numb. When he asked Stan if she was okay, "Just working things out behind the scenes, son," he said. "We just need to give her time."

Nora watched from the front porch while the dowser paced the property with a forked piece of willow. Stan and Elvis stood in the yard, a respectful distance away.

"He can really find water with that thing?" Elvis asked.

"That's what everyone around here says. He'd lose his reputation pretty quick if he couldn't."

"But do you believe he can?"

Stan looked at Elvis. "You're almost as tall as me, son. How the heck did you do that?"

Elvis grinned and straightened, making himself taller.

"I believe he's a cheaper bet than drilling in a dozen places," Stan said, finally.

After marking the spot, the dowser shook hands with both Stan and Elvis, making Elvis feel like an equal rather than a kid. He liked the man for that, and liked him better when the dowser approached Nora where she leaned on the porch railing, her thoughts held close as they had been so much lately.

"Mrs. Preston," he nodded to her.

"Yes," Nora said, coming back from wherever it was she had been. "Thank you for coming."

It had been still until then, but now a breeze started up, blowing a wisp of hair across her face. She tucked it behind an ear, and then seemed to collect herself: running both hands across her head to smooth her hair, straightening the cardigan where it draped across her shoulders.

"Everything passes," he told her.

"Thank you," she said again.

It was the sort of meaningless thing you'd say to anyone who's lost a loved one, Pink muses now, and easy enough for a person to look at another and intuit a sadness there, with all the clues present: the listlessness in her carriage, the absence of a smile. But for some reason, it was the right thing to say to Nora at that time, because she brightened in the days that followed, and came back, slowly, to her regular self. Had Stan or he said the same words, Pink doesn't think they'd have had the same effect. What was it about the words of a stranger that held more meaning?

"Lost his wife a year ago. Didn't work for a long time," Stan told Elvis much later. The two had the new well cover removed and were breathing the cold damp smell from deep inside. "Glad he's back, though."

The rain has stopped, the sky visibly brighter, now. From beneath his feet, the bleached smell of old concrete, no hint of the gas that once filled tanks under the ground. He wonders about Jo, the waitress. What was it about her that intrigued him so much? Something there, something behind the scenes he couldn't see.

In a crack in the concrete, a dandelion pushes upwards. Everything passes, he thinks, and shoulders his pack to head for the road.

Jo

How odd, the things that pass between strangers. It was like that fellow's life opened up just a crack, and what I glimpsed left me . . . something. Unsettled, I guess. It's like it's there, but I can't quite get a grip on it. What a weird day it's been. Outside, the wind keeps blowing and shifting; inside, it feels almost the same way. I feel as if I'm twisting in it, a dishtowel on a clothesline.

It's strange that Linda came to mind just then, in the middle of that odd conversation with that customer. Linda came not long after Genevieve died. The first time I saw her she was standing at the crosswalk at the end of my block. I thought her blue dress with the smocking was beautiful, and I thought Linda was a beautiful name. I can't remember if I told her so. I hope I did, because when she stopped being there at the corner when I came out to play, I felt so lonely. I can remember standing at the corner, this empty feeling right in my chest, and I remember thinking in that way you do, that's where my heart is supposed to be, so it must be that my heart is broken, because it hurts. I went home and told my mother, then, that I needed a band-aid for my heart, because it hurt. It was my mother who convinced me that Linda was imaginary. *You don't need a band-aid,* she told me. *You need to go and find some real friends to play with.*

Sometimes it feels as if I imagined the baby. Sometimes I think that whole time was a figment of some kind, a dream, maybe. Looking out at the sparkle of the sun on the wet ground, this feels real, but it also feels borrowed, like a bus stop or a train station. I can't tell if the bus has left without me, or I'm waiting for it to arrive.

Bob

I've been coming in to Cass's on a pretty regular basis for a long time, and I've seen her strays behind the counter from time to time. I've never figured out what criteria she uses for who she keeps and who she catches and releases, to use a fishing term. She sees *something* in the ones she keeps, that's for sure, and seems to have some sixth sense or some such thing about when they're ready to move on. Never once has anyone taken advantage of her; steal from the cash, or anything like that, and I would know. She's good to people, makes people want to be good back. I know I'm pretty happy having Cass cluck over me with a coffee and one of those cinnamon buns when I'm coming off shift.

And then there's Jo. Can't say what it is about that girl, or why it is that Cass kept her on, gave her a job. Everyone's got their reasons, I guess, and it doesn't do to question Cass about hers. Besides, I like the girl. Just something about her.

First day I came in, expecting Cass, and there was this tall red-haired girl behind the counter learning how to take orders. She was so shy, I just wanted to see her open up a little, you know? So I asked for a CCS.

"What's a CCS?" she asked.

"You mean Cass hasn't shown you how to make a CCS? Cass!" I called, "How long have you had this girl working here without showing her your specialty?"

Cass came out of the kitchen, wiping her hands down the thighs of her pants, which was ridiculous since she had a dishtowel flung over her shoulder at the time.

"He wants a CCS," Jo told her. "I know what a BLT is. But what's a CCS?"

"Huh. You better be careful what you ask for, Dudley," said Cass, and flicked the dishtowel at me.

It took a while before it came out that I'd asked for Cass's Carbon Special—what happens when she forgets and burns whatever she's got on the grill, like she did the first time she made me a ham and grilled cheese. We'd got talking, and before you know it she was bringing me this black brick on a plate, pickle on the side. "On the house," she told me. "Policeman's Special."

When Jo finally did take my order and make my sandwich, she called me Mr. Dudley—thought it was my name, asked Cass if Mr. Dudley wanted fries—before Cass let her know it was short for Dudley Do-Right. "It's a cop thing," Cass said, the two of us smirking and snorting, not very professional on the part of yours truly. By this time Jo was smiling. "First time all day," Cass whispered to me when Jo had gone back into the kitchen.

We've got along fine since, and I do believe Jo likes me well enough. At least she's started talking somewhat, and that's good: you need friends in this world. A little kindness goes a long way, whether it's small animals, or guys just this side of crime, or the strays that wash up at Cass's Roadside Café.

Cass and I have that much in common: looking out for people. One thing I've learned from this job, no point in being a hardass.

Before I was transferred to Middleton I was stationed in Vancouver, where for a summer and fall I was put on Commie detail. Must be just about twenty years ago, now, which tells you how long I've been here. Everyone was talking about the red threat, and we tailed everybody with a Communist Party card and a trunkful of pamphlets. I had a minor guy, J.P. Johnston, who was doing some advance work for the party leader slated to give a lecture on campus in a couple of weeks. He drove a yellow Dodge sedan, and we always joked it should be red. Johnston knew I was tailing him, of course, and after a while neither of us made any secret of the relationship. I felt no animosity towards the man. And I had no real direction to do anything but watch him and make him nervous, which I didn't, particularly. After a while, all that road, all those miles of nothing but trees sometimes, he started to feel more like a friend than the enemy.

I was following his taillights one evening, not too far outside of Hope. I was about a million miles away, thinking about I don't know what, when I saw him brake, saw the Dodge swerve, then disappear over the bank. I put on my flashers, caught up with his car in a second, in the process hitting the doe he'd unsuccessfully tried to avoid and finishing the job. The deer was good and dead and the impact had pushed her well enough onto the shoulder that I wasn't worried about another accident. Whatever damage the cruiser had sustained could wait. I could see in my headlights where the tracks went over the edge, and I pulled over, my light sending cherry-coloured beacons across the trunks of the trees. I called it in, and then went down over the bank, my boots sliding in the gravel. The car was down there all right, nudged up against a big pine but the ragged terrain and about a dozen saplings, snapped in his wake, must have slowed him down some. I found him groggy, blood on the steering wheel from the gash in his forehead, but conscious. He gave me a half-grin.

"Handy you were right behind me, officer" he said. "What kind of luck is that, eh?"

I held my handkerchief against his head. He looked pale in the light reflected off the trees from his headlights, and I reached across him to turn the motor off. I had radioed for an ambulance, and I told him that. He was shaking, maybe a bit of shock, and I saw a jacket on the back seat so I pulled it forward, tucking it around him.

"Thanks," he whispered. He grabbed my hand and held it.

We were there about fifteen minutes before the ambulance showed, but it seemed like forever. The car was making strange creaking noises, and something dripped. You could smell gasoline, but there was no flame, no sparks, and I didn't want to move him. It seemed as if something was broken, but I couldn't tell what.

"Should pay more attention to your driving," I told him, just to say something, extracting my hand and shifting on my haunches.

"Deer came out of nowhere."

"Well, they do that."

Above us on the highway a car went by, a whoosh, then another. I could hear the downshift of some rig, knew they'd be wondering what the cruiser was doing on the side with its flashers on, but thinking to leave whatever it was to Canada's Finest.

"It's not easy when you don't fit, is it?" Johnston said after a while.

"What?"

"You know what I mean." He was looking at me, looking inside me. I looked away and coughed into my sleeve while I kept the handkerchief against his forehead, hoped the blood flow was slowing, wondering where the hell the ambulance was. We heard the siren, then, still a ways off, but nonetheless obliterating all other sound while we listened to its wail. As it neared, he repeated what he'd said before. "You know what I mean." Eyes on mine.

When the flashlight from the local cruiser found us we were just there sitting in the awkwardness that followed, me with my handkerchief still pressed against Johnston's forehead. But when I looked up into the glare there must have been an expression of guilt in my face, of being caught out.

The officer thought he saw something between us, and this fed the suspicions that had been growing anyway. As I later came to realize, my colleagues had been talking about me for a long time. Whatever I said in my defence made no difference, which is why I'm now stationed in Middleton, have been for years against all Force policy, a dead-end posting if there ever was one. Which is how I came to find myself drinking coffee at Cass's Roadside Café most days of the week.

I used to mind, but not so much, now. It's just a matter of how you choose to see things, that's all. When Jo asks if I need a refill on my coffee, I'll tell her my cup is half full, my little joke with myself. Then I'll tell her to top it up anyway.

Wayward wind

One glowing ember
Dancing in playful danger
Rides a wayward wind
— Anonymous haiku

It was yesterday that Bob noticed him for the first time. It was in town, the hippie kid leaning against the wall of the local bar, a row of motorcycles parked outside. Bob was sitting in the cruiser across the road, watching; just keeping an eye on things. The guy who came up behind the hippie from the back parking lot walked into him as if he wasn't there. There was a mile of empty air on both sides of him, and Bob could hear the outraged "hey!" The man who turned with a smirk had short hair. He was wearing regular clothing: plaid shirt, jeans. Through the car window, the words were audible.

"Got a problem, hippie?" he tossed out. Then he saw the cop car, and ducked quickly into the cave of the bar.

The cruiser pulled up alongside. "Get inside," Bob told the young man.

"What was I doing?"

"Nothing. I just want to give you a bit of advice."

Bob let him off at the edge of town. "Most folks around here believe in live-and-let-live. Most, so long as you don't bother them, won't bother you. Don't care where you came from, or why. But the bar you were sitting outside of, well, you were asking for trouble. You didn't want to be there. Believe me. I just did you a favour."

Now, Bob sits in the cruiser thinking about the hippie. So many kids on the road these days. What are they looking for?

The cruiser is parked a little off the road where the brush is thick: Bob's waiting for speeders. Every car that passes is doing just under the limit, as if someone is up ahead tipping them off, but he knows the notion is ridiculous. He's well hidden, on a scrubby side road in a dip just past where the highway enters a straight stretch and the urge to hit the gas after all those curves, for most motorists, is too much to resist; he's been there himself.

He waits, and while he waits, he thinks about family: the one that doesn't speak of him, and the one he almost had. His wife, Marjorie, had him figured out early, when he still had himself fooled. Now, he has a friend in Bruford he meets every couple of weeks who works for the fire department. It works for both of them, the need for discretion equal.

The wind whips around the car, the humming as it skirts the car's exterior. What a day it's been: a squall here, and then, two miles up the road, not a drop. A car passes, a blue Valiant with dice dangling from the rearview mirror. He knows this car from town: Perry LaRivière owns it. He's never seen Perry drive so slowly. He'd like to stop him anyway, checks for a tail-light burned out or some other excuse, but there's nothing. He watches until the Valiant is out of sight.

Bob starts the ignition and pulls back onto the highway.

There is no quota, not really, but you should nail *somebody* over three hours running a speed trap.

As he passes a pullout he sees an older man looking over a map as he leans against the door of an old grey truck, vapour from his wet rain jacket steaming in the sun. Mountain weather, Bob thinks, accelerating. You just never know what it's going to throw at you.

On the left there's an overgrown skid track that leads to Howie's cabin. Recently empty, the cabin is already becoming a party place for some of the local teenagers. Bob drives partway in, then parks the cruiser to walk the rest of the way after calling in his whereabouts, letting dispatch know he'll inspect the place, do one more run through town, then be signing out for lunch. His concern about the cabin is as personal as it is official; he knew its former occupant well. Teenagers smashing beer bottles, making out: it's just disrespectful. As he approaches, it's clear there is someone here: a pair of boots outside the cabin door. The door is ajar, letting in late morning light and fresh air. As he approaches, a figure appears in the doorway.

It's that kid, the hippie he gave the ride out of town to, who, obviously aware he is trespassing, bolts out the door and around the corner.

"Hey!" yells Bob.

The flat Moroccan sandals on the kid's feet are useless on the forest floor; Bob can hear him panting, crashing, and then falling. He catches up easily and hauls Pink to his feet.

"It was abandoned," Pink explains. There are dead leaves and pine needles on his clothes, in his hair. "I didn't do any damage."

The older man looks at the younger in the morning light, filtered through a canopy of pines. "Why did you run?"

They walk back together. Bob pokes his head into the cabin and looks around, but doesn't enter immediately. It looks neat enough. The pack is still inside, a few things left lying around on the table, the bed. "I was just leaving," he says when Bob turns.

"The cabin belonged to a friend of mine," Bob tells him. "What's your name?"

"Elvis," a pause, while Bob raises his eyebrows, waiting. "Preston."

"Really?"

"Yeah. I know."

The sunlight is warm. Around them, the birds, quiet during the flight and capture, resume. There are crickets singing in the long grass in the clearing around the cabin.

"Been thinking of taking this cabin down," Bob says. "Partiers. Vandalism. It's a safety issue. It's Crown land, after all."

"No rides. I needed a break from the road," explains Pink, although Bob hasn't asked. "What happened to your friend?"

"Died," Bob tells him. "In the cabin." He watches for a reaction, but the kid is looking at the cabin with new reverence. "Wow. Sorry, man."

"Just going to check on it," says Bob. "See everything's in its place."

Pink watches the cop walk into the cabin, panicking inwardly. *Where's the weed? Where did I leave it? On the floor beside the bed? Did I put it away? Is it on the table? Oh, man, it's on the table. Shit.* He looks in; he can't help it, so when the cop picks up the baggie, Pink is there in the doorway. Pink sighs. There is nothing to lose. "Want a toke, man?" he asks weakly.

The cabin is a fairy-tale hideaway, its roof moss-covered, the smallest, most delicate yellow flowers growing up out of the soft green. It looks magical: the clearing, the sunlight, tiny multicoloured wildflowers in the grass. There are birds everywhere, their songs slipping about the branches. The scent of earth and pine is sweet. To Pink, anything seems possible. But the cop shakes his head, and Pink knows he's gone too far. He waits for it, but the tone, when the Mountie speaks, surprises him.

"I *am* a cop." Almost apologetic.

There is a long silence that Pink tries his best to read, but can't. The cop stands with the baggie in his hand, looking around the cabin.

"Time you headed off to wherever it is you're going," he says finally. "I never saw you."

Bob stands aside, then, and Pink moves past him and begins to pack up his stuff. His socks, drying at the foot of the bed, he stuffs into a side pocket. On the bed lies a heart-shaped rock that had been sitting on a shelf. Impulsively, he pushes it into the pocket with his socks. When he turns, packed, the Mountie is sitting on the one chair at the table, the bag in both hands, sifting the brownish green bud back and forth and looking at it closely.

"You ever smoked?" Pink asks, his voice coming out in a bit of a croak. It is a gamble; he can feel his heart speed up just a little. He's been given a break, there's no need to push it. Yet he's pretty sure that what he senses in the cop is curiosity. "Nobody's going to know. It could be, uh, *research*."

The cop appears to consider this. He hands the bag to Pink. Inside are rolling papers, the bearded fellow illustrating the cover looking more like a friendly sailor than anything else.

They sit on the step in a patch of sunlight. Bob—as he introduced himself—watches, mesmerized, while Pink—who, as a gesture of solidarity, offered the name he is using these days—rolls with long, expert fingers, tapping down the buds, forming a neat cylinder, licking the paper. The two ends twisted, Pink runs the whole thing lengthwise between his lips. Shooting a look at the cop, he lights the joint. "Like this." Inhaling, holding. Letting out the smoke with a soft exhale. "It's Thai," he says into the smoke. "Good weed."

The words Pink hears Bob mumble are: "against my better judgment." He doesn't appear to realize he's uttered them, so Pink says nothing. Bob coughs, and keeps coughing for several moments. The birds in the clearing fall silent, and then, one by one, begin to sing.

"Nothing's happening," says Bob to Pink, who is inhaling now, eyes closed. "Give it a minute," he croaks through a closed throat.

A few minutes later the joint is gone and the birdsong has taken on a new dimension for them both. They are quiet, sitting together on the step.

"Remarkable," says Bob.

"Uh huh."

"Like my head is full of something . . . woolly."

Pink grins and looks at him sideways. "Got any food?" he asks.

Bob does. He has one of Cass's cinnamon buns. It might be a little stale: he's been carrying it in the car since yesterday. Jo had chosen the biggest one to wrap in wax paper, so large she couldn't fit it in the brown paper bag. In the end, she'd just given it to him. "Too big for the bag," she said.

"A happy problem."

"Yeah. I guess it is." She'd given him a half-smile, then, and he'd felt the room light up the way it does when someone who doesn't smile often decides to. He was happier about that smile than the size of the cinnamon bun, but now, as he gets up to get it, he finds he's pretty happy about that, too.

There is an issue with depth perception as Bob makes his way to the car. Pink watches, knowing that, for Bob, his boots on the path are at that moment sharper, closer, and the mechanism of brain to motor function quite astonishing as a process, knows that Bob will be amazed he has never considered this before, and that as he does, he will start smiling. As the Mountie turns, grinning, Pink knows he's right.

Half the lukewarm coffee goes into Pink's blue tin camp cup. They sit in the doorway on the step, each leaning against one side of the doorframe. To Pink, the coffee tastes great, even if it's cold. To Bob, it's a whole different drink. But it's the cinnamon bun that really surprises him, and Pink laughs at the look on his face.

"It's a trip, eh, man?"

"Yeah," says Bob.

The sun, higher in the sky now, warms the clearing.

"It's like the road," Pink continues. "After a while it's not about getting there. It's about *going* there. Know what I mean?"

"No," says Bob. "Yes."

Bob starts laughing, and Pink, stoned, laughs too. It's a while before either of them can speak.

"Want another toke?"

"Yeah," says Bob.

They smoke in silence, and when the roach is finished they both lean back and look up at the tree canopy. There doesn't seem to be anything more to say, so neither of them speaks. The woods around them settle into midday. Pink lies back, thinking about Stan and Nora. What they might be thinking, wondering where he is. If he wrote them, what would he say? I'm hitchhiking with the wind?

"Where did you come from?" Bob asks, and Pink wonders if he was thinking out loud.

"Been here all the time."

"No, really. Before here."

He could lie, but he doesn't. "Washington State. It's a long story." There is a moment when Pink thinks about being in Canada, no papers, nothing. But then he thinks: I've just smoked a reefer with a cop. What have I got to worry about?

Bob plucks a piece of grass from beside the step and inserts it between his teeth. It was time to leave a long time ago. "That's the problem with this marijuana, obviously," he says aloud. "It makes you feel like not doing anything."

"Yep."

"You have parents?" Bob asks.

"Yeah. I'm adopted, actually, when I was six or so, by my aunt and uncle."

"And your parents?"

"Accident."

"So they took you in. What do they think of you being up here?"

"They don't know. I haven't been in touch."

The image of Nora, smoothing his shirt, adjusting his collar before he stepped on the bus in Pullman, so proud of his college scholarship. When he was in high school, Nora had sat with him evenings at the kitchen table, working through grade ten math problems right alongside him. "And Nora, with only grade nine herself," he once heard Kevin's mother say to a neighbour as he let himself in the back door to slip up to Kevin's room.

"I . . . dropped out of college. Nothing made any sense. I couldn't see why any of it mattered."

"Hmmmm."

"There was this girl I tripped with. Gorgeous eyes. Beautiful. In the morning she was packing up to hit the road, heading for Canada. I just . . . followed her. We got across the border on a Greyhound bus that took almost all of my money. When I woke up that first morning in the hostel in Vancouver, she'd taken the rest of it. I ended up working at the hostel, which is where I met Simon, who, I guess, started it all."

Bob leans back against the cabin doorframe. The sun makes him want to close his eyes, so he closes them, while Pink speaks; his words wrapped in something like cottonwood fluff. As Pink begins, Bob remembers, as a child, wanting to walk into the pages of the fairy-tale book, ride beside the prince on his horse. Listening to Pink's story, he feels as if that leap has occurred, the difference between listener and storyteller indecipherable. He is magically, wonderfully, in the moment.

Pink meets Limey Simon at the Vancouver commune he finds after spending a couple of chilly nights in Stanley Park, shortly after arriving in Canada. The Englishman is serving up a communal dinner at a table made from a door set on sawhorses. Nobody really knows where Simon came from, but one day after he and Pink smoke a few joints, Simon tells him. They're in an upstairs room in the big house on Venables, mattresses pushed up against the wall. The attic window is open, the evening breeze warm.

"It happened in Cheltenham, during my clergical training a few years ago."

"Clergical training?"

"Reverend Simon to you, mate."

"You're kidding."

"Nope."

"Far out," says Pink, settling back against the pillows.

"I was just finishing up my year and heading to the pub for a celebratory pint with my mates. I was driving an ancient old beast, then. You didn't really see hitchhikers out on those narrow lanes, but here was a black fellow waving me down. I fancied myself a progressive and so made a point of stopping, when some of my mates wouldn't have. Helping your fellow man is, after all, the point, isn't it?"

"Yeah. 'Course."

"So, right. I pick up this chap and he climbs in and I swear I could hear his stomach growling as soon as he's got himself tucked in. 'I have some apples in the boot,' I told him, but then I remembered I had taken them out. If this fellow was disappointed he hid it well, just smiled and told me he was going to meet his girl in London. 'I'm only going to Gloucester, to the pub,' I told him. That was okay with him. I apologized for the car—it was a horrible old thing that belched blue smoke and rattled like a tin can, more rust than metal, held together with holes, you could say—but he said he was just grateful for the ride, and if it came to needing a push, at least I'd have an extra set of muscles. Well, that made us pals if we weren't before, I'll tell you.

"Then he started telling me his story, just like I'm telling you this story, just like you'll tell your story to somebody else—" Pink, inhaling, holding, entertains the notion of stories within stories, like the disappearing picture on the tin can of hard candies: on the can a picture of another can, and on that can a picture of another can . . .

"—and by the time he was finished I wanted to take him all the way to Oxford. Getting robbed like that, by people who picked him up and whom he'd trusted, even taking the ring he was bringing to ask his girl to marry him. Leaving him sitting on the side of the road, half his stuff still in the boot of their car as they beetled off."

"You believed him?" even to Pink in the haze of the moment it sounds like bullshit, a story calculated to elicit sympathy.

"Well, I reasoned he was either as desperate as he said he was because he was robbed, or desperate enough to lie, and either way I was sympathetic. Compassion is what I'd been taught, after all."

"You didn't care about looking like an idiot?"

"It all gets sorted out in Heaven, mate," says Simon. "Anyhow, we're coming up to the pub and my mates are waiting outside the door, all of them messengers of the Lord but not a teetotaller among them. We'd raise our glasses in a toast: Let the Spirits be With You, we'd say. I looked at my passenger, feeling sorry for the long trip ahead of him. 'I'd like to take you all the way, mate,' I told him, but he said this was fine, he was sure to get a ride soon, happy in the anticipation of seeing his girl, however long it took. But I was thinking about him, stomach growling, arriving with nothing in his pockets and no ring to give her, and I pulled over across the street from the Queen's Head, my mates no doubt wondering all the while who the Wog was—that's what we called the blacks, we didn't even think about it—I had in the car. I had received a hundred pounds as a graduation present from my aunt. I had been off to buy a round and then a good suit and shoes to set me on my way. I gave it to him.

"'I can't take this,' he told me. 'Then consider it a loan,' I said. 'We'll meet in one year right here, at this pub.' I looked at my watch, 'Five-thirty.' "

"And did you?"

"Well, that's the story. A whole lot happened in that year. I wanted to come to Canada then, actually, but one thing after another seemed to get in the way. One of my mates got sick and I ended up taking over his parish for a while, a little rural village full of old ladies who thought I was far too young to know anything. It was a bloody awful year during which I made enough gaffes from the pulpit that the church had reprimanded me about as much as they were going to.

"Things going as they were, I started to think about the fellow in my car, and wondered how he fared. By then I was facing a sort of mutiny at the hands of the parish ladies, and so I wrote my superior and suggested a replacement for me might be in order, perhaps someone older, thereby saving him the trouble. And with not much money and no longer any vehicle, I found my way to the Gloucester pub on the appointed day, at the appointed time. I wasn't so much interested in the money, you understand. But I wanted to know if he was really the chap I thought he was; if I'd read him right."

"And?"

"He was standing outside, waiting for me. I was delighted to see him. 'Can I stand you a pint?' I offered. But no, he said, his wife and new baby were waiting for him. 'Where's your car?' he asked me, and I told him it had long given up the ghost.

" 'That's good,' he said, and I wondered why, but he went on. 'We got out of London,' he began. 'Good!' I said, and he nodded, continuing. 'No place for a wee one. I got a job at a tire shop, and then moved on to fixing autos up, selling them.' 'You've done well, then,' I said. 'Very well. I've brought your hundred pounds.' I was more than delighted, and pleased with myself for trusting my fellow man. Then he pointed to a pretty blue Mini across the street. 'It's in the glovebox.'

" 'Have I got to go take it out?' I asked, thinking he'd left my money in there. I was confused, because by now he was grinning from ear to ear. 'You can take it out now, or you can drive somewhere else and take it out, doesn't matter to me, mate.' And then I see he's holding out the keys. 'A good turn deserves a good turn,' he says.

"He had to leave. We said goodbye, and I realized after he'd sped off that I didn't get his name, but then I thought: as far as he's concerned, the book's closed, isn't it? But it never really is. It just goes on. Stories. Good turns. Perfect, really."

"Hey, what happened to the minister thing? Aren't you supposed to be in a church?"

"This IS my church. Well, the world is, I guess. I let the wind take me where I'm needed, and it took me here."

"The wind, huh?"

When Pink decides to hit the road a few days later, "Go with the wind, mate," says Simon over one last reefer, and they both laugh about it a little too long.

When he heads out to the highway, there's only one way to go: east. It's also the direction of the wind. Pink remembers the wind, the night of the fire, the pull of it. He begins walking in the direction of its gentle persuasion. It's all the plan he has.

They sit for a while, and Bob can feel himself coming down. This has probably been foolish. Definitely. This has definitely been foolish. What was he thinking?

"How do you decide when to stop?" he asks Pink.

"Stop?"

"Yeah. You going to just hitchhike around for the rest of your life?"

"I figure I'll know when the journey's over."

"How?"

"A sign, man. I'm just waiting for a sign."

Pink's cup, tied to his pack, bangs against the boots tied there as they walk up the path. At the cruiser, they pause, Bob's hand on the door, while Pink looks towards the cars passing on the main road, thinking of missed lifts. Bob drops him up a ways at a truck pullout, a good hitchhiking spot.

"Thanks, man," Pink says.

Bob nods curtly and pulls out onto the highway. Chances are excellent that Cass has a good soup on, and a BLT sounds just about right.

1:05 p.m.
Toasted BLT

The black and white car that pulls in is covered with leaves as the wind whips up again. To Jo, it looks as if a dust devil has descended to dance right in front of the door. Do they only spin in one direction? Clockwise, or counterclockwise?

Jo met Bob on her first day on the job. He made her laugh, she remembers. Something about a sandwich. He enters, brushing off the shoulders of his uniform. Jo likes him, and yet, cops can be so inscrutable, she thinks. They give nothing away.

"What's up, Jo?" he asks as he settles himself at the counter.

"Not much. Vegetable beef today."

"Okay. And a bacon, lettuce, and tomato. Can you do that?"

Jo shoots him a look that says: *Of course I can; what do you think?* and heads for the kitchen.

"Coffee? Did I need to say it?"

Jo re-emerges. "Sorry. Forgot."

As she pours his coffee, Bob feels the urge to talk. Maybe it's the residual effects of the dope. Maybe it's living alone, no real conversation today except at the detachment, before he went out to bust non-existent speeders. Maybe it's having just been at the cabin with Pink that makes him ask: "Cass ever mention Howie?"

"The guy that lived in the cabin? The retarded guy?" Jo has come across the cabin before, out walking one day after closing up, but, unsure if it was occupied, didn't approach. She'd asked Cass about it later, and Cass had explained that when she inherited the restaurant, she seemed to have inherited Howie, a relative of the former owner. Inheriting Howie meant seeing he had enough to eat, that he had what he needed, a duty picked up by locals between café owners, then happily handed back once Cass turned up.

"Howie—had his own way about him," Bob allows, now. "I'm going to take that cabin down. So it doesn't become a party place. Public safety issue. You know."

"Uh, sure." Jo pushes back through the swinging doors, pulls the bacon from the cooler, fires five pieces onto the hot grill, filling the air with the pungent, smoky smell.

"She ever tell you about that niece of hers, and Howie, what happened?" Bob calls through the window.

"No," Jo answers. On the grill, the bacon sizzles and spits. It's several minutes before she emerges from the kitchen, soup and sandwich in hand.

"You want to hear it?" Bob asks when she sets them down. "Got time?"

Jo looks at the empty restaurant and smiles. "Sure."

The mayonnaise drips out between the toast pieces, and Bob carefully wipes it from his moustache. "When I asked Donnie about it afterwards—that's Cass's niece—she kept talking about Derflops."

"About what?"

"That's pretty much what I said. But you know, she wasn't quite four years old, though she was smart as a whip: could count to twenty, and knew her ABCs. Still, between her and Howie, it was hard to get the whole story, but I managed to piece it together."

Bob takes another bite of his sandwich.

"It was October. I remember, because hunting season had just opened. And it must have been a Sunday, because Cass used to close on Sundays. Anyway, Cass told me she'd managed to convince Donnie to take a nap that day, Cass having been up late watching TV and drinking a little rye and ginger the way she liked to, and she was feeling like a nap herself. Donnie was used to amusing herself, but she must have got hungry because she wandered over to the restaurant, got herself a sandwich of some kind from the fridge. When Cass woke up and couldn't find the girl, she ran around calling at first, worried. Then she noticed that Donnie had taken her rock with her. It was a river rock, heart-shaped, that Donnie had kept on the shelf beside her bed since the day she and her mother—in a rare time of mother-daughter togetherness, far as I can tell—found it by the creek. Then, Cass found the fridge door open, and the drawer where the paper bags were kept, and she put it together. That's when she called me.

"She figured that Donnie might have wandered off to have a picnic in the woods. Cass told me she'd taught her that song, 'Teddy Bear's Picnic,' just that morning. If you think about it, it kind of makes sense, you know? I was about twenty minutes out, nobody closer. It's a big territory, and there was a domestic dispute that day, some sort of standoff had the detachment pretty busy. I told Cass to stay close to the diner, just keep calling for her. Didn't think she could get too far on those little legs of hers."

"Wouldn't she be worried someone had taken her?"

"Well, it's the middle of nowhere here, really, and about fifteen years ago. Different times. Bigger danger was that she'd wandered onto the highway. When I finally got there, Cass was running up the road calling and she was checking the ditch. Don't think I'll ever forget her face, the look on it."

"And?" Jo can imagine the panic, the desperate need to find the missing child.

"We started expanding our search. It was easier with two. Problem was, we didn't know how long she had been gone. We didn't know she was with Howie. Funny thing, we didn't even think about Howie, though it seemed obvious after."

"But that's where she was?"

"Yeah. I have to wonder what Donnie would have thought when she saw Howie. He was tall, quite a bit taller than me," says Bob. "But kind of like a big kid himself, and so she may have seen that in him, the way kids do, sometimes."

Jo nods, knowing what he means. As Bob speaks, Jo wonders when that childhood clarity left her, and where it has gone.

The man wore a brown plaid shirt and brown canvas pants hiked high on his hips. He didn't see Donnie at first, and as he went to his woodpile he sang a song: *She'll be coming 'round the mountain, she'll be coming 'round the mountain.* He sang it several times, then when he had his arms loaded up with pieces of firewood he turned and saw the little girl, and when he did he whispered: *when she comes.* And dropped them.

"Uh, oh," he said, like he was finishing the song. Then he walked back inside and shut the door. He opened it again half a minute later. "Little girl," he called out, looking down at the ground instead of at Donnie. "Little girl, who are you?"

"Donnie," she told him, then: "my name is Donalda Eve Sherbansky." She enunciated each part carefully.

He closed the door again. She could hear him singing on the other side: *She'll be wearing red pyjamas when she comes.* He opened it again, his head bent under the doorframe.

"I've seen you. At the restaurant. Do you want to come inside?"

Donnie held out the brown paper bag, and he nodded like he knew all along a girl would come to visit, and that she'd be bringing lunch. He stepped back and opened the door wide, and she walked over the sill and into a one-room cabin with a wood stove, a cot with a grey wool blanket against the wall, a scratched orange kitchen table, and one wooden chair. On the row of hooks by the door hung an oilskin raincoat, a plaid jacket, and a bright hunter's vest. There was a sink with a bucket underneath and shelves above holding tinned food and gallon pickle jars with teabags, sugar, flour. He turned over the empty wood box and sat on it carefully. Donnie sat on the wooden chair, her toes dangling above the floor. He looked at her paper bag and she opened it, unwrapped the sandwich, and gave him half. He took it, looked at it seriously, and took a bite.

"Turkey," he said, and smiled in its direction, his teeth full of white bread.

"Cass made it," Donnie told him. She watched him while he chewed.

"I have cookies," he said, his mouth full, and he set his sandwich down, crossed the room, opened one of the big jars and took out a crumpled bag of chocolate marshmallow cookies. "Derflops," he said, holding the bag open.

Inside, some of the cookies were broken, but she found a whole one and pulled it out. She hadn't eaten her sandwich, and she knew she was supposed to eat that first, so she set the cookie on the table.

"Why do you call them Derflops?"

"Just do," he said, and took one out of the bag and set it down carefully, opposite Donnie's. They ate their sandwiches quietly. He finished well before Donnie, then wet his finger and began picking up crumbs off the table. When it was clean, he put his cookie inside the cleaned area and waited for Donnie to finish.

"What's your name?" she asked him.

"Howie," he said, and began eating the cookie. Using his bottom teeth, he ate all of the chocolate off the marshmallow top—his teeth never nicking the spongy white surface—right down to the cookie base. Then, he nibbled off the marshmallow down to the little dollop of red jam. He licked this off, and began eating the base in spirals until he reached a centre portion too small to nibble. Then he popped it into his mouth. He looked up at the ceiling and smiled. "Your turn," he said.

Donnie took the cookie and put the whole thing in her mouth. It made her cheeks bulge out like a chipmunk, and she started to laugh, crumbs spraying out across the table. Howie started to laugh too, great, loud guffaws that filled up the room. Then he stopped. When he spoke, he spoke to the table. "I have Snakes and Ladders," he said. "Would you like to play?"

Donnie nodded, and he got out a worn board and a pair of dice. The long snakes were green, the shorter snakes pink. Donnie liked them better than the ladders, but you had to go up the ladders if you wanted to win.

They played several games. Sometimes, Donnie would get to the top of the board first, and sometimes Howie. As soon as the game was over Howie would clap his hands and move their men to the start again. But when the sun dipped and the light in the cabin changed, Donnie began to think about home. She didn't want to be in Howie's cabin anymore. She wanted to go home.

"I have to go," she said.

"Don't go," he said. "You can go up all the ladders. I don't mind." But she was standing up. "You can have another Derflop. Would you like another Derflop?" He put his hand on her arm. It was a big hand, covered in hair, and it scared her. "They're not called Derflops!" she shouted, backing up. "They're Mallo-Puffs!"

He stepped back, his hands in the air, backing up until the backs of his knees bumped into the cot. "It's okay," he whispered. "It's okay." And he began to sing at the ceiling, loudly, his hands over his ears. *And she'll have to sleep with grandma and she'll have to sleep with grandma and she'll have to sleep with grandma when she comes.*

Donnie, hand in her pocket, could feel the heart-shaped rock nestled there. She could see it in her mind, the way it was so perfectly shaped, pinkish-grey. She put the rock on the table, and she ran.

"Wait!" called Howie. "Wait, it's not safe!" As she ran up the path she could hear him calling, the sound of his feet pounding behind her.

She could see the highway through the trees when the shot rang out. She heard yelling behind her, and as she turned she saw him rolling on the ground like an animal, making a high-pitched noise, and she started running again, away from the sound. She remembered looking at her shoes as she ran, then seeing them rise off the ground as she was lifted from behind, something gripping her shoulders, and she screamed. The big hand that covered her mouth smelled of sweat and something sharp, like metal. "Quiet," said a voice urgently. "It's okay. Shhhh."

"Howie had followed her almost all the way back to Cass's before he was winged by a hunter. The hunter had caught a movement in the trees and assumed it was deer," says Bob. "Happens every year, accidents like that."

Jo has sat down, a bowl of soup in front of her. Bob's the only customer Cass doesn't mind her sitting down with.

"He was trying to follow her, to keep her safe. But he forgot his hunting vest. He always wore it in the woods, even when it wasn't hunting season, so he'd be seen."

"We always looked out for Howie, Cass and I. Cass saved him day-olds from here, and I'd drop by a couple of times a week. She'd go by and clean sometimes, although he kept the place pretty tidy all on his own. I used to bring him these cookies he liked, the chocolate marshmallow kind."

"He just lived there by himself? He wasn't lonely?"

"Didn't seem to be. Howie was nervous around people. He liked his own surroundings, where he felt safe."

"Seems kind of sad."

"Hard to say. I don't know how Howie came to be there, to tell you the truth, or what might have happened to him to scare him off people. You don't always know a person's history." Bob pushed his coffee cup forward. "Can you top me up?"

Jo, her soup finished, clears the dishes and refills Bob's cup.

"Thanks. So anyway, following Donnie was no small thing for Howie, I figure. And what happened was exactly what Cass and I had been warning him about."

They are both quiet for a few minutes, Bob sipping his coffee. Jo pours one for herself.

"The hunter who winged him drove him in his pickup to the hospital, Howie yelling all the way. The other one brought Donnie over to the café and told Cass he'd found her lost, and she was so relieved she didn't ask much. He didn't mention the shooting. I think they were probably just young guys, up from the city, pretty inexperienced. Neither stuck around after that, with Howie delivered to the hospital and Donnie brought home. Figure they didn't want trouble. By the time I circled back to find Donnie in Cass's arms, there was no sign of either of them.

"The hospital experience scared the daylights out of Howie. He wouldn't talk about it at all when I took him home. Before the hospital I could sometimes get him to come for coffee at Cass's. But after the hospital, he never went anywhere, just stayed in his cabin. But he talked about Donnie, long after she and her mother—Cass's sister—took off. I think he really missed her. I know he kept the rock she gave him. Funny, isn't it, how some people you wouldn't expect to have something special between them?"

"Maybe he just found someone to play with."

"Yeah, maybe. He kept hoping she'd come back to visit him, kept asking if I'd bring her, and it took me a long time to tell him that Donnie probably wouldn't be back. He didn't say much at the time, just started drumming his fingers on the table. He was still drumming when I left him.

"About a month ago when I went to check on him I found him dead, in his bed. He looked like he went natural, and not very long before; maybe a day passed at most. And those sandwiches Cass been sending with me, the day-olds? Found a couple of weeks' worth in a bin outside. You wouldn't believe the smell when I opened the lid. I don't think he could swallow at the end, figure maybe it was throat cancer. I did try to get him to hospital, you know, when he started losing weight. No way he'd go. That cabin was his whole world."

There's a moment in which they are both quiet. On the highway there is the whoosh of a car, not stopping, the destination of greater pull than the promise of pie.

"Never did find any relatives," says Bob finally.

"How could someone have no-one?" Jo cups her hands around her coffee to feel its warmth. "Everyone's got to have somebody, somewhere."

"You'd think so, wouldn't you? Couldn't even find a birth certificate."

Jo shivers. It feels cold in the restaurant, and yet the sun is shining.

"Gotta go," says Bob, leaving a five on the table. Then: "Glad you're here, Jo. You make a good BLT." He grins. "Cass always skimps on the bacon."

Jo

A bird is singing outside, the sound far larger than the bird; light splashes across the floor. A million tiny details spinning, and I stand here in the middle of them. How is it that one person's world can stop while everyone else's goes on?

In the house in Calgary, my mother and father go on with their lives. Eamon, wherever he is, snakes his way through the grass. I have no idea what happened after I left, and I don't want to know. It doesn't matter anymore.

My friends—the friends I had—attend their classes, go to parties, get drunk, wake up and complain about their hangovers, and speculate on whether or not they'll see the boy, again, who copped a feel in the corner by the bar.

What determines the size of someone's world: how small or how large it can be?

Genevieve sleeps, the press of earth above her, flowers growing.

Somewhere, my daughter sleeps in a woman's arms.

And I am sleeping in a cot in the back room of a trailer behind a diner on a mountain pass.

Cass

Sometimes I feel like all I've ever done is take in drifters. Seems like every kicked dog comes my way, every little thing that needs looking after. Archie's strays, cats from who-knows-where. Howie, of course, but he came with the place, part of the terms of ownership, you could say, and a kind soul in his way. Truth is, I suppose I like having someone to cluck over now and then.

Apple doesn't fall far from the tree, really. When we were teenagers the house seemed always full of kids with no place to go, living downtown like we did, and Dad gone half the time. There was always another loaf of bread, another jar of peanut butter. We never went hungry. If my sisters and I fought over who was wearing whose clothes, we were quick to lend a bra or a sweater to whoever showed up at the door looking lost. For all of my mother's gruffness, her husky voice and sharp tongue, there was a kindness there. Bottom line for all of us, there was that.

These days someone says boo! it's a capital offence. People need to learn to hear the words under the words. So when I tell Jo to get to work, like today, when I need a day off and I figure she knows the ropes well enough to go it on her own, and I say: 'bout time you started pulling your weight, don't you think? what I'm really saying is: I know you can do this and while you're at it you'll find out you have the smarts to look after yourself. A little hand up isn't a hand out. It's a way to say you know someone's got something to give, and they're worth a little investment.

Bob likes the girl, all right. Been sitting in there for over an hour, talking her ear off no doubt. Cops are always sitting down for coffee, like they've got nothing better to do. But there he goes, heading off at last to go catch some speeder somewhere, make his quota whatever that is, and now hellooooo sunshine: there's a yellow car pulled into the lot, lady dressed in yellow getting out, looks like an egg salad to me. Not just the colour, either. You get so as you can call 'em: hamburger & fries; slice of pie; cinnamon bun; eggs over easy. Whatever. This one's an egg salad sandwich if I ever saw one, not something Jo's likely to have any trouble with. Besides, there's a soap coming on the tube. Everyone needs a day off once in a while.

Rough winds do shake the darling buds of May.

— William Shakespeare

Evelyn keeps looking over her shoulder, although she can't quite remember why. It's a beautiful day, now that the sun's come out. The leaves on the trees sparkle from the recent rain; from the road, vapour lifts in fairy tendrils. She loves driving the Rambler, loves its butter yellow colour. When she dressed this morning in her yellow suit and hat, white gloves and pumps, she thought of the picture she would make, stepping out of her car at the library. "Pretty as a picture you are," Bryce would always say, and so she always tried to be. Then, as she appraised herself in the hallway mirror, she remembered about Bryce. Evelyn has a hard time holding onto thoughts.

Bryce doesn't like Evelyn to go very far. In fact, he forbids Evelyn to go very far. "This town is all you need, darling," he tells her, and she believes him. At least, she did until yesterday. In town there is a pharmacy, a hardware store, a small library, and a medical clinic. At the Fashion Shoppe, the clerk knows her favourite colours. There are a handful of restaurants, from the Tastee De-Light to the Lucky Dragon. The movie theatre that shows each movie for three days, by which time everybody who wants to has seen it. Evelyn knows the town, from one edge to the other, and that's all. It's enough; Bryce says so.

When Evelyn goes to City Hall to politely suggest the placement of more planters on the sidewalks, or to the shoe store for polish, or the greengrocer for tomatoes, everybody knows her by name. For Evelyn, there is an invisible wall beyond which she knows she must not go. So if Bryce asks her about her day, she will say: "Oh, I just stayed around town," and that's that. It's enough for Evelyn, because Bryce looks after her. Ever since she was picked up by the police.

Evelyn had always loved flowers. Blue hydrangeas, orange day lilies, roses the colour of a winter sunset. In her mother's flower shop, she would touch the cuttings as they lay across the table, cascades of colour and scent. As a small girl she would place a rose petal against her cheek, feel the innocence there; in her white-blonde hair her mother would pin the flowers whose heads had broken, and so could not be used in an arrangement. Her hair filled with the broken heads of flowers, Evelyn would dance around the shop, delighting customers.

When her mother died, the trustee set up an allowance from the estate under strict instructions as per the monthly allotment until such time as she was married, at which time the remaining funds would be released. This was because Evelyn's mother was unsure of her daughter's ability to handle money, and hoped that someday a good man would recognize Evelyn for the sweet girl she was. But until such a thing might happen, the allowance remained. Evelyn's mother had not anticipated the increased cost of living, and so things for Evelyn became difficult. She didn't mind the empty refrigerator; what she minded was the absence of flowers.

It started off simply enough: she would find flowers poking out from under a fence, but there always seemed to be nicer ones *inside* the fence. I'll just take one step, just one, she'd think to herself, and reach as far as she could with that one step, slender, pale fingers straining for the magnificent purple iris just out of reach. It became two steps, then three: tiger lilies, forsythia, calendula—as a child she wished she had been named Calendula—until a close call with a large Alsatian frightened her. Then she became attracted to bouquets. At the doctor's, the cut flowers on the receptionist's desk went into her purse, a large handbag she kept unfastened for the purpose. But the prettiest bouquets were at Frederico's, the nicest restaurant in town. Small, exquisite bouquets on every table. Evelyn could see them through the window. If she was walking by she'd go in on pretext to use the bathroom; as she slipped out she would just tuck one into her bag—there were so many of them, after all—and step onto the street as if nothing had happened.

Constable Bryce Smithson, as the investigating officer, took Frederico's statement. Of course there was only a reprimand: it was a small crime, and then there was Evelyn, being who she was and all. But later, after the file was closed, the constable arrived one afternoon at Evelyn's apartment door with the biggest bouquet of flowers the florist could make for him. It was obvious to Evelyn that he didn't believe the reports that she was "a little touched" as Dr. Croasdaile said when he came to her defence that day at the police station. Bryce asked Evelyn out for dinner that very night, and again the next night, avoiding Frederico's. He was besotted. "My delicate little flower," he called her, always afraid of what might happen to her "out there in the world."

At the wedding, the pungent perfume of hundreds of flowers

eclipsed the headiest scents worn by the oldest of old ladies; everyone in town came, if only to see the spectacle of someone actually marrying Evelyn Sallaway: after all, Evelyn was an odd duck at the best of times.

Evelyn loved the way Bryce would kiss her forehead as he left for work, saying: "Now stay close, my little rosebud." Every Friday, when Bryce came home, a new, fresh bouquet would appear on the table in the hallway, just by the door.

Evelyn hoped for children, little flowers she could nurture, but time passed, and none came. For a while, Evelyn was content to keep house, but you can only dust the mantel so many times. She tried hobbies: macramé, paper tole, coppercraft. After a while, there were bits of paper stuck everywhere in the house, knots in everything. The copper gave her a rash. "Volunteer work?" suggested Bryce. So Evelyn joined the Imperial Order of the Daughters of the Empire, but the thrift shop made her sneeze. She tried the Hospital Auxiliary, but got migraines every time she went into the building.

She was heading for the library one afternoon—another visit to the craft section, 745.5, she had it memorized—when she saw the young woman with the large packsack hitchhiking along the side of the road.

Evelyn thinks about her now, as the yellow Rambler crests a hill, the valley opening up in front of her. Just a little while ago it had been raining here as hard as it had been that particular day; Evelyn had felt sorry for the girl, and pulled over. The young woman, when she got into the car, looked positively drowned. Everything about her hung: straight, wet, black hair, dripping blouse, long skirt soaked at the hem, lace-up boots. Her packsack had drawings on it—peace, love—all bleeding in the rain. Normally, having somebody so wet on her clean upholstery would upset Evelyn, but that day she felt her heart race, her pulse quicken at this complete—*stranger*—in her car, somebody about whom she knew nothing. Somebody who came from somewhere else. Somebody who was going somewhere else.

She drove towards the edge of town, and as the rain came down around them the girl told Evelyn all about herself as she dripped on the seat of the car, and Evelyn listened, enraptured. She was going to meet up with friends at a big concert just south of the border. "It'll be really far out."

Evelyn thought she meant far out of town, so she told the girl she could only take her to the city limits. The girl didn't ask why, just told Evelyn that was "cool," which confused Evelyn, it being quite a warm day despite the rain.

When Evelyn's passenger explained about the bands that were going to be there, Evelyn wondered aloud at the notion that anyone would be grateful to be dead, and when the girl explained it more clearly, Evelyn told her gently that perhaps they should see someone who could help. She told the girl about the doctor she went to every week who listened so nicely.

When, at the edge of town, the girl thanked Evelyn and told her she was beautiful, Evelyn felt warm all over. "Peace," the girl said as she got out, and Evelyn thought that was such a nice thing to say. As she pulled into Garry's Gas & Grub to turn around she realized she had driven past the town's limits, past the limit Bryce had given her, and that nothing bad had happened. When she looked at the odometer she saw she had travelled exactly thirty miles, and so it was then that thirty miles became Evelyn's new limit.

The next time she picked up a hitchhiker—Ray, who was going to work on the new dams—she asked for a postcard.

"That's all I ask," she told him before she pulled back onto the road from the shoulder. "You agree to send me a postcard when you get to where you're going, and I'll give you a lift." She felt powerful, even a little dangerous, making this demand, but Ray looked at her for a long moment, and then: "Sure, ma'am," he said, and Evelyn believed him.

She never told Bryce about the postcards she kept in the back of the recipe card file in the kitchen. The Peace Tower; the Grand Canyon; a Venetian gondolier. On the back of a postcard of a hydroelectric dam, the words in block letters read: HERE'S THE POSTCARD YOU ASKED FOR. RAY.

Sometimes, they didn't understand, or appeared frustrated that she would only take them such a short distance. But once they were in the car and Evelyn told them about Bryce and the flowers, by the time she would pull over to drop them off they would promise to write. And they all do: Ray has been sending her postcards now for two years, even though she only ever asked for the one.

Evelyn, driving along the secondary highway, sees an old house just off the road that looks as if it hasn't seen paint in fifty years. It reminds her of the old fellow she picked up once, himself looking as dusty and neglected as that house. He started riding the rails during the Depression, he told Evelyn, and just couldn't settle down after that, even when times got better. Sometimes he follows the rail lines, other times it's the highway. "Been across the country fourteen times," he said. The postcard he sent her said "St. John's Newfoundland" across the top. Saltbox houses in deep yellows, rich reds, electric blues, colours like the richest of flowers. Big Ben, Peggy's Cove, a postcard showing a man and a trout that reads in red script: *Gone fishin'—in Lake Okanagan!*—they are equally exotic to Evelyn.

She strove for normalcy as she kept her secret. By day she went driving, looking for hitchhikers. She would ask them where they had been, where they were going, their futures stretching ahead like the road in front of her. Every evening she'd be sure to be waiting by the door for Bryce to come home from work, the house clean, dinner in the oven. Fridays, after he came in and kissed her on the forehead, Evelyn would take the fresh flowers and replace the old, careful to remove every leaf and petal in the new arrangement that wasn't absolutely perfect. She'd carefully place the vase—daffodils in spring, carnations in the winter, iris, gladiolas, yellow roses—on the hall table and then she'd fix him his drink, and sit, hands in her lap, while he told her about his day.

Then, two weeks ago, Evelyn was driving by Frederico's at noon and saw her husband eating lunch with a girl she had never seen before. "Oh, that's just Brenda," Bryce told her later. "She's taking over at reception for Charlene while Charlene's looking after her husband. You know, the fellow who had the accident at the mill," and he started talking about how the mill has been getting lax about the safety regulations, and how there'll be an investigation for sure, and then it was time for Evelyn to take the casserole out of the oven.

A few days later Evelyn was cleaning out Bryce's pockets to take his pants to the drycleaner, and found a hotel receipt. "I loaned my pants to Percy when he spilled coffee over his. He had an important meeting with the mayor, but I was just going to be behind a desk all day, so we switched," Bryce told Evelyn. "That must be Percy's receipt."

Evelyn thought nothing more about it.

But then came the day he wasn't home for dinner. In the past, if he had to stay late, he would always call. But this time dinner was dried out in the oven when Bryce hurried in, apologizing, telling Evelyn about a call, and emergency that kept him overtime, and then he stopped what he was saying and looked at the hall table. It was Friday. A tulip petal had fallen from the bouquet. The flowers were wide open, the way tulips are when their time is past, like open hearts. One touch, and they fall apart.

He had forgotten.

Evelyn pulls over to the shoulder. She takes a tissue from her handbag and dabs at her eyes, and then takes out her sunglasses, protection against the bright sun on the wet highway, and to hide the redness she's sure is there.

"No matter dear," she told him then. "It was a silly custom. These are perfectly good for another day."

He had taken her hand and spoken as if to a small child. "There are times when we come to a crossroads," he began, but she thought, suddenly, of the lamb in the oven. "Oh dear!" she had cried. "There will be nothing left of it!" and rushed to the kitchen, leaving her husband standing in the hallway.

When Bryce went to work Saturday morning—this morning, she realizes as she sits in the Rambler, hands worrying the hem of her knitted yellow suit—Evelyn got into the car with no thought other than to visit the library, walking by the falling petals on the hall table as she reached for the front door. She wasn't sure that bobbin lace mightn't be just a bit too finicky for her after all. Perhaps there was something else in the library, something different. But when she approached the building, hand on the turn signal, her fingers didn't move. She drove past. Kept going.

And now she is here.

When she picks up the long-haired boy with the forget-me-not eyes, she starts to tell him she can only take him thirty miles, and then stops herself. The rules have changed. "Where are you going?" she asks him, and when he tells her about the wind, she starts to laugh. She doesn't ask him to send her a postcard, this boy without a destination. "What a lovely thing," she tells him. "To follow the wind."

The hitchhiker explains how the wind has been changing all day, sending him in all directions. How the road is dry in one spot, then, a mile down the way, wet, as if the weather is playing tag, or hide and seek. This, too, delights her, and she feels lighter than she has for some time.

But when they reach the intersection of two roads, Evelyn pulls over. In her mind are Bryce's words: a crossroads. She doesn't know which way she should go. And there, she begins to cry. She has forgotten all about the boy, who sits, waiting.

She tells him about everything: about Bryce, and the girl in Frederico's, and about the flowers. When she runs out of words there is a moment or two of silence and then he gets out of the car, and she thinks he's going to try to get another ride; she doesn't blame him. But she sees he has left his packsack, and so she waits, looking ahead at the stop sign, thinking now that she'll have to hurry if she's going to be back in time to be standing there in the hallway, dinner in the oven, when Bryce gets home from work. It's what she is supposed to do, where she is supposed to be. After all, Bryce looks after her. She has travelled farther than she ever has. What was she thinking? And then she remembers.

She tilts the rearview mirror down to see her face, to see what she might look like after so much crying, and sees, in the mirror, the boy she has picked up walking back up the highway towards the Rambler. In his hands is a bouquet of wildflowers from alongside the road. Black-eyed Susans. Purple Vetch. Daisies. All sparkling from the recent rain. The bouquet fills his arms, leaving his shirt wet. He lays it beside her on the passenger seat, and Evelyn smiles as the car fills with colour.

"There are flowers everywhere," he tells her. "Maybe you should follow the flowers."

He waves as he heads off down the road heading east, following the bend in the treetops where the wind blows them. Evelyn looks west, and as far as she can see, in the ditches along the road, are flowers. They look as if they go on forever.

2:15 p.m.
Egg salad on white

There's the bite of tire on gravel, and as Jo turns, the slightest rise of dust, now that the parking lot is beginning to dry out in the heat. Pulling in is a yellow Rambler, the colour of butter. As the dust settles, it appears to fall around the car rather than on it, leaving it beaming in the sunlight.

Jo watches the woman in the car look at herself in the rearview mirror, adjusting her hair, her sunglasses, her white plastic earrings. The hair is white-blonde, arranged in a soft helmet, cut precisely at the level of each tiny earlobe. The glasses are large, and match: white frames, circular in shape. The pantsuit is pale yellow with white buttons, its polyester knit wrinkle-free as the woman steps from the car, placing white pumps neatly on the gravel.

By the time the door opens Jo has the coffee pot in one hand, cream in the other, but the woman asks for tea. She settles herself at the counter, setting her sunglasses and handbag neatly beside the salt and pepper, while Jo pours hot water into the metal teapot and sets it down in front of her, wanting, oddly, to spill some, to see the amber stain break up the relentless sunbeam of this customer.

"Special today is egg salad," Jo tells her, thinking of the yellow-and-white mixture in the refrigerator.

"That will be lovely." She tilts her head sideways, making Jo think of a small yellow bird. "What pretty hair. What's your name, dear?"

"Egg salad. Right," says Jo, not answering. She ducks into

the kitchen where she begins slapping the egg mixture on Wonderbread.

"My name's Evelyn," the woman calls through the window.

There's a beat in which Jo knows she's supposed to offer her own name. Through the kitchen window she watches while the woman opens her handbag and begins extracting post-cards, laying them on the counter in a precise manner. The result looks like a patchwork quilt. She carefully adjusts this arrangement so Jo can set the sandwich down, and then looks up, waiting for Jo to ask about them. "My *collection*," she explains, while Jo tries to think of something to say. She extends her hand, and Jo takes it. What else can she do? There is no pressure when their hands meet; it's like shaking hands with a butterfly. "Evelyn," she says.

"Yes, you told me."

"Oh, did I?"

Her eyes seem just a little wider than is natural; Jo can see the whites at the top. The effect is slightly startled and a little frozen, a deer caught in the headlights. She appears to be waiting.

"Umm. Jo."

She makes Jo think of a flower about to drop its petals, just past blooming. Jo looks at the postcards. Has she been to all these places?

"You're wondering about my postcards, I can tell," she says.

It's been a weird day all around. "I really have work to do."

"This is the Lion's Gate Bridge." She slides the postcard towards Jo. "Have you been there?" Jo shakes her head. "Neither have I," she says. Her fingers brush the image of a cruise ship passing under the bridge. "It's going to Alaska. Can you imagine? And this—this one is one of my favourites." She picks up a postcard almost tenderly. It's Victoria's Butchart Gardens; it says so in yellow angled script in the corner of a photograph of walking paths and flowerbeds.

"Where did you get all these?" Jo asks, because clearly she has not been to these places.

She leans forward. "Hitchhikers," she whispers. Now she's holding up a postcard, an aerial view of Niagara Falls, a Canadian flag on the upper right corner. Her voice has a soft lilt. "There were two of them, a boy and a girl, oh, not much older than you," she begins. "Brad and Susan. They were going there to get married. Isn't that wonderful? See? They've signed it, here." She points to the signature with a manicured finger. *To Evelyn, thanks for the lift,* it reads.

"This one came from Wayne. Oh, he was a one, I'll tell you. Tattoos *everywhere*. Well, everywhere I could see. He told me he'd just completed his time in prison, somewhere on the coast . . . I don't remember where, exactly. What for I'm sure I don't know."

"I should get to work."

"Of course you should. What am I thinking? I never think. That's what Bryce tells me." Evelyn's eyes fill with tears.

Now, Jo can't leave. She doesn't know what to say, or do. Evelyn is rummaging in her handbag, looking for a Kleenex, Jo thinks, but the handkerchief she extracts is embroidered with delicate flowers. There are tears falling on the top of the Wonderbread. She hasn't touched her sandwich or sipped her tea.

"Maybe you'd feel better if you ate something," Jo manages finally.

"It's just that I don't know where to go. I don't know where to go, now." Evelyn begins picking up the postcards, one by one. "I mean you, you have a home here, right? You have a place to come home to every day. I had a place, too. Every day, for eleven years."

"I don't live here. I'm just staying here for now."

Evelyn looks at Jo, doe eyes wide. Jo can't help it: she widens hers in spite of herself, and then blinks a few times. "It's just for now," she tells Evelyn.

"You must have parents. A home. Someplace to go back to."

"Not really."

"You're so young," Evelyn says, wistfully. "You have your whole life ahead of you. Do you know, I've never been anywhere. This is the farthest I've ever been."

Evelyn might look a little wilted, but she doesn't look all that old to Jo. The postcards are in her hand, as if she's forgotten they are there. Jo takes them from her and fans them out.

"Close your eyes and pick one," Jo tells her. "It's a game my dad used to play with me, when I collected animal cards in bubble gum packs. Whatever I picked, he said I could have as a pet."

She chooses the Butchart Gardens. Good, Jo thinks: it's someplace she can drive to. "Now, that's where you'll go. I think there's a map under here." Jo is sure she saw one in the box under the counter earlier. Sure enough, there it is on the bottom, a B.C. road map.

"You can keep it." Cass will never notice.

She tucks the postcard and the map into her handbag, and then fans out the other postcards for Jo like a deck of cards.

"Now you."

The card Jo picks shows a giant, happy potato. Welcome to Maugerville, N.B., it says. On the back a careful hand says: *I made it home. Appreciate the lift. Guy Robideau.*

"Thanks," Jo says, handing it back. "It was for you, anyway."

"What kind of pet did your father give you?"

"Pet?"

"When you chose an animal. Did you get to have a parrot? Or a monkey?"

"It was just a game."

Evelyn looks disappointed. Then she brightens, and picks up the plate. "Do you suppose I could have this wrapped? To take with me?"

Jo wraps the untouched egg salad sandwich in wax paper. Evelyn carefully counts out a small pile of quarters, one dime, a nickel. She pats the little stack, picks up the map and the sandwich, then reaches over and touches Jo's wrist. "So many kind people," she says. "First, there was that wind boy who gave me the flowers, and now you've given me a map." She laughs, an odd little trill. "I like games." She tucks the sandwich in her purse. "Would you have an extra pen in that box of yours? I'd like to write down the address here. I could send you a postcard."

There's usually a pen on the counter; Jo is sure that she had one, but now she can't see it anywhere. She ducks down to rifle through the box. There's a red pencil; that will do. As she stands up she hears the slam of the screen door and there is Evelyn, stepping into the Rambler.

Jo sets the pencil down beside the tomato paste can, the one that, up until a moment ago, held three plastic flowers.

Jo

My great aunt Bea was another crazy lady. My mother called her eccentric. My father explained that she was "one of the whisky aunts," three in all, who never married but lived together, and liked their drink. Warner, their brother, married Lucy, my grandmother.

In a way, Evelyn reminded me of Bea. Maybe it was her wide eyes. I remember visiting her after her sisters had passed away, there in the old house they had shared. I must have been about ten. My mother wanted to convince Bea to move into a home.

"She can't take care of herself anymore," I heard my mother tell my father. "She's getting stranger and stranger."

She was right. As we came up the walk to the old, two-storey house I loved, with the stained glass and the big front porch, I noticed something odd about the windows. From a distance, they looked as if they were filled with something grey and textured, like a wasp's nest. Then, as we got to the step, I saw they were bits of paper, and I thought maybe they were articles she'd cut out and taped to the window. But as we reached the porch, "Oh, my God," said my mother. In every window were hundreds of eyes.

She must have cut them out of magazines and newspapers, maybe even books. In the big bay window off the porch: eyes. In the smaller, parlour window: eyes. In the half-moon window in the door: eyes. Long-lashed eyes that may have once advertised mascara; wrinkle-lidded eyes, and the round eyes of babies; eyes that looked familiar, maybe a movie star I couldn't quite place; eyes that were not human: a horse, a monkey, a kitten.

We hadn't yet knocked when the door opened. Mum had no words, for once. She held out the bag she carried containing the groceries we picked up on the way.

"Oh, I don't need all this!" Bea told us. "I'm not eating so much these days, you know."

"Why are there eyes everywhere, Aunt Bea?" I asked. My mother looked at me sharply, but I remember she seemed relieved that I'd asked the question.

"What eyes?"

"In the windows."

"Oh. Those." She laughed, as if she was embarrassed, and then looked at them as if she'd never seen them before. Looking from inside the open door you could see the print on the backs of the cutouts.

"Why, it's so I can keep an eye on things, of course!" And she gave me a little wink, as if the whole thing was done just for me.

As my mother and Aunt Bea had tea at the kitchen table, I wandered the house. The light was dim because of all the paper in the windows. Backlit, each pair of eyes were superimposed with type, some with other photographs. In places, light poked in tiny fingers between the cutouts. On the *National Geographic* on the coffee table was a photograph of a young woman wearing a red headscarf. Her eyes were missing. At her bookshelf, I pulled out a book at random, a novel by a woman whose name I don't remember now, but I do remember that the author photograph on the flyleaf was also eyeless. Upstairs, I stepped into the bathroom, my favourite room in the house because of the huge clawfoot tub I'd been allowed to have lengthy bubble baths in when I was small. I sat on the toilet and looked at the door I'd swung shut behind me when I came in. On the full-length mirror that hung there: eyes.

When I came back into the kitchen, my mother's voice had risen an octave. "You can't live like this, Bea!" she was saying.

"Like what, Joyce?" Aunt Bea's hands were folded in her lap. My mother, distraught as she was, looked like the crazy one.

I asked my father later, when my mother was on the phone with her brother strategizing the removal of Aunt Bea, why she had to leave her house.

"When you get old, things start to go," he said, but he looked doubtful even to me at ten years old.

"What things?"

"Being able to look after yourself."

I didn't know what to answer. But I could remember that, except for the eyes, the house was clean. Aunt Bea looked healthy; she didn't look like she was starving or anything. Mostly, she looked happy.

Later, when the old house was sold and most of Aunt Bea's furniture had been crammed into the tiny two-room suite in the Home, we came to visit.

"They won't let me have my eyes," she grumbled. "It's lonely here without them."

The windows did look empty without Aunt Bea's cutout eyes. It seemed cruel to me that they refused my great-aunt this small indulgence: it was her room, after all.

When we were ready to leave, she gave me a book of animals, something someone had given to her. It was a childish sort of book for a grown woman that now I realize was because people thought she was becoming more childlike, the way old people sometimes do. My mother had gone ahead to speak to one of the attendants when Aunt Bea pulled me back inside.

"It's always good to have someone to keep an eye on you, dear," she told me, and tucked a piece of paper into my pocket.

"You know, eyes are the windows to the soul." She looked into my eyes. When I looked back, I saw not the eyes of an old woman, but the eyes of a baby. I don't mean the eyelids, or the soft, wrinkled skin: just the eyes themselves, blue-grey, round. Innocent. "When you look in someone's eyes, you are closer to God."

We picked up my father from work and drove home. Sitting in the back seat, I took the pair of eyes from my pocket and looked at them. The eyes that looked back were the eyes of a very old woman. I kept the book for a long time. Every page was intact: crocodiles, cockatiels, three-toed sloths: every one had both of their eyes. I often wondered if she meant for me to start my own collection.

Funny, I haven't thought of Aunt Bea for ages. She's been dead for years. Now I wonder if anyone is watching out for me. My mother wasn't; my father might have, if he'd opened his eyes enough to see what was happening. I have a child I'm not watching out for, who I have left in the care of people I hope will be better watchers than I would have been.

If I had looked into my daughter's eyes, what would I have seen there?

Archie

I come up over the rise and there's Bob coming the other way. Slow right down, of course. There's nothing like the sight of a cop to make your foot come off the gas like you've stepped on a hornet. Little farther along and there's that hippie kid thumbing the other way, same way as the wind's blowing this very moment, sure enough. *Hmmph*, I think. Wind's been all over the map today, like it can't decide *what* it's doing. Start off sunny, then wind out of nowhere, blowing all over the place, but cooling things down some, then a rain so hard it'd drown a fish, and now it's sunny again. Wouldn't be surprised if it snowed. Crazy mountain weather. Whole day's been a little strange, if you ask me. I keep going, foot off the gas. You just never know.

I start thinking about this wind thing. Growing up back in Wood's Harbour—when I was a teenager—we used to play this game, all of us piling into somebody's old car and we'd play left-right-straight-ahead. All of us—might be six of us—in the car would take turns telling the driver which way to go whenever we'd get to a crossroads or a turn of some kind. The game was better if the fog was right thick. The point was to get lost, which wasn't always easy since we knew the roads pretty well. But we did manage to get ourselves turned around once or twice, and there we'd be, end of a dirt track and up against a beach of silver sand as fine as talcum powder and the same colour as the fog around us. If the tide was out and we'd walk a little ways, you couldn't see the car, either. You'd think you were all covered up in a grey blanket. Sometimes I'd ditch the guys and walk out so's I couldn't see them. Just me and all that grey. You could imagine no school, no job, no chores, no nothing.

Thing is, being lost is only good when it's because you want to be lost. Maybe the wind thing is a little like that.

As I pass the rest stop there's a lady in yellow tying plastic flowers onto the antenna of her car. She's dressed nice, like she's going somewhere. The tailwind from the rig pulls a flower free. Glancing in the rearview, I see her catch it on the updraft.

Pink

Pink stands on the road's shoulder feeling tired: the adrenalin rush when he took flight, the risk he took with the cop, and the bizarre time that followed, then the lady with the flowers, and now here he is, standing on an empty highway in midafternoon, feeling like the day should surely be over for all that's been in it. Insect sounds in the roadside brush are a soothing lullaby, and Pink can feel his eyelids want to close.

A cat emerges from the brush. Pink wonders if the cat might once have belonged to the fellow in the cabin the Mountie had described; she's skinny, and looks feral, but when he crouches down she runs to him and leans her small weight against his leg, purring. As Pink strokes the tabby fur, running his hand along her spine, catching her tail as it lifts to meet his hand, he thinks about another cat, and another time.

Elvis was thirteen that year. He'd never learned to shoot, and Stan had let it go, eventually, to both Elvis and Nora's relief. Instead, Stan began taking Elvis fishing, something they both grew to like. Campfire evenings, Stan would tell the boy about his own childhood, his father quick with the strap, but quick, too, with praise.

"Scared the crap out of me sometimes, but he taught me how to do things well," Stan told Elvis. "No half measures."

Cleaning their catch, Elvis did his best to do it right, to make the cut straight, clean. Stan put his hand on the boy's head, ruffled his hair affectionately, and Elvis basked in the moment, feeling as if Stan really was his father.

As Elvis became a teenager he'd get through his chores, anxious to get together with Kevin, which, more and more, involved talking about girls and smoking stolen cigarettes. To Elvis, Kevin seemed vastly knowledgeable, and worldly.

They were sitting behind the back shed, blowing smoke rings and laughing, when they heard Stan yelling for Elvis. Quickly, they butted out the rollies that were cracking and sparking anyway.

"Gotta go," said Kevin.

"No, come with." Elvis tried to keep the pleading out of his voice. When Elvis was with a friend, Stan was often more relaxed, even jovial. "Please."

When Kevin and Elvis reached Stan, he was standing with a shovel at a scrubby spot at the far end of the corn patch, just before the field gave way to woods. The house, with laundry flapping on the line outside, stood in the far distance. Elvis could see Nora pin a sheet on the line, and although he couldn't see from this distance, imagined her humming through a clothes peg in her teeth, the way she often did. As he squinted, she turned to go inside.

"Need you to dig a hole," Stan was saying through his cigarette. "Right here." He handed Elvis the spade.

"What for?"

"The question isn't what for, son. Should be how deep? That's all you need to know."

Elvis cast a glance at Kevin, who smiled sympathetically, then quickly arranged his features back to seriousness. "How deep, sir?" He asked.

"Don't need two for this, Kevin." He looked at Elvis. "It needs to be this long," he held out his large hands, "this wide, and this deep. If you hit rock before two feet, start over. Do it well, now. No half measures."

He left, then, striding across the lawn. Kevin looked at Elvis. "I'll help," he said. "It won't take long. You go first."

The ground was hard, and there were a lot of rocks. It took four tries to find a spot where they could get down far enough, taking turns and sweating.

"What do you think it's for?" asked Kevin.

"Probably caught some poor animal in a trap, a skunk or something."

"Wouldn't he just throw the body in the woods, then?"

"I guess that would attract coyotes, and they'd go for the chickens. I don't know. Sometimes I think he just makes me do stuff to make some kind of a point."

Kevin leaned on the shovel. "What the heck kind of a point could this be? A whole afternoon wasted digging a stupid hole?"

"You didn't have to stay."

"You asked me to."

"So, go, then."

Kevin handed the shovel to Elvis, then, and headed back up the path that cut through the woods to his own place with a backwards wave. The hole was deep enough anyway, Elvis figured. He thought of Nora, maybe a glass of lemonade.

But here is Stan striding back across the big yard, carrying something in a bag. It's about the size of a cat, and Elvis thinks: skunk, because that makes the most sense. But then Elvis sees it move, and knows that Stan wouldn't be carrying a live skunk in a bag. When he reaches Elvis, he points to the bag.

"That was the last batch of kittens in this place," Stan says, pointing to the squirming bag. He's referring to the six kittens just weaned from the cat Elvis had begged to keep last winter; it had wrapped itself around his legs one afternoon on the way home from school, mewing winsomely. Promised to look after it himself, but he'd been so busy . . .

"Sick of them smelling up the place, spraying, screwing, fighting, yowling."

Elvis stares at the bag. Ginger, named for the yellow undercoat beneath her tabby stripes. Stan reaches his hand in, yelps, and then withdraws it, bloody scratches. This time, when he hauls out the cat by the scruff, claws slash at air.

In a moment, the cat is in the hole, which Elvis has managed to dig two feet down. No half measures. She's scrambling to get up, but Stan has one foot over the hole, pushing her back. Elvis turns to Stan, his mouth open, wordless. That's when Elvis sees the raised .22.

The shot is quick, catching the cat across the back of the small head, between the ears. There is the arch of the body, then the cat leaps twice more in a futile escape attempt, the moment of panic greater than the mortal blow. Elvis's breath is stopped in his chest, and around him, a roaring.

"Fill it up," Stan tells him, throwing the bag on top of the twitching body.

Pink, at the side of the highway, picks up the cat, feels her bones under her fur, absorbs the vibration of its purr through his shirt. What sort of lesson was he supposed to learn? To look after things? He has never made sense of the incident, choosing, instead, to bury it in the same way he has buried the cat: deep enough to keep the coyotes out. As long as he avoided that part of the yard, he could keep it there. And yet, in a stray tabby on a mountain road, here it was again.

The cat bats a paw playfully at the soft hair on his chin. Gently, he puts her down on the shoulder. "Sorry. Can't take you with me," he says. There is no traffic, and Pink sees, down the road, a sign he recognizes as pointing to a rest stop. Someplace to take a nap, maybe. He starts walking, and the cat follows anyway, as if knowing this to be salvation, if only she can love enough.

Ill wind

Except wind stands as never it stood,
It is an ill wind turns none to good.
— Thomas Tusser (c. 1515–1580)

Carson hasn't stopped driving for hours. When he finally does stop, at a pullout picnic site on some mountain pass, he feels as if his bladder is about to burst. It's all he can do to get his fly unzipped, and so when he's peeing against the signpost advertising a roadside café somewhere up the way, his back turned to the highway, the gushing arc of urine is quite visible to the woman in the yellow Rambler who drives by, waving gaily at him while he looks, trapped in the moment, over his shoulder. His hands, when he zips up, still display a tremor. To his horror, when he looks down he sees there is a spatter of dried blood across the back of his right hand.

He spits on it, rubs it against his white dress shirt. Then, appalled by the pink smear, he takes off his shirt and stuffs it into the ash at the bottom of a rusty metal box intended for family barbecues. He sits on the picnic table, shirtless, head in his hands while above him the afternoon sun approaches the tops on the trees. Not far away, the hot car engine settles. He is just grateful to not be moving. He has been driving for hours, his gas tank now almost empty.

Carson startles when he hears a sound behind him. As things come back into focus, he realizes the sight he must be: dress pants, Italian leather shoes, dishevelled hair, shirtless. The hippie with the backpack doesn't seem to notice.

"I was napping over there," he points to a grassy patch off behind another picnic table. "No rides." He pauses to appraise the Jaguar with the Washington plates and whistles. "Which way are you going?"

Carson shakes his head.

"You okay?"

"Yes. No. I can't give you a ride."

The hippie backs away, eyes wide, a nervous smile on his face in which Carson can see the expression he, himself, must be carrying. "Hey, man, no problem. Just asking."

A sob escapes Carson's lips. He didn't know it was in there.

"Hey. You okay?" says the hippie again, and now Carson is sobbing in earnest. His words, when he begins his story, begin as runoff and expand to landslide, tumbling debris down a mountainside.

The education of Carson Weymouth Jr. began when his father decided to teach him a lesson in commerce. Everyone in Carson's grade three class was talking about the new *Action Comics*, and a hero with special powers called Superman. Carson asked his father for money to buy the issue he'd seen at the store, the issue on which a man in a red cape was picking up a car. He told his father how all the kids wanted it, and he wanted to be the first to own one. As he said this, he knew his father would approve of his drive to be first.

"How many are for sale at the store?" Carson Sr. asked his son.

"I don't know," Carson shrugged. "I just want to buy one. It's only ten cents."

"I'll loan you ten cents, son. But nothing comes for free. You'll pay it back with ten percent interest."

"How will I do that?"

"First, go back to the store and count how many are there."

So Carson went back to the store. At the magazine rack, Jimmy and Pete had a copy open, heads touching as they looked at the page. "Pow!" Carson heard Pete read aloud. Carson had just time to count five copies still in the rack, plus the one becoming slightly crumpled in Jimmy's sweaty paw, before Mr. Stamatelakis shouted at them all to pay up or leave.

When Carson reported back, his father gave him sixty cents. "Buy them all," he told his son.

"What for?"

"You'll see."

Carson sold each comic for fifteen cents. In 1938, at nine years old, it occurred to none of his friends that another store somewhere else might stock the *Action Comics*, and besides, the desire to own one was far too great. They paid, but they grumbled. Carson didn't mind: he made thirty cents and, after paying back his father with interest, had enough left to buy the last two *Ace Comics* in the rack, the new one featuring Blondie, Jungle Jim, and Felix. Before long, all the kids bought their comics from Carson. Next, he hired Tommy Jachowics from the grade two class to buy up copies as they came in, and paid him a cent per copy. At a profit margin of four cents, Carson was averaging sixty-five cents a week. By the time Mr. Stamatelakis put a stop to it, Carson had eleven dollars in his bank account. His father laughed when Mr. Stamatelakis called to tell him about his son's unfair trading practices. "You'll be more discreet next time, boy," Carson's father said later.

At the collegiate, fourteen-year-old Carson found a March, 1946, copy of *Bizarre* magazine in his math teacher's desk while waiting for Mr. Duckworth to discuss his marks. He'd intended to make his case by citing his father's hefty endowment to the school; now, he discovered some hefty endowments in the pages of the magazine that was secreted inside a file marked "statistics" in the bottom drawer. He didn't wait for the instructor, who was late anyway.

Carson made a fortune that year renting the magazine, with its illustrations of large-breasted women with their hands bound, to his dormmates. The fines for any pages found stuck together were particularly large.

Later, in university, Carson learned a great deal about media spin while editing the campus newspaper, a lesson he later applied when "encouraging" financial pages columnists to plug particular companies and hint about the downfall of others. As shareholders pulled out, Weymouth & Son swooped in.

"It's all about building equity through acquisition," his father told him. "It's all about getting yours. Because if you don't get yours, some other bastard will."

If pressed to say what it was he did in his work, while at a cocktail party or during the champagne-and-schmooze intermission of a cultural event, Carson would be necessarily vague: brokering mergers, for example, and most would leave it at that. There was no question that the Weymouth force was successful. "Enforced mergers and hostile takeovers" would have been closer to the truth. "Kill the competition" was the credo.

There was only one other person who moved inside the

circle of father/son trust. Jamieson T. Sibley had served overseas with Carson's father, and whatever had passed between them at that time had sealed a pact of brotherhood. Beyond these three, with regards to the outside world, no trust existed. Carson was often unsure if Sibley—J.T., as he was called by insiders—and his father entirely trusted *him*. There were times he felt as if a piece were missing, but nothing he could quite put his finger on.

As the empire grew, there were casualties. J.T. and Weymouth Sr. exulted in these. But then came the day, when, at a stockholders' meeting, Carson's father stopped speaking, in midsentence. Around the table, men in suits assumed a pregnant pause, and waited for the delivery.

"What he delivered was a spray of saliva across the table," Carson explains to Pink, as the hitchhiker has introduced himself. "I think he was sputtering, trying to get the last word out. Then he fell, face forward, across the profit report. Massive stroke. He was only sixty."

"Sounds like Karma to me."

Carson looks at him blankly.

"Sort of an ethical cause-and-effect."

"Hmmm. Well, after that J.T. took me under his wing. He needed to, really. I had a hard time with the loss of Dad, couldn't quite see my way without him."

Pink looks at Carson sympathetically. "I'm sorry. About your father dying."

"Thank you."

They sit for a few moments before Carson continues.

"'We'll keep the Weymouth name strong,' Sibley told me. 'We'll honour your father's legacy.'"

"And did he?"

"In his way, I guess he did."

Carson, business-savvy, streetwise in the financial world, was temporarily numb after his father's death. His anchor loose, he moved through his days like a ship without course. Carson and Sibley were photographed more times than Carson could count: the handshake; the paternal arm around his shoulder. If Sibley advised him, Carson followed the advice. If there were papers to sign, Carson signed them. Sibley doubled Carson's personal holdings in a year, showed him new ways to use his power.

Sibley told Carson he felt honour-bound to complete the education Carson's father had begun before his untimely death. He said this as if Carson was his own son, the son he never had, and Carson, bereft, flattered, embraced his new "father." In fact, Sibley was more fatherlike than Carson's own father had ever been: over the next few years he made sure Carson joined the right clubs; they played racquetball on Wednesday afternoons. Afterwards, they'd go to the executive club. Carson would watch while J.T.—"call me Jamie, boy," he told Carson—set the climate for a deal down the road, how he knew just the right word to say. He'd raise one eyebrow at Carson, acknowledgment of their private understanding.

"I didn't know until yesterday, when I was awakened by a phone call. A reporter. He wanted my comments on the Securities Commission freeze on my assets. That's when I knew I'd been framed. And who had set me up."

"Yeah?"

Carson seems unaware that he's talking to a traveller with long hair, a backpack, and what are, most likely, entirely empty pockets. He rambles on as if to himself.

"I had been accused of insider trading. I had a couple of hundred cash in my wallet. No idea what I would do next. I went out, locked the door behind me, took the elevator down to the lobby."

As it turned out, the reporter who broke the story had his own insider information, and, eager to beat the competition to the scoop, jumped the gun. The story should have broken in time for the late edition at best. This was something Carson found out later, listening to the news on the car radio. The reporter's name had been vaguely familiar; it took Carson some time to recognize the name as the same as a financial reporter he'd once paid off, then cut off when demands got too high. He'd threatened the man with exposure, eventually seeding rumours in the right places to ensure the reporter would have difficulty finding work in the future.

It no longer mattered: all Carson could see was a wall of fog in front of him, and in his ears, a roaring. He could hear a voice in his mind speak of lawyers, but he knew instinctively how far Sibley's influence would have spread, how thoroughly he'd been framed.

In the lobby it was as if nothing had happened; businessmen came and went, the morning busy as usual with the first stirrings of commerce. Carson, still engulfed in fog and roar, could barely fathom the normalcy of the scene. The sun came through and lit up the atrium—the plush seats, the mahogany tables, the lush ferns. It came as a surprise that everyone didn't yet know. He looked at the cuffs of the fine Italian suit he now had no business owning, almost expecting them to unravel as he watched.

Walking into the door of the lobby washroom, then, Carson saw Sibley.

"Of course, he hadn't expected me to know anything yet. He had orchestrated the whole thing so as to be on a jet for London when the news broke." Carson laughs, an odd giggle. "Goes to show you. You can't trust anyone."

Pink shifts uneasily.

"My stomach felt sick; I thought my bowels might give way. I ran to the bathroom and spent a long time sitting in the stall. When I came out, Sibley was at the sink; he saw me behind him, framed in the gilt mirror. We stared at one another for a moment. Then he seemed to collect himself: 'There's my boy!' he said. He was jovial. Slapped me on the back. 'Are you sick, boy? You don't look well.' He said it with such fatherly concern, I almost thought maybe I'd misread it all. Then I saw this—gleam in his eye. I hadn't seen it before. I must have had that look myself from time to time, honed over all those years. It was a look that said you'd pulled one off. That someone was going down. This time, it was me."

Carson didn't think about what he did then, didn't know he was about to grab the potted palm from the countertop until he had it in his hands, knocking Sibley across the head with it, putting everything he had into the swing. Sibley went down, cracking the back of his head on the edge of the counter, sending a spray of blood across the white marble basin. It was then that Carson ran.

"I don't know if I killed him or not. Oh, God, I hope I didn't kill him. What if I did?"

Pink isn't sure what to say. Finally, "Maybe you didn't," he manages.

Carson nods. "It's ironic, though, isn't it? Our unofficial company motto: kill the competition. Oh, God." Carson covers his eyes for a moment, and then rubs them as if they are painful. "I got in the car," he continues. "I had a full tank of gas, and some cash. And here I am."

"Now what?"

"Now, I don't know. At first, the only thing I could think of was suicide. I was thinking of jumping. The quickest. Most painless. It seemed the only way. But I have never been decisive: it was always my father and Sibley who really made the decisions. When it came right down to it, I couldn't make up my mind."

Carson and Pink both look at the trees across the road, the way the afternoon sun, now behind a thin haze of clouds, looks as if it is perched on their tops.

"Here's the thing. I'm thirty-six years old. Never had a wife, a family. My parents are dead, and I have no brothers or sisters. What I had was a lot of money. And now I don't have that."

"So now what?" Pink asks again.

"Now?" Carson says again. "Change my name, I guess. Begin again, somehow. Funny thing is, just now, talking to you? I feel almost—free. Because it's all over. That life. Isn't that odd?" Carson looks at Pink like a bewildered child.

"Not so strange, man. There's a song about that, you know the one: freedom's just another word . . ."

Carson shrugs. "I don't listen to popular music." He giggles, an edge of hysteria. "Didn't. I suppose the rules have changed, now. I mean, anything goes."

"Well, anyway. You want to give me a ride?"

"You want to ride with a criminal? A possible murderer? An exile on the run?" Carson looks at Pink. "Hey, are you a draft dodger?"

"No. I don't know. I left before my number came up, but you know, it was all pretty much over anyway. Lucky, I guess." Pink is quiet for a minute; some of his friends weren't so lucky. He looks at Carson, thinks about how easily money can buy a ticket out. Some of the time, anyway. "Man, if you don't want to give me a ride, that's okay. I'd better get going."

"I never do anything for nothing, you know. Everything has a price."

"I don't have any money."

"Then give me a name."

"What?"

"I mean, you made up *your* name, right? Nobody called you that. Don't tell me otherwise. I want a name. A fresh start."

"You want me to give you a name."

"Yes. What's my name?"

Pink thinks for a minute.

"You said you felt . . . free."

Clouds gather, the air chills slightly, and Carson "Freedom" Weymouth Jr. shivers.

"I'll give you something else," Pink says, digging into his pack. In it is the t-shirt Carson will be wearing when he pulls into the parking lot of Cass's roadside café a half-hour from now.

3:20 p.m.
Coffee, black

The silver Jaguar glints in the afternoon sun as it pulls into the lot, and Jo puts down the newspaper she's been reading to watch its driver emerge. American plates. A movie star, maybe. Certainly somebody rich. Doing what, exactly, at Cass's Roadside Café? But the man who emerges is wearing a Pink Floyd t-shirt.

"Nice car," she tells him as he opens the door to the diner. As he enters, he glances over his shoulder, then around the room before settling on Jo.

"Actually, I'm selling it," he tells her. "Trading it, maybe. For a truck?" He seems uncertain.

"Why do you want to do that?"

He giggles, a childlike sound. "Just want a change, I guess. Yes, that's it. Do you know anybody? I'd make a deal. A good one."

Jo shakes her head. "What can I get you?"

"Just coffee, please. Black."

"Something else? Cass makes great cookies."

Carson begins to laugh then. He laughs for long enough that Jo finds herself glancing towards the trailer, where Cass is apparently taking the longest nap in the history of the world, or she's into one of her soap opera marathons. As Carson's laughter subsides, "Everyone should get to have dessert," he says, and starts up again.

Jo pours his coffee. What else can she do?

"You know, it's not like me to talk about myself," Carson says, wrapping two hands around the cup. "I've always kept my cards close to my chest. Second nature, really. But there was the hitchhiker just now, and, I don't know. I mean, after this morning. What have I got to lose?" He starts laughing again, as if he's just cracked a knee-slapping good joke.

"What hitchhiker?"

"Oh, just a guy." Carson pulls at the hem of his t-shirt, holds it out, and looks at it. On the front, two businessmen shake hands. One of them is in flames. *Wish You Were Here* it reads.

Carson looks around the café, takes in the Jesus hands, the Fanta sign. He reads the slogan on his cup: *You should be dancing*. His face falls into an expression of bewilderment. "This will take some getting used to."

Jo leans against the back counter, arms crossed, watching the customer sip his coffee. "What did you mean, everyone should get to have dessert?" Like he said, she thinks, what have I got to lose?

"Well, I'd just had this—shock, I guess you'd call it. A fright. So I ducked into the kitchen of the hotel I was in—ran right past the cooks—and out the back door. And that's when I met these girls."

Uh, oh, thinks Jo. She glances again at the trailer.

"Two of them, dressed like . . . hippies, I guess you'd call them. You know, long hair, backpacks, sandals, that sort of thing. Not people I usually talk to. There was a restaurant worker about to throw out leftover desserts into the Dumpster. The Chancery Bay Hotel is the best in the city. These were éclairs, petit-fours: dainty little desserts on doilies. Chancery Bay is known for its high tea. I never thought about what they might do with food that wasn't absolutely fresh, but of course, they couldn't serve anything but the best to their clientele."

Jo thinks about Howie, and the day-old sandwiches Cass

would send over with Bob. Nothing was ever wasted at Cass's. What couldn't be eaten, if it wasn't to be disguised in one of Cass's Today's Special casseroles, became dog food or chicken food, or generally fed to something.

"He asked if they wanted one, and they asked for them all. He just shrugged his shoulders and left the trays there, telling them he'd get them a couple of boxes. When they had loaded them up and the fellow had gone back inside, my curiosity got the better of me. I guess I startled them, coming out of the shadows like that. But when I asked them what they were going to do with all those desserts, 'Follow us,' said the girl with the earrings. So I did."

Carson pushes his empty cup forward, and Jo fills it.

"The part of town they led me to . . . I'll tell you, I was shocked. I was also—not in my right mind, you understand. Because of this thing that had happened. So I suppose I sort of stumbled after them, as much because I didn't know what else to do as anything. It was early in the morning, not yet even eight o'clock, when I think about it. A lot had happened really fast. On the way, they introduced themselves: the girl with the earrings, she was dark-skinned with black hair, which she wore straight and parted in the middle—like yours—her name was Angie. The other girl, with the blonde hair, was Susan. They explained to me that they had spent the night in the park. They were looking for food. Restaurants are always throwing out food, the better the restaurant, the more they waste, she said. They weren't actually looking for desserts. But now that they had so many . . . It's funny. They didn't even ask what I was doing there, or why I wanted to follow them. I wonder why."

Because you look shell-shocked, thinks Jo. Because you look lost. Even in a suit. Or half a suit.

"The streets we walked down: faded signs and burnt-out neon of seedy hotels, free clinics, strip clubs. In some of the doorways were piles of clothing—and I realized to my absolute horror there were people inside the clothing. Street bums. Rubbies. Winos. Words I'd heard used, but that I never attached to a real human being. When the first one rolled over and stretched . . . *well.*"

"I remember my father drove me through the Southeast, once," Jo offers. "So I'd be grateful for what I had, I guess. My mother was furious with him when we got back." Jo's not even sure what city he's talking about, but the scene is clear in front of her. There had been a garbage strike at the time. What she most remembers was the smell, which served to underline the inescapability of the situation for the residents of the street.

Carson nods, but carries on as if ignoring a non sequitur. "I sat on a bench in a scrubby patch of park the size of a postage stamp and watched those two girls offer desserts, still on their paper doilies, to each person on the street. They did it with such—*kindness.* And humour, with this little flourish, like they were all at the Chancery Bay. But not like they were any better than the people on the receiving end, you understand. They'd just open the box and people would choose one—just one—and then take the box and offer it to the other people around them before handing it back to the girls. So polite. It's not that polite in the boardroom." He looks at Jo, and his eyes are full of wonder. Like a small boy, she thinks. "I'd forgotten that people could actually look after one another."

Jo refills Carson's coffee again, and he nods gratefully.

"One old man was very close to where I sat. He was curled up against a wall, eyes closed, and when I noticed him at first, I didn't know if he was just resting, or dead. I actually thought he might be dead. Beside him was a grocery cart full of odd items, cans and bottles. He opened his eyes when he heard people stirring around him. He had the bluest eyes I've ever seen. Then he looked at the dessert that Angie was holding out to him, picked it up, and took a bite. As with any good éclair, the Bavarian cream squirted out the sides. He laughed—and so did I.

"The girls were having a pretty good time with it all. The desserts were gone, so they flattened the boxes and put them beside the overflowing garbage can. I'd been pretty quiet up until then. I asked Susan why they did it."

Jo is leaning on the counter, chin in her hands. "What did she say?"

"She said: '*Everyone* should get to have dessert.'"

Jo sends him on his way with a bag of Cass's cookies. She leans in the doorway in the afternoon light and watches the man in the dress pants, Italian leather shoes, and Pink Floyd t-shirt carrying a brown paper bag who smiles thinly as he gets into his car.

Before he left, he'd sheepishly told her his name was now Free.

"Does that sound silly?"

"It sounds—liberating," she told him. "It sounds like something someone would want to be."

"That's what *I* thought."

Now, as the Jaguar turns tentatively from the lot, Bob's cruiser pulls in. There's a lurch, and then the Jag is on the highway and picking up speed.

Jo

"Higher class of business you're getting here these days," comments Bob as he walks in, screen door banging behind him.

"Yeah," I say. "No thanks to Cass's influence."

Bob nods towards the trailer. "What, she left you to yourself all day?"

"Guess she figures I can handle it."

"Of course you can."

"Anyway, I don't think there's been two people in here at the same time all day," I tell him, but he's looking at the highway, where Carson's car had turned.

"There was something that came in this morning. Asking for our cooperation. I should call it in, that might have been the car."

Should I say anything? That guy certainly looked nervous, but he never said anything specific. If he's done something, it'll probably catch up with him without any help from me.

"Cass has fresh cookies," I tell Bob.

When I was small, my dad taught me about taking responsibility for your actions. It was after I got caught taking money that had been left for the paperboy. I guess I was ten or so, and Todd, who delivered the *Herald*, was twelve. I never liked Todd; he lived on Farnham and curled his lip when he talked. A couple of years before, when I was eight and he was ten, I was walking home from Nick's corner store with a *Donald Duck* comic book. He was coming the other way on his bicycle and as we passed on the sidewalk he skidded to a stop, almost knocking me down. He snatched my comic, crumpling it, and looked at it, sneering. Then he tossed it back. "Oh. *Donald Duck*. Kid's stuff," he said, and dropped it for me to pick up while he rode away. When I got home, "What did you buy with your allowance?" my mother asked, and I was too embarrassed to tell her, suddenly, that I'd bought a *Donald Duck* comic book, which I had smoothed out and then rolled into a tight cylinder that I held against my side. It was a terrible thing, I suddenly realized, to be a kid who still read *Donald Duck*. What had I been thinking? Later, in my room, I unrolled the comic book, but I couldn't enjoy it anymore.

My mother would put the money for the month's newspaper delivery in an envelope and thumbtack it to the door. Inside would be the charge, plus a fifty-cent tip. What I began doing was taking one of the two quarters meant for Todd, who didn't deserve them both, in my opinion. Then I would go to Nick's and buy a *Ripley's Believe It or Not*, having moved up from *Donald Duck*.

I'm not sure how my mother caught me. I was too embarrassed to ask, the temperature in the room suddenly rising, a noise in my ears like a big truck passing on the freeway. But she turned me over to my father, the look between them saying how deeply disappointed they were in me. At least, that's how I read it.

My father told me a story about his own childhood. Until then, it hadn't occurred to me he *had* a childhood. He and his friend Jerry had been playing with fire, he told me, in back of a neighbour's barn. They started with little piles of brush. They had a contest—a dare—to see how big they could let it get and still stamp it out. I can see them, killing themselves laughing while they melted the soles of their boots. When the brush fire got too big and ignited the mouldy bale of hay leaning against the barn wall, and that, in turn, went up in sheets of flame, both boys took off. They hid out until dinnertime, watching from the woods as the fire brigade arrived, in awe, I guess, of what they'd done, but fascinated, too. Then they went to their homes pretending they'd spent the day hunting crows with their slingshots.

When questioned, my dad told me, he made his eyes go wide and pretended to know nothing about the fire—his first mistake, he said, because you'd have to have been a hundred miles away or unconscious to have missed the plume of smoke and the sirens. That, and the fact that his shoes smelled like burnt rubber and the bottoms of his pants were black and caked in ash, were dead giveaways.

Dad and Jerry had to work for the fellow who owned the old barn for the entire summer. Even though the barn was really worthless, nothing stored in it anymore, and ready to be torn down. *His* dad—my grandfather—told him that even though the barn wasn't long for this world, it belonged to someone else. That you have to take responsibility for your actions, and that it was up to the barn's owner to set the price.

I told him I didn't think it was fair to have to work a whole summer—every day for two whole months—for a falling-down barn. "Fair? Fair is a place where pigs get ribbons, Jo-girl," he told me, sitting on the end of the bed in my room while I leaned against the headboard, hugging a pillow. "You do something bad, you don't get to set the penalty. You just lost all your rights."

I had to pay Todd back every quarter I'd stolen, in person, in front of his mother, and apologize. It was horrible, because

Todd's lip never stopped curling the whole time, and I knew he would tell his friends at school, which he did. Much later, when I liked Terry Mitchell and it must have shown as I hung around in his general proximity in the cafeteria, I heard Todd tell him: "That little thief has the hots for you," sending me scurrying to the girls' washroom to cry in the stall.

Because I had spent the money, I had to borrow it from my dad and pay him back, and that meant a variety of jobs that, in turn, kept me away from my circle of friends who gathered at one house or another on the weekends, so that when I finally returned to the group, debts paid, new alliances had formed and I was now the odd person out. Worse, I didn't want to tell them the truth about why I hadn't been around, so I told them I had to do chores. "Your parents are really cruel," Patty said, the others nodding and, hoping to be re-admitted into the fold, I agreed, feeling guilty for this new betrayal. So it was, then, the beginning of my future of being a loner, a chain reaction I never could have predicted when all I wanted was a *Ripley's Believe It or Not* comic book.

Dad told me, that day in my room, that taking responsibility for your actions also means showing you've learned your lesson. At the time, I just wanted him to go away. I just wanted *everyone* to go away. It took me a long time to pull the lesson from the punishment. Now, I'd give just about anything to be a kid again, with Dad sitting at the end of my bed giving me some boring father/daughter lecture.

If I could talk to my father now, what would I say?

It's not like I think Bob was really going to run out and arrest the guy in the Jaguar. Bob doesn't seem like the kind of guy to run out and arrest anybody, cop or not. And I don't even know if there's something to arrest the guy for, except that he looked like someone on the run shooting for—freedom, I guess. I figure if there's anything to catch up with him, it will eventually. He might as well have time to eat the cookies.

Everyone should get to have dessert.

Cass

Every so often I've got to take a lazy day, and I suppose this is the one. Jo knows to call me if it gets busy, but you can just tell when it's not going to. Some days, everyone comes in a clump, other days, it's one by one by one. Jesus, day's almost over now I come to look at it. Well, she never did call me, and that's a blessing. Because right now, Dirk is about to make off with Sofia, herself married to Brad who is for sure a good-for-nothing, although I'm not at all sure that Dirk is a better choice. I could tell Sofia a thing of two about men, but from the look of her she'd not likely listen to me.

I like the soaps. I like the way you can see good and evil so clearly. Even the music changes when the sleazy guy starts putting one over on the innocent girl, lying to his wife, that type of thing. You know who to like and who to hate. It's not always so easy in real life.

I've managed to stay free of a man, pretty much, my whole life. That is, free of a man telling me what to do. Bob says that makes me one of those feminists, but I don't count myself in with the bra-burners. I'm just not about to compromise anything for some man, that's all. I'm thinking of my own mother, here. Forget it. And Archie? Archie's a buddy, and a good one. That's all. Otherwise, he keeps his nose out, mostly.

When I was a little younger than Jo is now—still in high school, in fact, so maybe too young to know better—I met Bruno Scarpelli. Dressed nice. Talked smooth. Had a way of touching my face, just along my jawline—I had a jawline back then—that sent shivers right down to my toes. He had chest hair when none of the boys I knew had chest hair, and combed and greased his black hair into a ducktail. Mum hated him, but what did she know? After all, she'd married Dad, and where was he? Bruno said that when I finished high school, we'd travel. See the world.

Three o'clock in the morning one night there's a tap at my bedroom window. By now we'd moved to the main floor apartment of a house downtown, and we got to use the basement for storage, but I had made myself a little room down there so I could get away from my sisters, get some privacy. I've always loved my privacy.

So anyway, Bruno taps on my basement window and wakes me up out of a deep sleep, annoying, but it's thrilling, too. No way he could come in without waking everyone up, and no way he could fit that bulk of his through the casement window, but I was skinnier then. I threw on some clothes, stood on my dresser and wiggled through, crawled out onto the grass and then flipped over onto my back, looking up at the big black shape that was Bruno, the night stars all around him. He pulled me to my feet and gave me a deep, long kiss that just about melted my kneecaps. Then he told me he needed my help.

I'd have done anything he asked. Anything.

There were two guys I'd never met in the Chev idling on the street. The dome light was busted—you could see the wires dangling—so I couldn't see them very well. Bruno drove, and I sat beside him up front, feeling special, like I really was his girl. *Bruno's girl.* The guys in the back made a couple of cracks but Bruno told them to shut up. I felt protected, then. I was Bruno's girl, and he was looking after me.

We drove up to the back of a pawn shop. Bruno told me the guy had ripped him off, took his watch and sold it and now wouldn't give him the money for it, even though he had the chit. He told me it was his dad's watch, God rest his soul he said, and that he just wanted to take what was his due, nothing more. That he had been planning to use the money from the watch to help out his mother, who was sick. To buy her medicine. The guys in the back saying, yeah, this pawn guy has ripped off other guys. He was a bad character, they said.

Bruno had been teaching me to drive in empty parking lots, around and around, using the row of streetlights down the middle like traffic cones on a test course, weaving in and out. He said he'd give me a car for graduation, had a buddy who worked at a wrecker, could fix one up for me nobody wanted anymore. So I knew how to drive well enough, I guess.

I was behind the wheel when the alarm sounded. I saw Bruno run towards the car, his buddies right behind, then saw the tall one fling something back into the open door. The blast was like a furnace, heat and noise, and I was down under the dash, Bruno beside me, hauling me up by my hair and yelling DRIVE! I stepped on the gas, the back door swinging where one of the guys had opened it then fell and rolled when the car lurched off, I could see him on the ground in the rearview, but I couldn't see the other guy at all, just a lot of smoke. We must've driven right by a sleeping cruiser coming out of the alley at eighty, and he was on our tail in no time, me shaking and crying, Bruno yelling FASTER! We came around a corner and ducked down another alley and Bruno yelled SLOW DOWN and I hit the brakes and he was out and running down a gap between buildings. When the cops pulled up it was just me in the car, the passenger door open, car all pitted up with whatever it was that exploded from the back of the pawn shop—glass and metal and wood and stuff—and stolen, to boot. And on the floor of the passenger seat the duffel bag with a bunch of jewellery and stuff from the smashed display case the cops found in the wreckage, but not of any great value because all the good stuff was in the safe with the money.

I got three months in juvie as an accomplice. I was supposed to finish my high school there, but I never. I met some girls who scared the pants off me, and encountered some stuff I'd rather not relate. I did learn to look after myself, and expect nobody to look after me. Mum about wrote me off; when Dad left me the diner, that was the final straw, because she never figured I deserved it after all the shame and trouble I'd caused, never mind how he came by it in the first place. "Serves you right for listening to some good-for-nothing hoodlum," she told me when she got to the police station, and that much I listened to even if I ignored the rest of her ranting and raving.

So when Archie brings me a stray now and then, I know a thing or two about mistakes, I figure. Enough so that when Cantha was screwing up, I could see it clear as day just as if there was that music like in the soaps, you know? Telling you what's going to happen by getting all spooky. Could see the good and the bad in Cantha like I wrote the script myself, except I'd never have written a little kid like Donnie into a show like that. Not ever. Now she's grown up herself, gotta wonder if she learned how to be, or how not to be. Wonder if I'll ever know.

Wind shift

When the wind blows, the cradle will rock
— Nursery rhyme

I'm on my way back to Cass's. Screw-up with the load I'm scheduled to pick up from the mill and Cass is closest, always say take the path of least resistance, right? On the way up the hill I see that hippie on the side of the road, waiting for a ride in the other direction. Laugh to myself, because he's gone just about nowhere all day with that crazy rule he's following, but he's determined, I'll give him that much. And sure enough, wind's blowing the way he's trying to go. So I give him a wave as I pass and he raises his hand in return. Crazy kids.

I'm rounding the bluff where the rock face goes straight up on one side and the other side is cliff all the way down to the lake way below, when I see this guy waving me down. The highway's full of freaks these days, and that's a fact, but the truth is, I don't mind them much. They kind of add a bit of colour. I pull the rig over and leave my door and the two windows open when I get out, hope to cool off the interior some with the wind blowing through. Been sticking to the vinyl all afternoon.

Well, the fellow tells me he's got a bus with an overheated radiator down a side road, and his wife's pregnant, and could I help them out. I got a can of water and a little time and it's not anything I wouldn't want someone to do for me, though I admit there's a moment when we're walking down that road and there's no vehicle in sight and I'm wondering if there aren't maybe six of them waiting in the bushes to jump me, and wishing I'd closed up the rig at least. Then I see this painted-up school bus, all—what do they call it?—psychedelic. Big yellow daisies and hearts, looks like a kid painted some of it. Across the front it says, where the route would have been posted, Magic Bouncing Baby Bus. It's got its hood up, steam all over the place.

The girl is sitting in the grass. Her hair is up in a kerchief, her long skirt all spread out around her. She looks like she's got a basketball in there.

"You paint your bus up for the baby?" I'm trying to be friendly. She looks kind of worried or something. "It's just a radiator overheated. We'll get it fixed up for you, don't you worry."

"Melissa's a midwife," the husband says, looking at the bus. "A mobile midwife."

I guess I look a little blank.

"She does home births."

"What happened to hospitals?" I ask, but I don't get an answer because the husband hauls off his t-shirt and balls it up around his hand to take the radiator cap off and I yell "Whoa!" because I can see it's going to have to cool down some before he tries something like that or I'll be taking him to the hospital—and that's a bit of a drive, out here in the middle of nowhere. He steps back, hands in the air like I'm going to shoot him, his right hand still all wrapped up. "You gotta give it time to cool down. Don't be opening that now."

Michael and Melissa, their names are. Michael looks like those pictures of Jesus, long hair and a beard. He's wearing some kind of rawhide vest, looks homemade. Melissa's hair is really long, brown waves right down her back to her fanny. She must be sitting on it all the time. I look at the bus, wonder how these people wash.

But they're nice enough young people, I guess. I point to the water can, though, tell them they can keep it. Get up to head back out to the highway, back to the rig. But: "Don't," says Melissa. "Please. Would you stay and help us get it going? Please."

That's when Michael tells me Melissa thinks she's in labour and that the midwife lives about eight miles up the road from here. Ross Creek Road is a forest service road, I tell them. There's no houses up there.

"In a teepee," explains Michael.

"I've been feeling funny all morning. I just want to get to Carole-Ann's." She smiles at me. "Even midwives need midwives."

Michael looks at me, then at the steaming engine, then towards the highway. "Can't take my rig up that road," I tell him. "Don't know how you were going to get that bus up there, but maybe. Thing is, I've been hunting up there, so I know. Can't turn around, even, not 'til you're practically at the top."

There's a CB in the rig, I can call for help, I tell them. They shake their heads. No ambulance. "We want a natural childbirth," says Michael. Well, I don't know, it's all new to me, but live and let live, that's what I say.

So I sit with them on a hunk of concrete there in the weeds, thinking things'll cool down pretty quick and I'll see them on their way. Melissa's from way down in Tennessee, she tells me, learned the baby business with some sort of hippie caravan, so now she goes around helping deliver babies. That is, she tells me, when she's not having her own. This is her first.

Michael's from Toronto. They met at some big concert

somewhere, thousands of people. "It was a trip," says Michael, "but the biggest trip was meeting Melissa."

We sit waiting for the rad to cool down. I keep looking at the girl, big as a house. I sure as hell don't want to be around any baby being born, and I wish they'd let me call on the CB or just let me the hell go, but I feel like I should stick around because I don't want it on my conscience if they don't get the bus up and running, and wind up having the baby here in the middle of nowhere.

We sit together in a little circle, me on the berm, Melissa on the step of the bus and Michael on the ground at her feet, and they start telling me about helping babies be born, and half the time it's more than I want to know thanks very much, but I listen anyway at first to be polite and then because I've just never heard the like, and I suppose I'm kind of fascinated, you know? The way you get sometimes, reading some of those *Enquirer* stories. Two-headed calves, aliens. It makes you feel weird, but you can't stop reading.

Those two, they travel around in that bus and how they know about who needs them is word of mouth or some kind of hippie jungle drums, I guess. But they know where to go. They just came from helping in the delivery of a baby boy, and when they talk about it their eyes kind of glaze over.

"It was far out, man, so . . ."

". . . wonderful, so holy, like . . ."

". . . something spiritual, like . . ."

". . . a miracle, this little . . ."

". . . boy, when he turned pink, and you could actually see the blood . . ."

". . . rushing from his chest into his arms and legs and he looked like . . ."

". . . Krishna, his little arms and legs . . ."

". . . weaving like a sacred dance and it was so . . ."

". . . beautiful."

Well, it doesn't sound very medical to me and I tell them so. "Whatever happened to hospitals?" I ask them. "You know, doctors."

Michael shakes his head. "That's no way to have a baby, man."

Melissa describes the lady in labour, with the father, brothers and sisters, friends all around, like it's some big party. Seems a little personal to me, should be private. Not a place a man should be, somehow. Makes me think of a Stanley Cup party, like this spring when everyone jammed into our little living room to watch the Habs win. Imagine having a baby in the middle of something that.

The wind has died again but the rad's still hot so we sit for a while together and I decide I don't mind them so much. So they dress funny. So what?

"My mama was a midwife," Melissa tilts her head, picks a daisy and twirls it in her fingers. Her voice is singsong, that funny accent from the South. "And my grandma, too, although later she changed her specialty, you could say. I was born at home, and my brothers and sisters, too. We lived in the Blue Ridge Mountains on a small farm. I was the youngest, so I never saw any siblings born, and Mama didn't ever take me to births because I had all the older ones to look after me, and I suppose it was just easier for her. I only ever went on a visit with her once and I had to play outside the whole time, but that was okay with me because I saw a litter of puppies being born in the barn and I remember being disappointed when later Mama told me that the lady had had only one baby, and that was hard enough. I thought it would be better to have puppies, and then you could play with them right away.

"Then Papa died and Mama started midwifing more for the money and the trade goods. My sisters got married off and my brothers took the farming part on and so I started going with Grandma on her visits. While Mama specialized in births, well, Grandma, by then, she specialized in deaths."

Melissa peers around to the front of the bus. "Think that's cool enough yet?" she asks me. "I think we should get on the road." Michael and I look at the front of the bus. I can see the heat rising in waves, making the trees behind look like they're melting. "Don't think so," I tell her. "Few more minutes, we'll give it a try."

"You okay?" Michael's hand is on her belly again.

"Think so. I'm not getting real contractions yet. I just feel like I . . . I just want to be there, you know?" There's a tremor in her voice. She looks at me, eyes all soft. "Can you stay a little longer?" She's agitated, and I tell her sure, I can stay a little longer, get things fixed up.

To distract her and pass the time, "Tell me about your grandma," I say. She takes a big breath, lets it out, and goes on, hands clasped tightly around the daisy.

"Grandma would go help someone who was about to die. She organized everything: say it was an old auntie, she got the relatives who hadn't spoken for years talking to her and to each other. She could mend a rift in a family like it was an old shirt just needed a button. If people were too grief-stricken to make the arrangements, she did that. She knew when the dying wanted their kin around them and when they wanted to be left alone; even if they couldn't talk anymore, she knew. She knew when there were days left, when there were only minutes. And when the person finally went, the first thing she'd do is open all the windows to let the spirit out of the room. To set it free on its journey."

The wind, which had died for a bit, has come up again, and I think: that's good. Things'll cool down faster, now. I want to get going, because some old gal letting spirits fly out of windows is just a little—well, just a little too hippie, I'm thinking, 'til I remember Melissa's a little girl in this story and her grandma an old lady, and this was way before hippies and psychedelic painted buses were all over the place.

"Where were you born?" Melissa asks me. Wood's Harbour I tell her, and then I realize that's not what she means. I realize I don't know if I was born at home or in a hospital. Not something we ever talked about, and I certainly don't remember, but the more I think about it, the more I think I probably was born at the house. Like her, I was the last born. Doris must be fifty-nine this year, Betty fifty-eight, and me come along almost ten years later. Never said anything about it, though they must have had some recollection of the event. Most likely they were sent to a neighbour's, I figure, or Aunt Maddie's when the time came. Never thought to ask, and that's what I told her.

"How a baby is born, and where, and who is there to greet the baby, and what those first moments are like," explains Michael, "That's the most important thing. The first thing a baby knows affects how it sees the world from then on in. If the first thing is a bunch of strangers and bright lights and a slap, if the mother's all doped up, can't even relate to her baby at the beginning when it's most important, well, it's not much of a first impression of the world, is it?"

"What if something goes wrong?"

"It did, once," says Melissa quietly. She begins plucking

petals off the daisy. "I had just started apprenticing. Laura tried everything. It was a Christian family, everybody praying and praying, the mama losing energy and blood and getting weaker and weaker so she couldn't push anymore but then finally she found the energy—I don't know where but I guess they were praying for it—but by then the baby was dead. I'll never forget the way that mama wailed, and then the family praying in the next room started wailing too, still praying: 'Lord Jesus Save his Soul,' and the grandma saying 'Get the priest, we need to baptize him.' Laura just trying to get the placenta delivered so we wouldn't lose the mama, too. And then I did what I knew how to do, which was open the windows to let the spirit out, like I'd been taught.

"The grandma shouted: 'What are you doing?' because there was a real storm happening outside, wind and rain and even hail, and I explained I was letting the baby's spirit out. 'Get that witch out of here,' the grandma hissed and Laura nodded I'd better go, and I guessed the storm outside was better than the storm inside at that moment. I went out and stood in the rain and cried, listening to the sound of the windows being shut up tight."

The daisy is in pieces, Melissa's lap full of petals. She brushes them off and picks another one. Michael leans against the side of the bus, eyes closed, one hand resting gently on Melissa's bare foot. "Cool enough yet?" she asks, looking at the hood of the bus. I take Michael's t-shirt and walk over. When I turn the radiator cap I jump back just in time to miss the hissing steam that shoots out. "Pretty soon," I say.

Then, when I come back to the bus I see water dripping off the bottom step and I think *can't be the radiator all the way over here* and then I realize it's come from the girl. The daisy is on the ground, and she's breathing heavily, hand on her belly. Michael's on his feet, then he's helping her into the bus while I stand outside, grasshoppers going off in the long grass and a can of water at my feet and now the radiator is quiet and probably cooled enough to open up but I don't think we're going anywhere because from inside the bus comes a wail that makes every hair on my arms stand straight up.

A second later and Michael's at the door. "You gotta try it *now!*" he yells and when I crack the radiator cap I have to jump back for the arc of hot water comes spitting out but after that it's just a quiet hiss and I get the water in it, wait 'til it settles, put some more in and all the time these low groans coming from the bus.

"Okay!" I call, and Michael yells: "Key's in the ignition!" and there's nothing to do but climb in and try to start the thing.

But it doesn't start. I crank and crank her but it's not catching, the motor groaning and Melissa groaning, and me groaning with the frustration of it, all of us groaning. After a while the engine's not even turning over, and there's sweat running down my face and I know I've run the battery down on top of everything else. I realize I've been cranking the thing for twenty minutes at least.

There's no time for a boost. The sounds coming from the back are big, bigger than anything, and over them I hear Michael calling for me to come. I sit with my two hands on the steering wheel and look out at the day. The wind has whipped up something fierce and it's blowing all around us. I see the daisy Melissa picked fly by. Michael calls again, and there is nothing to do but go.

It's dim in the back. In the front part of the bus there is a small stove and sink with a pump faucet and a bucket beneath.

Banged-together cupboards, their knobs tied together with big elastic bands. Most of the back is taken up with a bed. Michael has a sheet spread out between Melissa's open legs. She's naked, and I don't know where to look. "It's not supposed to be this fast," she's gasping, and Michael reminds her to breathe. "Don't you tell *me* what to do!" she shouts, like she's a whole different person than she was a half-hour ago, and Michael jumps back like he's been burned.

His hands are trembling and he holds them up as if to show me how scared he is, but "She says to wash them" he tells me. "You need to get me a bowl of water and the soap and a towel—over there."

I pump the water but of course it's cold. I can hear Melissa giving Michael directions when she's not moaning or panting and I bring over a bucket of water and the Sunlight soap and have to turn around in the small space and reach back for the towel, kicking the bucket with my foot and spilling some. My own hands are shaking.

The wind's blowing all around us but inside it feels like the outside doesn't exist. There's Melissa, propped upright on a bunch of pillows with a bunch of sheets under her, her legs almost underneath her, now. Her chest is hanging right out there. Huge nipples. Different situation, I'd feel differently about seeing something like that. There's Michael, right in front, and he's rubbing her legs up and down and saying things like: you're doing great, baby, while she breathes and pants and pauses and starts breathing again. And there's me, pressed up against the sink and wanting to leave and wanting to see this in that twisted way you do like wanting to see a crash at a stock car race. I can see her belly tighten all over like a drum, and I can see between her legs, everything, and I don't even think about sex, not once. And this all goes on for what could be a day or could be a minute, I can't tell anymore.

"It's coming. It's coming too fast. Melissa! Is it supposed to come so fast?" Michael's voice is high, like a girl's.

Over his voice comes Melissa's, and I think: that's courage. That's real courage, because she's somehow got ahold of herself and she's actually calming him down, giving him instructions: "Support underneath, where it's bulging," she gasps. "With your fingers. Okay, I'm gonna push, now."

The sound is animal. There is nothing human about it. It goes on, and on. I look away. I don't want to see this, and I might throw up. I feel dizzy, and at the same time I feel embarrassed for being sick and dizzy. The sound stops, and there is heavy breathing. Then: "Hold my hand," she commands, and I do what I'm told, moving up towards her in the cramped space, so now I'm right beside Michael, my legs losing their circulation under me, the bulk of me taking up what feels like way too much space. I look at our hands, where she's cutting the circulation faster than my own feet are going to sleep. My fingernails are dirty. In a moment, the ends of my fingers are white from the pressure.

"I can see the head! Oh, Melissa. I can see the head!" says Michael, then: "It's going back in."

"S'okay. I'm going to push again in a minute. You have to feel for the cord."

"What?"

"The cord," she gasps. "You have to put your fingers right up inside. See if the cord's around the neck."

"But—"

There's that sound again, that animal sound.

"I don't know. I can feel the neck I think. I can't tell. There's no cord. I can't feel a cord. I think it's okay. But it's all blue. Melissa. Everything's blue."

She takes her other hand, the hand that's not holding mine, and she reaches down and touches the top of the baby's head, a blue bulge in all that red. "Okay," she gasps. "You're sure? Okay."

The sound begins again, the longest yet, getting louder towards the end. She reaches down and touches again. The bulge is bigger.

"Okay Michael, listen. You have to gently take the head when it comes out and feel for the shoulders. Then you have to ease the shoulders through. You have to turn them a little, you—"

Another animal sound, and sweet Jesus there's the head, all misshapen and awful like something out of the *Enquirer*, slimy and bloody and the wrong colour, and then the shoulders and the sound of hard breathing and—then there is a wet sound, like nothing I have ever heard.

"A girl! It's a girl!"

"Let me see." Melissa's voice is husky, like someone else, but I'm not looking at her, I'm looking at the thing in Michael's hands. It's horrible, ugly, not human. It's covered in white slime and underneath it's blue and there's a bulbous twisted thing coming out of its belly.

"Michael, you have to clear her nose. Suck on her nose and mouth."

I feel my stomach flip.

"She's still blue. She's not breathing. Melissa."

"Mouth to mouth. You know how. Rub her chest." She is the only one in control, here. I do believe I am going to faint. I lean against the wall of the bus, eye to eye with a Grateful Dead poster, wanting to be anywhere, anywhere else. Michael does what she says, I can hear him breathing, little puffs, listening. Is it a minute, or an hour?

"Keep. Going. No, give her to me." And now Melissa's on her side and the twisted thing snakes up from between her legs to the blue baby, almost hidden beneath Melissa's long brown hair. She's breathing into the baby. I can hear Michael saying ohmygodohmelissaohmygod but I can't see him because I can't take my eyes off Melissa. She looks around, sees me.

"Open the windows." Almost a hiss. "Open the windows *now*." I don't think, I just do what I'm told. I start opening them, all of the sliding windows down the length of the bus. I start at the back, moving forward, and after the fifth window I know why I'm doing this and a sob comes out.

When I get to where the baby is, lying on its back in the crook of Melissa's arm, Michael pushing with two fingers onto its tiny chest, I am about to open the sixth window and I can't look at it, I have to look at the window, I have to follow instructions, my face all wet, a roaring in my ears, and then I hear it, a tiny cry.

There is laughter as the small voice gets louder, crazy laughter. When I finally bring myself to look there is a pink, slimy baby in her mother's arms and I step outside into the sunshine and throw up, finally, into the tall grass at the side of the road.

I sit there on the concrete for a while and drink some from the water can even though the water tastes like old metal and rust. I don't want to go inside, now. It's not the place for a man, at least, not this one. It's private, that's all.

After a bit Michael pokes his head out. "She delivered the placenta," he says. "Want to see?" he asks, and I can't think what to say to that, then I realize to my relief that he means the baby. I do. Can't come this far, after all.

I come in and there are fresh sheets under Melissa and the baby's all wrapped up in a little flannel blanket. "You can touch her," she says and I reach out a finger, which looks huge and coarse. Dirty from the rad cap. She is pink, now, and cleaner, and she looks like a tiny old man. Touch her little hand and she curls her fingers around mine. Never felt a thing like that before.

We get the bus started after just a couple of tries. Maybe it was just flooded, I don't know. They want the midwife to check things out, don't care if they can't get the bus turned around after. They just want to get there. Melissa gives me a hug and a big sloppy kiss on my stubbly old cheek. Michael thanks me too, and I can't say I'm used to being hugged by a man but I take it because there was just a baby born, after all. Michael's still a little shaky, and Melissa teases him about whether or not he should drive. I'm a little shaky myself as I watch the bus with all its crazy colours head on up the Ross Creek Road. I forgot to ask them what her name is.

When I get back to the rig the wind's died down again. Before I climb in I look down the drop-off by the shoulder, a tumble of boulders with this one scrubby little pine tree growing sideways out of the rock like some kind of miracle. Life, when it wants to, can grow just about anywhere.

Jo

There's a lull in which no-one comes in the diner, and I decide to clean up under the counter, something Cass probably hasn't done in the last two decades. When I pull out the box-of-many-things, I find a nest of miscellaneous stuff so much like a packrat's nest, I think for a minute that's what it actually is. But no, it's an eight-track tape disintegrating into spaghetti folds. Good thing: Cass has told me a tale or two about pack-rats. The tape goes in the garbage, as well as half a deck of playing cards and several bottle caps: Hires, Crush, Pepsi. There's a photograph of Cass and Archie, in younger, thinner days, which I put back in the box after noting the smaller girth of the trees around the diner. There is a handful of emergency candles—hard to find way back there if the power did go out—and, in the corner, a baby's bottle.

It's glass, with flattened sides. The nipple is old, its rubber breaking down, powdery. What baby lips touched it, once? What small hands held it?

There were nights when I felt the baby kick and roll, an alien thing inside me. At the end I slept with four pillows: under my head, at the small of my back, between my legs and, finally, one to wrap my arms around. In the morning, the baby would wake up with me, stretch inside me. I could imagine it yawning, eyes squeezed shut.

The papers were all in place. "You can change your mind," the social worker said, "but we don't encourage it. You've certainly been responsible, keeping up with your appointments, eating well. Not every pregnant teenager is like you've been, let me tell you."

Change my mind. I thought about it every waking second, and dreamt about it every night. Then I'd think of the basement apartment, with its mis-hung cupboards, its damp bathroom. Upstairs, the bull terrier barked all day long.

Irresponsible conception, responsible pregnancy, irresponsible fantasies, responsible conclusion. Does each responsible action cancel out the irresponsible one? If so, where does that leave me, now?

Change my mind.

Which would have meant acknowledging that my daughter had a grandmother. *Has* a grandmother. Now, my mother doesn't ever need to know. Not my mother, not my daughter. Just me, in the middle, girl with a secret.

Whirlwind

A people without history
is like the wind on the buffalo grass
— Sioux saying

Pixie settles herself on a rock. It's almost time to go back to work, back into town. To make her Monday shift at the co-op, she really needs to get going. Who knows what the rides will be like? But the old woman is speaking, and she can't seem to leave whenever the old woman speaks.

Pixie met the old woman one day in the spring, when she caught her stealing bananas. Pixie had just started at the co-op, and so she wasn't at all sure what to do. Besides, the woman looked—odd. Long skirts, layers and layers of clothing, greying hair in braids, wrapped around her head Scandinavian-style. Round, lined face; blue eyes.

When their eyes met, the woman put a finger to her lips. Shhhhhhhhh. Pixie nodded once, corkscrew curls bobbing, and continued stocking the lettuce.

The woman was there when Pixie emerged from the side door at the end of shift. It was a spring evening, the days just getting longer, the air warm. There was a pink tinge to everything, Pixie presumed it was from the sun beginning to set somewhere on the other side of the building.

"What have you got there?" The woman's eyes were fixed on the two bags Pixie held in either hand, groceries she was taking to her attic apartment just up the hill.

"Umm. Groceries."

"Apples?"

"Yes . . ."

"Carrots?"

"Can I help you in some way?"

The woman smiled, a million creases around her eyes. "*Yes*," she said, clapping her hands.

Pixie couldn't say why she followed the woman to the lookout, amazed as she did at the old woman's agility in contrast to her wrinkled face. "Best place for a picnic," the woman had told her, "and the best place to watch the sunset."

At the edge of the trees a coyote emerged and watched them while they ate. The sun dipped over a mountain range that faded to the palest purple, making Pixie think of a colourized postcard like the ones her own grandmother had collected. There was nobody waiting for her back in town, wondering where she was, an effect of being a little odd herself. She was glad to have gotten the job at the co-op, where eccentricities tended to be embraced, or at least overlooked. In fact, sometimes she thought her coworkers didn't even see her. She looked at the woman and asked the question that was in her mind at that moment.

"Why am I here?"

At which the old woman began to laugh.

The old woman sits across from Pixie now; she's dressed in a man's shirt, her various skirts and socks are the same earthy tones as the log on which she sits. The lookout where they had their first picnic isn't far away, perhaps fifteen minutes' walk at most. The canvas tent behind them is braced with branches lashed together; there is a good woodpile, and a neatly dug latrine out back. The campsite has a hidden feel to it, as if it could not possibly be discovered by chance by hunters or hikers, although she can't say why this is so. Pixie doesn't know how long the old woman has lived here, but Pixie herself has been here every weekend throughout the summer, arriving with sleeping bag and groceries after work on Fridays, heading back into town on Mondays. Once she knew the route through the bush, it wasn't as far as she'd thought. If the weather was bad, she could usually thumb a ride. When her co-workers would ask about her weekend, Pixie would be evasive. "Winter comes, think I'll move to that old cabin," Grannie told her once. She assumes it's the cabin near the diner, but she isn't sure.

Now, "Guess you're going soon," Grannie says.

"I'll be back next weekend."

"You need to bring me tea. And sugar. And I want some bananas."

"Okay."

"And you need to do something else for me."

Pixie shifts on one haunch. "What?"

But the old woman is settling the way she does when she's about to begin. Pixie tucks her knees up, tiny feet perched on the rock, hands clasped across them. There is often a story at about this point. She likes mulling the old woman's words as she makes the trek back to town. The tales are myriad and colourful: philosophies and fables, myths and parables. Strange creatures: minotaurs, cyclopses; extraordinary adventures, noble deeds, clever tricks and double-crosses. Some, she recognizes; others could be an old woman's fabrication, or rooted in a place unfamiliar to Pixie. She is fascinated, their tellings satisfying a new and surprising desire.

"In the beginning," the old woman begins, "there were the Little People."

"The pixies," says Pixie. Her own grandmother had once told her stories about pixies. It was her grandmother who had given Pixie her nickname in the first place.

"If you like. In Africa, Abatwa. Some are called Asparas, whose job it is to keep science from challenging the spirit world. Ha!" The old woman laughs for a moment at the absurdity of this. "Brownies, some call them. Seelies. Ghillie Dhu, with their clothes of leaves and moss. Kul, the water spirit who helps the northern people find fish. The Mazikeen, the Ohdows. The hooved Polevik, the Yakshas, the Sidhe."

"How do you know all these names?"

"Mythological Studies. You think I've lived up here my whole life?"

Pixie had wondered. This was the most the old woman had ever offered about any previous life. She wants to ask more, but the old woman is speaking again, and Pixie has learned not to interrupt too often.

"Do you ever wonder that everywhere, the world over, there are tales of little people. Do you think this could be a coincidence?"

Pixie shakes her head. She tries to imagine Grannie at a university. Studying, or teaching? She can imagine neither, here in the woods, the wind blowing the treetops all around them. She shakes her head again and leans forward on the rock, hoping to coax the old woman to continue.

"So. Before anybody else, there were the little people. These creatures had a favourite colour. You'd think it was green, being spirits of the forest and all. But actually it was blue."

Pixie shivers involuntarily. Blue is her favourite colour. Grannie is eyeing her. "Someone walking on my grave," Pixie says, shrugging.

"You shouldn't believe nonsense like that," says the old woman. "Anyway. They loved the colour blue, and here's why: because they were navigators. They navigated by the pale sky at dawn and the bright blue of high noon, the deep evening blue and the blue-black of night. They navigated by the evening star, that twinkling blue star that appears in the west. They navigated by the lake and flash of minnows, and by the river and its fast blue water. They charted their courses by watching the flight of the Mountain Bluebird and the Stellar's Jay, and mapped routes by fields of forget-me-nots and wild iris."

"I know: they lived on blueberries."

"Did I say that?" But crows' feet gather at the corners of her eyes. You never can tell about the old woman, what she'll find funny, what will make her clam up. Perhaps this is what keeps Pixie coming back: to unravel the enigma that is Grannie. She's wondered at her own motivation more than once. Pixie is glad when Grannie continues.

"In the beginning, the little people told the animals where to go. Where to catch the best salmon, where to hide a new fawn, the route to run when lightning strikes and sets the trees alight. They were the ones who charted migratory paths for geese and caribou, told the trout to swim upstream and the mountain goat where to place his feet on the rocky ledge.

"Then the Indians came, and the little people had to tell them how to follow the animals and the weather. It was hard work, sometimes: these new people thought more about what they did, and they didn't always listen to the whisperings of the little people because their heads were full of thoughts. Still, the little people got through most of the time.

"Before long the Indians figured out all on their own how to navigate by watching the seasons and the animals, and the little people could relax. But it's a good thing they had the Indians to practise on, because when the white people came they were altogether deaf to the whisperings of the little people. Actually, the first thing the little people did when these new people came was tell the Indians to steer clear. It was something about the way they didn't listen, couldn't even hear the wind—which was how the little people sent their messages—because they were making so much noise themselves. Because there was so much noise in their heads! They were thinking about new things, shiny things, things that made life easier.

"The little people felt they'd failed as navigators, so they had to try a new approach. They tried talking to the new people while they slept, but the new people would wake up and stretch and laugh and tell one another what funny dreams they'd had. Then they'd forget everything they heard and go about their day, which mostly involved killing animals and pulling up trees and generally making a mess of things. Occasionally, it meant shooting at the Indians and eventually it meant telling them they could no longer follow the paths the little people had taught them about weather and animals. It meant making them all live together on a patch of land with a fence around it and a whole bunch of rules they made up to give the Indians a better life. It was a bad time."

There is a pause for long enough that Pixie wonders if she should collect her things to leave. Sometimes, the stories end midway, and she has to wait until the next weekend. This is always dissatisfying, making Pixie feel out of sorts for the week; she doesn't like it. The wind blows, and the old woman watches it sway the trees.

"You want the rest," she says, finally, fixing Pixie with a blue-eyed stare.

Pixie nods.

"You like a good story." A statement, not a question.

Pixie waits.

"That's good. That's what we have. It's *all* we have to leave our children."

The wind blows, a crow caws from high in a red cedar, and Pixie holds her breath. The old woman continues.

"Some gave up. Some stopped sending their messages on the wind, went back to their forest hideaways and sparkling brooks and peat bogs and whathaveyou. But one persevering little sprite, frustrated with a cocky young man who thought he knew everything, thought she'd give it one last, good blow, and—" the old woman inhales, holds her breath, and then blows as hard as she can. "*Blew* herself right into his ear!"

Hands clasped around her knees, Grannie leans back laughing. Pixie laughs, too. It's hard not to laugh, she finds, when the old woman laughs.

"And then what?"

"Well, it was murky inside, as you can imagine. Messy and cluttered. But that sprite got to work and cleaned out the cobwebs, and next thing you know that young man was telling people how to live. And they were listening."

Grannie is quiet, and Pixie figures this is the end of the story. They stopped like that sometimes, abruptly. But the old woman isn't quite finished.

"Sometimes people need steering. You can call it intuition, or luck. A dream, maybe. Right place, right time."

"What about coincidences?"

"There *are* no coincidences. What have I been telling you? Little people. It's the little people."

"Is that the end of the story?"

Grannie sighs. "There's no end to the story. We are all stories, layers and layers of stories. We are vessels for stories. Put them all together, they make a new story, but blink, and the story changes again. That's the best thing about them."

Pixie imagines a street full of people shaped like jugs full of swirling liquids of different colours. Sometimes, bright splashes spill out, catching the sunlight as they run down the pavement.

"As for this vessel, it's time for my whisky," says the old woman now. Above them, in the stand of cedar, the crow cackles.

Now Pixie is on the highway, walking. After having a shot of whisky in a cracked china cup, the old woman had dozed off. Pixie sat beside her for a while on the mossy ground, listening to the crow and the soft breaths of the old woman. At one point, as she looked at the sleeping wizened face, one eye opened and focused on Pixie where she sat. The lips moved. "Get lost," they told her.

At the co-op Pixie ties her green apron around her and begins refilling the carrot bin. On the other side of the fruit display she sees a man about her age, long hair, eyes like a husky. He looks hungry. Without thinking, unaware she is about to speak, she thrusts a bunch of bananas towards him.

"On the house," she tells him. "Special today. Good food for the road."

***

Pink looks at the girl speaking to him. She is small and bony and all one colour: brown hair, brownish, almost coppery skin, clothes in shades of brown. She's holding the bananas like they're an offering. Pink takes them from her almost without thinking.

"Who says I'm on the road?"

She just smiles, small teeth. "Don't worry," she tells him. "It's going to be okay."

"What is?"

The girl gives him a look as if taking in his weariness, dishevelled hair, road dust, and the evidence of miles. "There's a place I think you should go."

Pink is confused. Is she flirting? What does she want from him? But she's pulled a brown bag out from beside the mushroom display, and from someplace she's produced a pencil, the old, soft, carpenter's kind like Pink remembers Stan using, and he is flooded with nostalgia, regret. He watches her make marks on the paper, but all he can think about is Stan and Nora, and the day Stan took him into the workshop out back and together they drew up plans for a wooden go-cart. With a pencil just like that. There were times of kindness, Pink remembers. He can smell the wood shavings on the floor, see the jars and tins of nails and screws lined up at the back of the bench, see the way Stan looked at Pink when he said, "You're really going to go places, now."

Go places. He doesn't think this was what Stan had in mind.

"Here." The small brown person hands him a little map. There are no words on it, but he can see the highway and, near the top, a little drawing that looks like that diner where he met the red-haired girl, Jo, and he realizes, with a swept-under, drowning sensation, how much he wants to see her again. The feeling is overwhelming, and he blinks to bring himself back to the co-op where he stands, bananas in his hand.

It's a bit of a hike through the woods, she explains, but it's worth it.

"What's worth it?" Pink asks, but she continues.

"There's an old cabin not too far from here," the girl pokes her pencil at the diner. "Looks like the path ends there, but you'll pick it up again." Pink recognizes the cabin where he smoked the joint with the cop. "And at this fork here there's a rock shaped like a toad," she tells him, tapping the pencil on it, "a big toad," and by tapping and pointing she tells Pink how to get to a lookout point.

"Best place for a picnic," she says, "and the best place to watch the sunset." She holds the map out to him, but he doesn't take it.

"I can watch the sunset from anywhere."

"Suit yourself," she says, tucking the bag into her back pocket. "But I told you, this is the best place." She turns, and begins restocking the green peppers, but she watches him from the corner of her eye. He leaves with the bananas she has given him, and nobody stops him.

Pink, back on the highway, tucks the bananas into the top of his pack after pulling one off the bunch to eat. Sweet and starchy, it's just the thing, just as the girl in the co-op had told him. The wind is blowing the opposite way to the route she had drawn on the map. He begins walking against it anyway, feeling the cool of the air blowing across his face.

***

Her shift over, Pixie walks on the highway shoulder in the direction of the diner she had indicated on the map. The late sun lights up her curly hair; she watches her shadow grow long in front of her. A silver Jaguar passes her, going in the opposite direction, and Pixie turns to watch it crest the rise she's just descended like a spawning trout and disappear over the other side. In the momentary quiet of the empty highway, she can hear, distantly, the sound of an engine turning over, again and again, but not catching. There is no other traffic for a while as she walks, the flat of the highway giving in to a rolling rise until she is sweating in the residual heat of the day, the sound of cicadas in her ears. An RCMP car passes, and she gives the driver a wave, but the officer doesn't appear to see her.

4:25 p.m.
Glass of water

"Don't you want to order something?" says Jo to the small person who comes in on foot, looking for all the world like a leaf that's just blown in.

"Just had a banana," the girl says, showing two rows of tiny white teeth. Like a monkey, thinks Jo. "Just a glass of cold water, please."

"We don't generally just serve water."

"Well, you don't charge for it, do you?"

"Of course not."

"Oh, I know," the girl looks at Jo, and for a moment Jo can see in her the old woman she will one day become. "Nothing for nothing. But there's always something to trade."

"What do you have to trade?"

"I have a story."

"Right." There have been enough of those, thanks. But Jo sets the water down on the counter anyway. It's still a half-hour 'til closing. Meanwhile, she might as well start sweeping up. Cass doesn't like Jo to do this when there are customers in the restaurant, but a small, monkey-like person with a free glass of water is hardly a customer. As she picks up the broom, the wind picks up, blowing the door open and showering the entrance with bits of grass and leaves. It must not have been closed all the way.

"You know the fable about the North Wind and the Sun?" asks the girl.

Jo closes the door. She has to lean into it against the sudden force of wind.

"It's an Aesop's fable. Old. Older, maybe."

Than what? Jo thinks. Aesop. She remembers something about a fox and some grapes. She begins sweeping, while at the door, the wind rattles.

"There's this contest, see? Between the North Wind and the Sun. About who's stronger. And the North Wind says that he's stronger, because he's so powerful. He sees a man walking along wearing a big old cloak, and he says to the Sun: let's see who can get the cloak off this guy."

The girl stops and takes a long drink of water. Jo begins sweeping under the tables, listening. How can so much stuff blow in from the parking lot in one day? She picks up a black feather, thinking: crow.

"Two crows, good luck," says the girl, pointing to a second feather in the corner under the counter. "I suppose two feathers mean good luck, too." She leans over and scoops it up. When she hands it to Jo, it is with a flourish, as if this is a grand gesture. Jo holds it with the first and looks at them before handing them back.

"It's twice as lucky to give luck away," says the girl approvingly, tucking the two feathers in her back pocket. "Now, where was I? Right. So the North Wind blows and blows but all that happens is that the guy wraps the cloak tighter around himself. The harder he blows, the harder the guy holds on. Finally, the North Wind is all puffed out and needs to take a breather."

Jo looks outside, expecting to see the wind die, but it's blowing harder than ever.

"So then the Sun tries her stuff. She pushes away all the clouds so she's the only thing in the sky, and she climbs high so she's shining down with everything she's got, warm, but gentle, too. And you know what happens?"

"He takes his cloak off."

"You've heard the story," says the girl.

"Well, it makes sense."

"Of course it does. What doesn't make sense is why we can't seem to remember when we really need to."

"Remember what?"

"About kindness."

The girl pulls the two feathers out of her back pocket, then, and hands them to Jo. "If I give these back to you, then the luck just doubled again," she says. "I figure I'm lucky enough. Just got a free glass of water, anyway."

"For the price of a story."

"Stories are always free."

The girl exits the way she came, in the manner of a dry leaf twisting in a breeze. The wind *has* died down, Jo sees, but the sun has dipped below the mountain and won't be warming anything more today. On the floor Jo sees a piece of brown paper that wasn't there a moment ago when she started sweeping. Picking it up, she examines the map drawn there in soft pencil; it must have fallen out of the monkey girl's pocket when she gave Jo back the crow feathers. The diner is there, and a path that snakes through what Jo knows to be the woods running past Howie's cabin. The route continues on, eventually ending at a drawing that looks like a cliff, a childlike sun setting over mountains. She's about to toss the map into the trash with the sweepings from the floor, but instead tucks it in her own pocket.

Gale force

Suddenly there came a sound from heaven,
As if a rushing mighty wind.
— Acts of the Apostles 2:2

Pink stands by the side of the road at the edge of town eating a banana. There are perhaps two hours 'til sunset: time enough to get somewhere. He could spend the night in town, but he'd rather head out and find a good campsite, maybe even find the lookout the strange woman in the co-op told him about. It was close to the diner where he'd met that girl this morning; he could hike in for coffee in the morning and see her again. Who cares what the wind is doing? He's still got a couple of dollars tucked under the insole of his shoe.

It baffles Pink that he's spent the day travelling in what amounts to circles. As he stands, thumb out, he finds he can't quite remember why he'd decided to hitchhike in the direction of the wind—a romantic notion, that was all.

A dusty red pickup truck pulls over. Pink can't quite see the driver's eyes under the ballcap. "Thanks," he says as he climbs in after throwing his pack into the open truck bed amid bungee cords and cables. He notes a single rifle hanging from the rack in the back of the cab. A hunter, probably. The driver grunts and pulls back onto the highway.

***

Jo is just finishing mopping the floor, the string mop wrung through the red plastic bucket, when the Fairlane pulls into the lot. *We're closed* mouths Jo through the glass door, expecting the indignant rattle of the handle, but the door opens; Jo has forgotten to lock it.

"I just—I just need to come in for a minute."

"We're closed. Really."

"It's been a long time since I was here."

Jo looks at the woman who stands in the middle of the floor scanning her surroundings. She's in her forties, tall, thin, with reddish-brown hair and a wide mouth. She's well dressed, Jo sees: dress pants, blouse, low platform heels. She tugs at the hem of the print blouse nervously.

"Cass around?"

"Cass?"

"She's still here, isn't she? She hasn't moved or something? This is still her place, isn't it?"

"Yeah. Yeah, she's still here. She's in the trailer." Where she's been most of the day, thinks Jo. "I just work here."

The woman looks at Jo for a long moment, making her nervous. "Look, do you think I could have a cup of coffee or something?" she says finally.

"We're closed. Sorry."

"Please."

There's maybe a cup or so left in the urn. "It's probably pretty bad by now."

"I don't mind."

The woman sips her coffee, wincing slightly. She's at the

counter on the swivel stool with her legs crossed, cigarette in one hand tipped backwards, smoke rising.

"It's just by coincidence that I'm here. I'm on my way to a sales meeting. I sell Avon. At least, I'm trying to. I figure it's in the family genes. My father was a salesman, too." The woman uncrosses her legs, reverses them, crosses again. With her finger she begins making pictures in the wet circle where her coffee has dripped. "I'm just starting, though." She looks at Jo again, a few beats too long, and Jo, uncomfortable, looks away. "How old are you?"

None of your business. "Almost nineteen."

"You have beautiful hair. Do you straighten it?"

"What? No." *Who is this woman?*

There is no wind at all; it is as still outside as it is in the diner, and the woman at the counter exhales into the silence. Looking through the front windows, it appears to Jo as if nature is holding her breath. Inside, every sound is amplified: the creak of the stool under the shift of body weight; the nervous tinkle of the spoon stirring an already-stirred cup of coffee.

"And how *is* Cass?"

"Cass is—fine. Who did you say you were?"

"Just an old friend."

"Do you want me to get her? I can call her. She's shouting distance, just out the back door."

But the woman doesn't want Jo to call Cass, not just yet. Jo looks at the Fanta clock: it's fifteen minutes past closing. Something has knocked the plastic Jesus hands. They point at the door now, and Jo thinks *please, God.* It's been a long, strange day.

***

"Nice day," says Pink above the growl of the truck. Trying not to be obvious, he checks out the driver. Hair curling over the collar of a workshirt. Sleeves rolled up reveal prominent biceps, and several tattoos. "Thanks for picking me up."

"Uh," grunts the driver.

Pink waits for him to ask about a destination, but he doesn't. So: "You going far?" he asks.

"Nope."

A semi passes, a whoosh. Into the receding sound, Pink tries again. "Well, I'm happy to go as far as you'll take me."

"You got an accent." Not a question.

"My mother and father were from the States," says Pink, wary. It's not a lie.

"They live here, now?"

"They died," he offers, truthfully.

The driver looks at him for the first time. "Recently?"

There's something in his look, in the tension of his jaw, Pink thinks. He's dressed casually, not a hippie, but not a redneck, either. *Buddy*, says his ballcap. The truck feels as if it's going too fast, and Pink tries to see the speedometer without Buddy noticing. The hands gripping the steering wheel relax, suddenly, as the driver notices the speedometer gauge and exhales, letting off on the gas as he does. The needle drops.

"Sorry," he says. "Sometimes I just get kind of caught up. I forget. It just comes over me."

The tone is apologetic, and Pink is relieved. Maybe this ride is going to be okay after all. He settles himself into the worn upholstery of the bench seat, realizing that, up until now, he'd been sitting on the edge. "No problem," he says, and then continues conversationally into the residual tension. "You get all kinds of rides. People are good, though." He remembers Stefan and Thérèse. "Most of them." He's chatting away nervously: about the rides, about the weather, and then he finds himself babbling on about how friendly Canadians are.

"What?"

"Umm—"

"Where are you from again?"

"Umm, Washington. State, I mean. Just up for a visit."

Buddy grunts. "Let me tell you something," he says, and Pink thinks: "Oh, no."

But Buddy doesn't say anything for a while, like he's thinking. Ahead, the road is a silvery ribbon. There is little traffic in either direction, the sky a flat, unbroken cerulean, the trees the deep green of summer. Finally, Buddy says to the windshield: "My dad used to take me fishing in Washington. Curlew Lake. Know where that is?"

Pink doesn't. Buddy looks at him, eyes narrowed.

"Just where are you going, anyway?"

Pink doesn't want to say he's going where the wind takes him. It's the sort of thing that could set someone like this off, and anyway, it suddenly seems like a long time ago. Before he can answer, Buddy grunts another question.

"How old are you?"

"Twenty-one."

"You look older. Thought you might have been one of them draft dodgers."

"Yeah. Guess I was lucky."

There's a yellow road sign, a vertical line with another line running perpendicular to it. Pink catches it in his field of vision. A road on the right. Just as it registers in Pink's mind, the truck spins onto it in a flurry of shoulder gravel, and Pink grabs the dash to keep his seat, his finger gripping the gritty surface. "Whoa," he yells, but they are tearing down the road, careening at the bends. He thinks of opening the door, of rolling, but they are travelling too fast. He hangs on, heart pounding.

***

"I have a daughter your age," says the woman, now. "Having a kid is like something pulling at you, all the time. Even if you don't see your kid for years and years, it's always there. Pulling at you. I can't explain it. When you have a child, you'll know."

Jo can feel the pull in her womb. She can feel the pull across the mountain range she has crossed to be here. She imagines an umbilical cord, snaking along highways.

"Give me your hand," the woman says, now. "No really, just for a minute. I can read palms. I can tell you how many children you'll have."

Jo tucks her hands behind her back.

"Come on. What harm can it do?"

When Jo extends her hand, palm down, the woman takes it gently in two hands. With her thumbs, she pushes up the sleeve of Jo's shirt ever so slightly, then turns Jo's hand over. "Right," she says, and exhales, a release of air that is not quite relief, not quite disappointment. Tracing the lines on Jo's palm, she tells her: "You've had disappointments, but things are about to get a great deal better. You'll live a long life, and—" the woman cups Jo's hand until it makes a fist, then examines the lines below her littlest finger "—you'll have two children."

Jo takes her hand back and tucks it in the pocket of her jeans.

"You have no idea how far down you can go," the woman is saying now. "I hope you never do. I hit bottom, about as far down as you can go. At that point, you either wind up dead or you find a way back up."

"You did?" Jo's not sure if she's asking about the bottom, or the return trip.

"Yeah, I did. I don't know what set me off that time, besides the usual. Yes, I do. I do remember. I was sharing a basement apartment with a roommate. I guess she was my friend. I wasn't too choosy in those days, to tell the truth. We made a little money any way we could. Things I'd rather not say, now. I wasn't very choosy in that regard, either. Janis and I, we were on this kind of party whirlwind. Woke up sometimes, no idea where I was, who I was with. Didn't really care. One time I woke up in a bathtub, some old geezer sitting on the toilet taking a crap."

Jo winces.

"Sorry. Anyway, Janis—my roommate—got really sick with something, I didn't know what. She was burning up, and I didn't know what to do, so I leaned against the wall beside her mattress and started telling her stories. She had a forty-ouncer under the mattress and I knew it was there and she wouldn't know because she was pretty delirious, so I started drinking it to pass the time, and while I did the stories kept coming. Every story I could think of from when I was a little girl and even a few I made up. I knew Janis wasn't hearing me, and I just kept telling them anyway. Stories, all night long, and it was a long night, I'll tell you. Thumbelina. Cinderella. Jack and the Beanstalk. People like us who got lucky. Stories where the good, poor people won in the end. That's when I realized I hadn't felt like a good person for a long time. I knew if I could just get my hands on some magic beans . . . just one break and I'd be a better person.

"In the morning, the bottle was empty and Janis was dead. I didn't know what to do. I hadn't called the hospital because it hadn't occurred to me she was that sick, and anyway, people like us didn't go to hospitals. I didn't know if she had family, didn't know anything. The rent was way past due and the landlord had been by, oh, felt like every fifteen minutes over the last few days. I had the shakes and needed something to drink but I thought maybe I'd make myself a coffee and just think about what to do. No food in the place but I scraped some instant out of the jar and lit the gas, but I was shaking so much I dropped the jar and it knocked the eviction notice off the counter into the flame and I watched in a kind of dream when it lifted up and caught the pile of flyers."

***

They reach a pullout, a place wide enough for trucks to pass, and Buddy spins the truck around so it's facing back the way they came. The air is grey with fine dust, the trees, close on either side, covered with it. Pink's breath comes in gasps. He wants to run, but he's shaking too hard.

"Why the fuck did you do that?"

Buddy's palm whacks the steering wheel. He turns, lips in a sneer. "You guys really piss me off."

Pink's hand reaches for the door handle.

"You just sit tight and listen to me. You owe it to me."

Pink doesn't know why he owes this guy anything, but he's

not about to argue, and there's nowhere to run. The engine settles, clicking sounds. It's hot in the truck, and the dust as it falls is choking.

"When I did my tour it was neighbours helping neighbours, fighting the Communists. That's what we were doing. But mostly I joined up because of my friend, Jerry. Summers at Curlew Lake, our families went every year and there would be Jerry each summer, up from Boise. When he wrote he'd joined the Marines, I joined, too. Surprised? There was more of us than you'd think. Wanted to do some good in the world, fighting the Commies. I'd seen the TV news, I knew what was going on over there. I looked around and there were too many of these hippies—" he looks at Pink, who can't seem to take his eyes off the square jaw, the shadow of stubble there, watching the lips move "—just messing up the place."

He reaches across and flips down the glove compartment, pulling out a pack of Export 'A' while Pink shrinks against the seat. Maybe if he just listens, the guy will settle down. There's nowhere to run anyway, the narrow trees a cage around them. "I was in school, man," he says, his voice a croak. Maybe he should just keep quiet.

Buddy lights a cigarette, the cab filling with blue smoke that wafts out the half-open windows. "I had some stupid idea I'd meet up with Jerry and we'd go over together, but nothing like that ever happened. Boot camp was hell but it was exciting, too. All of us, waiting to see action, charged up with the thought of it. Some guys who were drafted wanted out, pretended to be pansies, and maybe some of them were, I don't know. But the guys I was with: *semper fi*. I was the only Canadian. They thought that was great."

Pink tries not to cough, but the smoke is choking him. He rolls down the window all the way, afraid he might faint, or throw up.

"Listen to me."

"I'm listening."

"You better be."

Pink coughs, then stifles it.

"My dad was a war hero. Distinguished himself on the battlefield during World War II. That's what I wanted to do. Like him, you know? But when we got there, there *was* no battlefield. Just a lot of jungle and people who all looked the same: you couldn't tell the allies from the enemy. We burned down a village once because they'd been helping the NVA, feeding them. Damn gooks. Then they're crying because those squalid damn huts are gone. And because their cows were shot up, but that was just a bit of sport and serves 'em right since they were feeding the enemy. You gotta scare them or they'll just keep doing it. It's a war, for Christ sakes. They knew the rules. Half the time out there I don't even know where I am. You just have to hope your C.O. knows where you are, and that's all there is to it.

"Except one time we found our C.O. just outside camp. He was stabbed about fifty times and his lips were sewn shut. Guess what was inside."

Pink doesn't want to guess. Buddy stares at him from under the baseball cap.

"Fucking gooks. I've heard all that bullshit about U.S. atrocities, but I never saw anything like that. Used to threaten to cut their ears off. Vietnamese have this thing about ears. Won't go to heaven without all their parts. Heard some guys collected them, but I never saw it. Meanwhile our guys are getting blown into a million pieces." He raises his voice. "I'll tell you what I did see, though."

***

"I looked around and I saw the place like I was taking a snapshot, you know? Click: there's Janis, and the bottle on its side, and the circles of dirt around the light switches illuminated in the flicker of burning paper, and then the kitchen curtains went up and the air turned orange and grey, made me think of a war zone or something. The smoke drove me out. I stumbled out into the alley and just kept going."

"What about your friend?"

"Well, she was dead. There was nothing more I could do for her, and nobody I could call that I knew about. Although I suppose everyone has somebody. A mother. A sister. I think the landlord had her name, if she gave her real name. I don't even know what it was. It's a fear though, isn't it? That you die, and there's nobody to identify the remains.

"I guess I was running, thinking about that, about who would care if I kicked off, who would notify my—my sister. It's the last thing I remember thinking."

***

"I saw a couple of guys put themselves in danger to get a medic for a little kid who was sick. Those gooks were glad we were there, the good ones, that is. What if we hadn't been there? Where would they be?" He doesn't want an answer; his voice has begun to shake. "Met these two guys coming off a landing pad with a poncho full of something, asking where to put it. Inside was something that looked like ground meat. He'd been alive that morning, probably joking with his friends. Somebody would have to tell his family." Pink can tell that Buddy, staring through the windshield, is seeing the contents of the poncho. "I just told them where to take him. What else could I do?

"It was eleven months but it felt like a lifetime. No sleep, counting days by the big red horse pill you had to take for malaria. Jungle rot every-fucking-where. I lost thirty-five pounds.

"This one reporter shadowed our unit for about three days. 'It's a people's war,' this idiot said. 'You can't win it because you'll always be outside it.' We told him to go find some Commies to sleep with. Jesus. He hadn't seen the things we'd seen. Jesus. Wanted to kill that fucker, just for being so fucking self-righteous."

Buddy's voice has dropped an octave, and it sounds hollow. "Every sound wakes me up. The dog farts, I'm up and swinging. I can smell blood from a cut on the other side of the room. I smell diesel, I want to puke."

Pink's palms are sweaty, and he shifts in his seat. "Sounds bad, man," he says. He means it. The pain in the cab is palpable.

"What do you know about bad?" Now the jaw is thrust out, two inches from Pink's own. Pink can see the blood vessels in the whites of his eyes, hot breath. "You don't know nothing, hippie." Pink holds his gaze, afraid to look away. He feels as if he might be having a heart attack, and this frightens him more than the face in his. *Breathe*, he tells himself. They stay like that for one beat, two. Then: "Freedom isn't free. There is always a price to pay."

Buddy sits back, exhaling, as if exhausted.

"That's what's so fucking ironic. Your kind runs up here to get out of fighting for your country, and I leave mine to fight for yours."

***

"What happened?"

"I passed out a few streets over. Smoke inhalation, the booze, hunger. Fear. I sure had no fight left. Someone took me to the hospital, what I should have done with Janis. I guess I wasn't so far down that I didn't have enough humanity to cry, but I wouldn't talk, I just cried and so they probably thought I was a psych case. Which I suppose I was. There was one social worker, Barbara, kept coming back, took me on as a personal project, I guess. When she first asked my name, you know, I couldn't even remember. Later, when I did remember, I thought: why do I want that old name? It seemed like an opportunity. To start fresh.

"You changed your name?"

"Eve. My mother's name. First thing, when I started the program, I went to ask her permission."

"And?"

"And I couldn't find her. She'd moved, I guess. No forwarding address. And you know, that wouldn't have mattered any time in the last twenty years, but now. Now, there's this hole. I need to say *sorry.* I need to get her blessing. Whatever her shortcomings—Christ knows, she wasn't much of a mother sometimes, but she was my mother—I need to look her in the eye. I need us to see each other, you know? I mean, really see each other. I need to hear her say sorry, sorry to me, but that's not the point. That's not what the program says."

"Like a twelve-step kind of thing?"

"That's the one. I can't quite fathom the Jesus stuff, but the rest of it makes sense."

Jo knows, now, why she's here. Who she is. The photographs in the box. The woman pulls a pack of cigarettes from her purse, lights one, exhales through pursed lips, smiles apologetically.

"And now you need to see Cass."

"Now I need to see Cass. See if she'll forgive me."

"Forgive you for what?"

***

"Then, when we finally get back and land in San Diego and there's a bunch of people look just like you *jeering* at us. *Baby killers!* They're shouting. What do they know? It's a fucking war. I never killed any babies."

Knuckles white on the steering wheel.

"That was bad enough. At least the U.S. vets get benefits when they come home. Medical care. Education. The military looks after its own. Even if a bunch of hippie freaks are spitting at you, you know you did right, and your country recognizes you for it. Canadians? *Nothing.*"

Pink musters his words. "It's not about the soldiers, man. It's about the war. It's not personal." He can see this is a big misunderstanding. Nobody hates these poor guys for having been misguided by the American war machine, he thinks. You have to hate the machine. That's what they said on campus, especially towards the end. People spitting, yelling at soldiers? "I never saw anything like that," he says.

"Just because you didn't see it doesn't mean it doesn't happen," Buddy continues. "I come home and there's nothing. Not. A. Thing. No homecoming, no benefits, no acknowledgment that I rotted in that stinking jungle for eleven months for a just cause and saw my buddies shot to hell and now I can't sleep or keep a job or a fucking relationship—" he pauses, takes a breath, says in measured words: "and it's your fucking fault." A fist strikes the steering wheel. "Now get the fuck out."

***

"Forgive you for what?"

The timing is beyond cliché. The trailer door bangs, and Cass lumbers across the gravel, a glance at the Fairlane in the parking lot.

"Jo?" she calls as she opens the back door. "Everything okay? It's past closing."

"Someone to see you," says Jo, and gets up, a wave to say she's leaving.

"Please stay," whispers the woman. Pleading.

"Cantha?"

***

Pink doesn't need to be told twice. As he steps out, thinking the long walk back is preferable to this, he turns to see Buddy emerge from the driver's side. Holding the rifle. Motioning him back, towards the shadows in the trees behind the truck.

"Move."

Pink moves, Buddy behind him. He can't see, but he can hear the footfalls behind him as he steps into the shade. He hears a click, raises his hands feeling, ridiculously, like he's in a bad movie and it should be funny, but it's not.

"Turn around."

Pink has his back against a large cedar. He can feel the rasp of bark, smell the familiar smell. Backlit by the thin wash of sun from the road behind him, Pink can't discern the expression under the baseball cap. Behind him, the truck's image wavers, a mirage. It's not really there. I'm not really here. Life is a dream.

"You want to know what it feels like to have a gun pointed in your face?"

"No."

"It feels like *this*."

Pink can't speak, can hardly breathe. The muzzle of the rifle is six inches from his face.

"Here's the thing," Buddy is saying, not moving. "I could shoot you right here."

A pause.

"Couldn't I?" Shouting.

"Yes," agrees Pink.

"So why shouldn't I?"

Why not? Pink scrambles for words. "Because it wouldn't accomplish anything."

"I'd get a shitload of satisfaction."

There's nothing to say to that. A moment feels like an hour. Pink closes his eyes, waits for it. He opens them again.

The gun lowers. "You're not worth it," says Buddy. "That's the thing." He spits out the words. "Just another dumb-fuck hippie."

Pink realizes his knees are shaking, and that all at once, they're not going to hold him up. He sinks to the ground, bark scraping as he slides down the tree.

"I didn't shoot you, but I could have," spits Buddy. "Go do something with your fucking useless life."

Pink hears the receding footsteps, the sound of the door being opened, closed. He hears the engine come to life, the gears shift, tires crunch. He leans against the tree and listens to the birds, first one, a great distance off. Then another, closer, answering.

***

"Cantha?"

There is an embrace, more a melding of bodies, one tall and skinny, one short and round, but the smile on each face is identical, eyes shut tight against the emotion of the moment. Cass is the first to push away.

"Where's Donnie?"

"Oh, Cass."

"Where is she?"

"She's all grown up by now. She's as old as your waitress, here. A woman."

There's the sound of brakes, a diesel smell. Cass glances at Archie's rig pulling in, but her eyes fix again on her sister.

"Where is she?"

Archie swings down from the cab, pulls his t-shirt down, and fits his ballcap on his head before starting across the lot. To Jo, he looks younger; there's a spring in his step.

"A lot has happened."

The door swings open, and Archie, grinning, says: "Guess what just happened?

Cass holds up one hand. "*Where is she?*"

"Cass, a baby was just born, a girl. I was *there!*"

"I lost her a long time ago, Cass."

Jo's hand is on the handle of the back door when she hears Archie's voice, full of wonder. Then she hears Cass speak, all twisting pain, in a voice that makes the hair on Jo's arms stand on end.

"What kind of a woman loses her baby?"

Jo

What kind of a woman loses her baby?

On both sides of the road are trails. I don't know where they go, and I don't care. Crashing through brush. Crashing through thoughts coming too fast to dodge their rocks and thorns.

When I finally slow down, my breath comes in ragged gasps. Leaning against a pine, I wrap my arms around it, feel the bark on my cheek. The forest stops whirling; things settle into their places: my shoes on the ground; the scent of the pine tar dripping down the trunk, sticky under my fingers; the chatter of a squirrel somewhere in the branches above.

My mother. Me. *What kind of a woman loses her baby?*

Archie, so full of excitement at the birth he witnessed, at the miracle of it. That's what he called it: a miracle. It was so unlike Archie, the word in his mouth, I almost wanted to laugh, except for the knife in my chest.

A miracle. And a birth without sorrow, or regret.

And what am I supposed to do, now? That's been the whole problem, all along. I hoped I'd just spend a little time at Cass's, work a little until I could get a sense of direction. Find my feet, and then get on my way. Leave everything else, all that stuff, behind me. I didn't expect it to follow me.

The tree I lean against is a cedar, rough, reddish bark. I look up into its twisted branches, swaying at the top. I could just stay here, under this tree. If only I could just stay here.

When I bring my head down I see, for the first time, the

remains of an old woodpile under a decaying tarp. Then the outline of a cabin emerges from the dusk as I stare. There's a roof that's really more moss than roof. Howie's cabin. The brown paper bag is still in my back pocket. The lines in soft pencil tell me the way to go.

Pink

The light is fading by the time I haul myself up from the base of the tree. Buddy tossed my pack out of his truck bed before he took off, and I picked it up from the dirt of the road, everything intact.

Do something with your fucking useless life.

He should get some serious help.

Of course, I'm the one hitchhiking in circles.

What if he comes back? He's not coming back. Is he? My knees are jelly; when I hold my hand out, it's shaking. I don't want to be on this road. There's a path, heading off into the trees but still heading in the direction of the highway.

Do something with your fucking useless life.

I walk down the path for a while, not really caring where I'm going. It feels safer in the woods. It's a while before things start to look familiar, which is no surprise the way the trails twist and turn through the forest around here, hikers, hunters, I don't know. Ahead is the cabin where I smoked a joint with that cop. Man, I wouldn't mind running into him now. Guys like Buddy shouldn't be running around with loaded guns in their trucks. At least, I think it was loaded.

It probably wasn't even loaded. Jesus.

Nobody's been in the cabin since I was there, I can tell. By the front door, a roach ground into a rock. I can see the path heading off back behind the cabin. It's the same path I took off down when the cop arrived, not that I got very far.

Another five minutes, and what do you know? A big rock, moss all over the top, squatting in the trees like a big old toad.

Windblown

Grey-eyed Athena sent them a favourable breeze,
a fresh west wind, singing over a wine-dark sea.
— Homer

The view, at sunset, is spectacular. Mountain ranges fade into the distance in subtle shades of green, blue, and purple. The sky shifts from rose to gold, blue to turquoise, and the clouds, lit from beneath, send fingers of light heavenwards. The air is fresh; there is the slightest wind, and it feels delicious on Jo's skin. She waits for something inspirational, something poetic, to come to her.

She hears the snap of twigs that tells her someone is approaching. She turns her head, heart in her throat, waiting to see what might emerge from the trees. She is barely breathing, ready to spring and run if she needs to. In the reddish sunset glow it's hard to make out anything at all in the shadows.

***

Pink walks quickly; the light is fading. Pretty soon, he won't be able to see the path. If it's a nice spot, as the girl at the co-op said, at the very least he'll have a good, quiet place to bed down and sort out his thoughts. He still feels shaky, his knees not quite as they should be.

Follow the rules, Stan's voice in his head. He remembers Nora's voice, when, conspiratorially, they'd open the cookie tin before dinner. *Rules are meant to be broken* she'd tell him, winking, while breaking her own. It occurs to Pink now that even if he makes up his own rules, they're still rules. Follow the wind; follow the rules. It amounts to the same thing. What happens is that the rules, whatever they are, keep changing.

When Pink was six—when Pink was Elvis—there was that first night at Stan and Nora's. Big swaths of memories are missing, but that night, he remembers, he was bundled up in Stan's plaid flannel pyjama top. It came to his ankles, and Nora, clucking, did up the very top button under the collar so it wouldn't slide off his shoulders. "Poor dear," she said. "Reminds me of Robby. Isn't he a lot like Robby?" and Stan said: "Now, Nora . . ." It was years before Pink learned about the son his aunt and uncle had lost.

Lost: it's such a strange way to put it. Like he was misplaced. As if he might turn up later. It was Kevin who told him, surprised Elvis didn't know, that Stan and Nora's only son had drowned. It was not clear who was supposed to be watching, who had turned away for just a moment, assuming the other had his eye on the little boy playing at the edge of the creek. Nora grieved; Stan, angry, blamed the circumstances, Nora, and himself.

Growing up, he'd hear people say: poor Elvis; you know he lost his parents. He can hardly remember them and yet, when he cast his mind back, he can feel a hand on his forehead—a fever, perhaps—that he's sure wasn't Nora's. He can see the outline of a man chopping wood, rubber boots and canvas pants, white undershirt, the whack of axe on wood, and he knows this dim figure to be his father, the familiar limp as he moved from chopping block to woodpile.

Lost. Kevin lost his life in the war in Vietnam. Pink can imagine the sniper bullet as it hit his friend's chest. If Buddy, instead of pointing the gun at him, had actually taken the shot . . . Pink can see himself, slow motion, falling against the tree, arching the way the cat's body had arched as it fell against the side of the hole when Stan shot her. Would word get back to Stan and Nora? After all this time, the way he left, would they feel the loss?

What was he thinking, listening to that weird person at the co-op, and then heading off on this hike to some lookout, with bananas in his pack and not much else. But he's here, now; nothing to lose. Ha! He is without money or identification, lost in his jacket in a Volkswagen van that could be anywhere. Couldn't get across the border if he wanted to, now, and all at once this is important. Family. *Freedom's just another word for nothing left to lose* goes the soundtrack in his mind. He starts to whistle nervously against the growing dark.

Abruptly, the light changes. There's a clearing up ahead; he can see the sun glowing red through the trees, knows it to be smoke in the air, a fire burning somewhere giving the setting sun its strange fiery glow. But it's beautiful, too, and as he approaches he thinks about the two sides to everything.

There's a person sitting on a rock at the edge of the lookout, the landscape dropping away beyond. In silhouette, he can't identify age or gender, so he approaches cautiously, then, irrationally and as if he is approaching a wild animal, he reaches his hand over his shoulder and pulls the bananas from where they sit at the top of his pack, tucked into the strap.

***

Jo stands to meet the figure emerging from the trees. How stupid to have left herself with her back to a sheer drop. The figure—she can tell it's a person—is holding something out in front. Oh, man. What is it? She thinks about the novels she's read: *her throat constricted; her heart pounded; she broke out into a sweat.*

She is all of those.

The voice is timorous, not at all like a killer.

"Banana?"

It's so ridiculous, she laughs.

***

They sit together on the rock, a safe foot or so between them. The flush she felt when she first saw him is back, but the morning feels like a long time ago. She looks at him, wondering how it came to be that they are both here, on this rock, watching this sunset, like some sort of B movie plotline.

"It's quite a coincidence," he says.

"Someone once told me there are no coincidences."

"What do you think?"

"I don't know. Weird stuff happens. Strange patterns emerge. *They hear a voice in every wind, and snatch a fearful joy.*"

Pink looks at Jo, who is gazing across the mountain ranges, watching the subtle shifts in shade and colour in the dying light. She turns when she feels his eyes on her. "It just came to me. From my English lit class, about a million years ago. Thomas Grey, 1700s."

"Well, anyway," offers Pink, after sitting with this for a moment. "Someone told me it was a nice view."

"I thought you were going to tell me the wind blew you here."

"Up until an hour ago, yeah, I guess that would have been my answer."

"What happened?"

"Stuff. Just stuff."

"Me, too," says Jo.

They're quiet for a bit. The evening star sharpens above the horizon. Pink decides not to talk about the guy in the pickup truck. After several minutes, he speaks.

"There are all these weird choices to make. It's hard to know, sometimes, what the right ones are. Sometimes I feel like I've never made a concrete decision in my life. Unless you count the idea of hitchhiking with the wind."

"Well, it *was* a choice, right?"

". . . that brought me here. For some reason, I'd like to think." He thinks for a while about the day: it's been a long one. Stefan and Thérèse, the flower lady, the guy he gave his shirt to, the girl at the co-op. Just stuff blowing around, or something else?

Jo looks at his profile against the darkening sky. His nose is crooked, his chin a little weak. He's just a guy. This morning was a long time ago.

"The reason I left," he's saying now, "was this thing that happened. I'd done most of a year at college but I was flunking out. I was going to lose my deferment. I didn't know they were going to pull out troops, it just seemed like Vietnam was going to go on forever. Some people I knew had left for Canada, and I was starting to hear stories about how easy it was to come up, you know, so many points at the border. There was even a manual about how to get in. I wouldn't have a college degree, but I had my high school transcripts back at Stan and Nora's, and a buddy who said he could get me a letter promising me a job at some bookstore in Vancouver. I'd gotten these letters from my friend Kevin, from Vietnam, lots of blacked-out stuff, but it was still there, in his words. The misery. No way I was going over.

"So I went back, took the bus from Seattle to Pullman, turned up at the house without letting them know I was coming. I came in, Nora and Stan sitting there at the table in the kitchen, and I just sat down like I hadn't been away and told them what I wanted, and why. I don't know, it didn't even occur to me that they hadn't risen to greet me; that Nora hadn't done her usual fussing over me, Stan wasn't there with his comments about the length of my hair.

"Turns out, my timing was, um, ironic. They had just heard from Kevin's mother who had called, crying, to tell them about the telegram.

"Stan flew off the handle. I mean, he really flew off the handle."

Pink remembers the scene with Kodak clarity: Stan, the colour rising upwards from his collar; Nora, hands flapping.

"You got the same candy-ass genes as your father. Know how he got out of the war? You know how?" Stan's face about an inch from his. Hot breath on his face. "Shot himself in the *foot*. Told my sister when she met him it was a war wound, but I found out. Witnesses. Disgusting. Weren't for him being married to my sister, would have blown the whistle, got that medal withdrawn."

"It doesn't matter," Pink started to say, meaning: it was a long time ago.

But: "You're just like him. Good for nothing. Hopeless."

Nora, crying, against the stove in the kitchen.

"When I think about Robby—"

From the direction of the stove, a wail. Anguish. Pink wants to look, but he can't seem to take his eyes from Stan's.

"Get out. You're no child of mine."

Now, sitting at the lookout with Jo, "How could he just cut me off like that?" he asks.

"What happened then? You just left?"

"Yeah. Just like that, walked right out. Thing is, I keep wondering if maybe he—if maybe he regretted it. He always had a temper. I mean, Stan could be really decent, I think he was a good father to me, but sometimes something came over him. I don't know if this was one of those times, if maybe now he wishes he hadn't said that, or if he really meant it. And then there's Nora. When I walked out she came after me, grabbed me and turned me around and hugged me. She told me: 'Thank God you didn't go,' but I was still so mad at Stan, you know? At what he said. Shocked, and confused, because I didn't know that about my father. So I hugged her back, but then I turned and kept walking. I still had my pack on my shoulder. I hadn't even set it down."

They are quiet in shared regret; it's palpable in the chilling air.

"I think about going back, you know? But it just seems too—risky, I guess. Emotionally, you know? And too much time has passed, now. What would I say?"

Jo doesn't speak for a while. She's thinking of her mother

and father, the distance between them, and now, the distance between herself and them. It is almost dark, but Pink can see her profile limned with the last light.

"Where are you going now?" asks Jo, finally. She waits for the answer, watching the red fade from the sky. To the north, dry lightning, like distant warfare.

He looks at her, and she's beautiful. It's the only word in his head. He reaches over and touches her face with the tips of his fingers.

She jumps up. It's nearly dark, now. *Eamon*. It was so stupid to come here by herself. What does she know about this person? She can't see which way to run. "Fuck off," she tells him. It's all she can think of.

He's on his feet, too. "Hey, I'm sorry. I'm really sorry. Please."

She doesn't know what he means by please. Please what? She stands, panting. She won't get very far in the dark. Pink has his hands in the air, like he's under arrest.

"I didn't mean anything. I'm sorry."

Sorry, she thinks. There's so much to be sorry for.

She sits a little ways away. She's aware of stars coming out, more visible each second as the night turns indigo. Neither speaks. Nothing seems clear. For Pink's part, he's rehearsing in his head what to say, wishing he could undo that moment, wondering how to get past this one. Above them, the stars multiply.

"Are you cold?" he asks, finally. He has no idea how much time has passed.

Jo realizes she is shivering. On any June night in the mountains the temperature drops. She shakes her head, no. But in the end it's the cold that drives them together, leaning now against the rock, the unzipped sleeping bag drawn around them. Their shoulders touch, but that's all.

Pink extends his arm. "Satellite," he says, and they watch the tiny point of light move through the stars. "Do you ever watch the meteor showers?"

"Meteor showers?"

"Shooting stars. We used to go out into the hayfields, my friend Kevin and I, and lie on our backs and watch them. The best time is about three in the morning. He was the dedicated one, always made sure he set his alarm, and then he'd come over and wake me up. That started when we were nine or ten. Later on, we'd just stay up drinking until then." Pink laughs, then grows quiet. "He was killed in the last days of the war."

"Sorry."

"We should watch them together next time. Do you want to?" His voice in the dark has brightened. It reminds Jo of a little boy.

"Yeah," she says. "Sure." In this moment, it actually seems possible.

There are crickets in the tall grass. They've been singing their night songs for some time, but now Pink hears them as if for the first time. They are fervent and persistent. They know exactly what they are doing, just being crickets in the night. It seems simple, and perfect.

"I'm going to Vancouver tomorrow," he says suddenly. He knows it's true. "Come with me."

"To do what?"

"I don't know. Get my bearings."

The lightning is all around them, now, but there's no accompanying thunder, just the flash, illuminating the trees, their faces, then gone. The wind has come up, blowing across the lookout, pushing leaves and grass about them in dark waves. The outline of the mountains is barely discernable against the black of the sky awash in stars. The storm has moved on. Jo can't see Pink, but she moves a little closer. He feels the increased heat of her body and remains still, as if in the presence of a small, wild animal. Over the next few hours, in the safety of the darkness, they talk, their words weaving patterns in the night.

In the morning they are rolled up together in the sleeping bag, Pink's face pressed into Jo's hair, her chin nestled into his collarbone, the rib of his t-shirt making lines in her skin. His arm has encircled her waist in the night, a finger tucked in a belt loop; her hand rests on the side seam of his jeans. At some point in the night, both have kicked off their shoes. As they pack up, Pink, on a whim, leaves the last three bananas on the rock.

When they finally leave the lookout, the air is full of poplar seeds like tiny, perfect parachutes, and the sun is rising, illuminating the mountaintops.

5:45 a.m.
Sandwiches to go

Archie's in the La-Z-Boy, feet on the coffee table, snoring. The Fairlane is gone, the parking lot empty. Cass is curled on the couch, afghan tucked around her, oblivious to the morning sun streaming through the windows of the trailer. The air smells of stale smoke. Jo looks at Cass thoughtfully. A good person. Kindness. As she stands there, Cass opens one eye.

"Late night," she says.

"Looks like it."

"Wondered where you were. Thought maybe you'd taken off home."

"Still here."

"Maybe you *should* go home." She coughs twice, opens the other eye, and then closes them both. "Tomorrow, I mean. Might need a little help opening up today. But then, might not even open." Cass pulls the afghan over her head. "I'll be in later," she says, gravel voice muffled.

As Jo turns to leave, she hears Cass's voice again from beneath the blankets, as if speaking from a place of half-sleep. "She had a birthmark. I'd forgotten about that."

Jo remembers Cantha, when she asked to read Jo's palm, carefully turning her hand over, then the soft exhale.

In the back room, Jo pushes her things into her pack. Sitting on the cot in the early morning quiet, she sees the photograph album lying on the rumpled blankets of the cot. Jo can imagine Cass and Cantha, two sisters, looking at the shared photographs that shaped their lives. She wonders about Cantha's daughter: foster care, perhaps adoption. A family, maybe, who wanted this red-haired little girl more than anything, wanted her at least as much as Cass did. There is the unfolding of events, Jo thinks. And sometimes, there is reconciliation. She hopes that Cass and her sister found it. For the first time since she arrived at Cass's, the tears come.

Pink will be here soon. She'd asked him for some time alone before meeting her at the diner. He sat on the rock at the lookout, back to the vista, and watched her cross the clearing and enter the woods. She knows because she turned twice to look back before the trees embraced her. She had been on the path less than five minutes when a sound made her start. A pheasant, beating its wings. The rush as, flushed from the bushes, it rose and flew, disappearing over the lip of the hillside where the forest dropped away.

The pen is in her hand. In the end, the note Jo leaves says simply: *I'll send you a postcard when I get to where I'm going.*

Pink isn't yet there when she gets to the diner. She pulls a couple of day-old sandwiches from the cooler, food for the road. She feels strange standing there, in the middle of the restaurant, empty tables around her. The plaster Jesus hands are on the same crazy tilt, pointing towards the door. She goes to straighten them, and then stops herself. Their direction seems appropriate: salvation to go.

A rattle at the front door makes her turn. Pink is there, pack on his shoulders. Ready for the road.

Windtails

He that observeth the wind shall not sow,
and he that regardeth the clouds shall not reap.
— Ecclesiastes 11:4

Jo opens the door, the sign rattling against the glass. She glances guiltily towards the trailer, but it has the air of a sleeping house.

"You ready?" asks Pink. His eyes are full of Jo, and the road ahead. Possibility. Promise. It's all good, he thinks, standing in a patch of sunlight that slants through the open door. Life is good. "Actually, I have something for you," he says. He found it at that cabin in the woods, he tells her. Jo remembers Bob's story, about Howie, a little girl, and a heart-shaped rock. She takes it from him, feels it warm in her hand, and then sets it carefully in the centre of the counter with its empty row of swivel stools.

"It's good to leave something behind. To say goodbye, you know?"

Pink nods: whatever. He's just anxious to be going. He wants the road, wants to start walking in the cool of the morning, put Cass's a mile or two behind him while they feel the rush of trucks passing by their outstretched arms. He looks out at the trees, at the wind blowing east. They are going west. Against the wind, but who cares? If the rides are good, they'll be there well before nightfall. "Let's go, then," he says. The café is hot, the air close, the sunlit patch widening as the sun rises. Suddenly, it's stifling. "Come on." Pink has the door open. He watches her straighten, smile. She's beautiful, he thinks.

On the road the air is fresh and cool, the breeze slight. Mare's tails skitter across the sky, blown by winds higher than a bird can fly. The day is perfect.

They cross the highway and Pink turns to smile at Jo, but she's looking the other way. Down the highway. East. The way the wind is blowing, treetops bending gently.

"Vancouver's this way."

"The wind's blowing east. Towards Calgary."

"What's in Calgary?"

"The end of the story. And anyway, it's the way the wind's blowing."

"It doesn't matter. It was a stupid idea. Something to give me some kind of direction, that's all." Pink believes he can see movement in the trailer across the road.

There's the sound of a car approaching from the west.

"We should start walking. Let's go." He touches her arm.

The kiss she gives him is like the brush of a leaf. It's so quick, so fleeting, he's not even sure he feels it, and, confused, he turns to kiss her properly, thinking she needs reassurance before they can get on their way.

She's running, *loping*, across the highway, to the other side.

She's there with her thumb out when the first eastbound car crests the rise.

Acknowledgments

Thanks to those who provided seeds for the tales within this novel, or who answered my questions when I needed details to flesh something out: Ross O'Connell, Stephanie Fischer, Helen Blum, Mary Keirstead, Margaret Stegman, Linda Mennie, Trish Miller, Wendi Thomson, Pat Rogers, Doug and Faye Hergett, Pietro Comelli, Norm Pratt, Johan Mayrhofer.

Special thanks to my mentor through the Humber College creative writing program, Shaena Lambert, for her insight and encouragement; to Verna Relkoff, editor extraordinaire; and to my writing group, who saw more versions of some chapters than I (or probably they) care to count: Jennifer Craig, Joyce MacDonald, Susan Andrews Grace, and Rita Moir. Thanks to the readers of various drafts: Steve Thornton, Irene Mock, Cyndi Sand-Eveland, Kathy Witkowsky, Jacqueline Cameron.

Thanks, of course, to my family, and especially to my children, Alex, Tam, and Annika, who are inspirations in themselves. Finally, thanks to Phillip Jackson for the story: the one I used in the book, and the one unfolding.

Morty Mint prefers I call him a friend rather than an agent; here, I will thank him sincerely for being both. *Far From Home* was first published in Canada under the name *Wind Tails*; thanks to Kim McArthur and the team at McArthur & Company for believing in me. In the U.S., thanks are due to Maya Rock of Writers House Literary Agency, and to Emily Krump of HarperCollins/Avon for her support and enthusiasm throughout my south-of-the-border journey.

Thanks also to the Columbia Basin Trust through the Columbia Kootenay Cultural Alliance, who provided financial assistance for the writing of this book.

FROM

ANNE
DEGRACE

AND

AVON A

Q&A with Anne DeGrace

The stories in *Far from Home* are each distinct and yet interconnected. How did these connections come to you?

I really do see people as vessels full of stories, as Granny tells Pixie. These stories include the stories of one's life, and the stories we collect as we encounter the stories of others. They all touch us in some way. At times, it's obvious: we're touched by something, and it changes the way we see a person or situation, or even ourselves. At other times it's less obvious; it's the layering of stories that slowly, over time, changes us. In *Far from Home* I started with Jo and Pink: two young people in search of something. I also had a number of stories and characters in my back pocket, so to speak. With each new character who entered the story I thought: who is this person? What do their stories mean to them? How will they touch Jo, and how will Jo, in turn, touch them? As I wrote, the characters and their stories—just sketches at first—grew through the telling, and then took on another dimension at Cass's Roadside café. For Jo, the stories she picks up are subliminal, but the reader knows the true story.

If there's one thing the travelers who come through the diner have in common, it's that they are all misfits in some way. Do you see yourself that way?

We all see ourselves as misfits in a way, I suppose, or perhaps we like to think of ourselves that way, because I sets us apart. When does "different" become simply "odd?" It's a fine line, and one that fascinates me. I love eccentric people; I seem to surround myself with them. They are the out-of-the-box thinkers, the artists, the wacky scientists for whom the world seems just a little more colourful, its spark burning just a bit brighter. I wouldn't say I'm a misfit, but some days, I aspire to be one just for that reason.

What are your thoughts about the connections between people? Do you believe in coincidence? Does everything happen for a reason?

That's a great question. The practical side of me believes in the randomness of all things, and I admit I take some comfort in that. I am delighted by serendipity, and the magic of coincidence. And then there's the random serendipity of coincidence that is so pointed there's nothing to do but sit up and say: *Wow. Obviously, there's a lesson to be learned, here.* When that happens, it's hard to imagine there was no orchestration involved. And so I suppose I was playing with that in *Far from Home*: the convergence of seemingly disparate people propelled by unusual circumstances that, encountered by one person, change that person's view of the world. The nice thing is that we don't really need to know if life's serendipities are random or divine in order to appreciate them.

At one point in the book Eunice says: "You know what I've figured out? That life keeps slapping you in the face with a lesson 'til you learn whatever the lesson is you're supposed to learn." I really believe that.

Many of the characters in the novel express a certain amount of longing, sometimes regret. Is there a message here?

I try not to write with any overt message in mind. To me, fiction—like all art—is a reflection of what we see around us. There *is* longing in the world, from the abstract—longing to belong, longing to be loved—to the concrete: longing for a warm bed or a hot meal. It's pretty universal, just as regret is something everyone experiences. By exploring a theme through writing, I suppose I learn something about it on a subtle level. There are other themes in the book as well, you could say, such as optimism or hope, or the value of the journey, rather than just the destination.

I don't think about it all that much when I'm writing, honestly. There's just a story I want to tell. But I like that themes do emerge in the process. I suppose a painter experiences the same thing, when, through layered applications of paint, an unexpected quality emerges.

The characters in *Far from Home* come from different backgrounds. Do you have to do a lot of research into things like midwifery or dowsing?

The short answer is that the amount of research I do is just enough. Research, in itself, is very seductive. It's awfully tempting to go deeper and deeper into the minutiae of a subject and never write a word. Writers of period novels, or political or scientific novels, really do need to know their subject. You can't fudge the details, because someone out there is an expert and they'll call you on it. Literary license is a wonderful thing, but you can only push it so far. So I try to make sure I know my stuff, but not spend so much time researching that the book won't get written. One thing I always do is ensure I have plenty of readers who will catch my mistakes, so if there weren't cell phones in 1977, Archie had better not be talking on one.

What about those readers? Are they friends? Other writers?

I have a writing group to whom I owe a great deal. Each brings something to the critique I hadn't anticipated, and we often wind up with lively discussions about whether a character would say a certain thing. They ask me hard questions that need to be asked. When we're finished critiquing one another's work, we have a "staving artist" dinner: soup, bread, cheese, and wine. I wouldn't trade it for anything. I believe anyone who wants to write, at any stage, should find a writing group. When the first draft of a manuscript is finished, I have several writers and friends, in addition to the group, who give me feedback.

Have they ever told you to start over?

(laughing). Yep.

When do you write? Do you have a set time?

Not really. I admire writers who, say, get up at 4 a.m. and write 'til 7 a.m. every morning. When my kids were all still at home—I was a single mother—I had the computer in the living room, partly so everyone was forced to interact with one another. I think in too many families, kids wind up sequestered in a "computer room" or in their own rooms. But the other reason the computer was there was because there really wasn't another place to put it. Consequently, I wrote whenever the thing was free. I often wrote when the kids were at school, but if I was on a roll, I became very good at tuning out whatever was going on around me, short of a house fire. It drove the kids crazy, in a way, but they got used to it, and there doesn't seem to be any lasting damage. And I got the book written.

You write on a computer, then. Do you ever write longhand? Does it come easily?

Sometimes it does, and then—this is going to sound a little flaky—it's as if the muse is sitting just above my right shoulder feeding me words that travel through my fingers and out onto the keyboard. I imagine this thing to look something like Gizmo the Gremlin, only perhaps green and more disheveled. Other times, Gizmo's off starring in some '80s movie and I'm left with paralyzed fingers. That's when bizarre things happen in my house, like a sudden cleaning of the cupboard under the kitchen sink. My house is never cleaner than when the words won't come. I never write longhand. I can't read my own handwriting after about five minutes.

Did you always want to write?

When I was a kid, I wanted to be a visual artist, a painter or an illustrator. Writing surprised me by being a more comfortable creative medium, as I discovered when I began writing a regular column for a newspaper about the local arts scene. It's not always easy to erase a line or paint over a canvas, but words are endlessly malleable, and I love that. I love that if you come back to your words a day later, they have suddenly acquired their own distinct personalities, somewhat separate from their writer. It's lovely. I'll look at something I wrote, delighted to make a new, vaguely familiar acquaintance.

I admire all creative people. I revere the dancers, the actors, the filmmakers, the painters, the musicians. If I could choose any art to be something I did well, it would be music, for its ability to evoke emotion so immediately. You have to pick up a book, but you can catch a song when you're riding a bus, and it becomes the soundtrack for your day. Without even expecting it, it can warm your heart, or make you cry. As a writer I try to do the same thing—it just takes me three hundred pages to do it!

It sounds like music is important to you. Does it have any influence on your writing?

Funny you should ask. An early draft of the novel was set during the Vietnam war, at the height of student protest and the Civil

Rights Movement. So my personal soundtrack included songs like Joni Mitchell's *Woodstock*, Blind Faith's *Can't Find my Way Home,* and Neil Young's *Ohio.* I let David Crosby sing to me about the Chicago Seven while I wrote. When I re-set the story in 1977—in part, ironically, to regain my original sense of direction—I had to update my playlist! So my new soundtrack became the kind of AM radio tunes I imagined Jo would have listened to around that time: *Wish You Were Here* by Pink Floyd, *Fly Like an Eagle* by the Steve Miller Band, Fleetwood Mac's *Go Your Own Way*, and *Long May You Run* by Neil Young and Stephen Stills. I could clearly imagine Jo wiping the counters at Cass's while, on a tinny two-knob plastic radio in the kitchen, Bruce Springsteen sings: *Baby, you were born to run.*

When you read, what makes a perfect novel for you?

I want a good story, and I want characters I care about. There doesn't need to be a lot of action, but there does need to be enough depth to make me think, and make me care. I can admire a writer for the crafting of the story, or the character development, or my need to turn the page. But the very best writers are painters with language. Or master chefs. They make me want to eat the words, to savour them. These are the writers I admire most.

Any advice for up-and-coming writers?

Trust. It takes a tremendous amount of trust—in yourself, in the story you want to tell—to be able to write. If you can trust, you're halfway there.

On Being a Story Vulture

Where do the seeds for story ideas come from?

It would be lovely to say I dream them, or they come from some sort of divine inspiration. The truth is (and I try to be truthful, even in the midst of writing fiction which is, after all, lies) the seed for *Far from Home* first germinated in a bar.

It was my birthday, and a full moon, and several friends and I had been out cross-country night skiing in the mountains where I live. Our favorite bar has a fireplace and a cozy atmosphere, and it was just the thing to warm toes, never mind imaginations. I'm not sure how the conversation came around to hitchhiking tales, but somehow it did, and everyone had one.

Stephanie talked about the hitchhiker she loaned money to one New Year's Eve in Germany, with a plan to meet on the same night, a year later, in an Irish pub. She showed up, he didn't, but the nice thing about fiction is you can make a story end any way you want. Perhaps it was the mention of an Irish pub, or perhaps it was just another hitchhiker story in a night of tales of the road, but it was Ross's story that came next, and to which I really owe everything. Ross had been sitting in a pub with a mug of Guinness in hand when a traveler collapsed onto the bar stool beside him. His only rule of the road, this fellow told my friend, was to hitchhike in the direction of the wind. He was relieved to be sitting there at last, he said. Because the wind kept changing, he'd been circling Dublin for three days.

What a notion, to let the wind take you! What freedom! Unless you find yourself going in circles, and we've all been there in life. And of course, sooner or later decisions must be made, because, as the Vietnam vet Buddy tells Pink, freedom isn't ever really free. Ultimately, we all have to face those things that bind us to the earth: our loved ones, our pasts, the choices we make.

Most of the stories told that night, as well as the stories related to me subsequently—like Helen's story about the person who collected both hitchhikers and their postcards—found their way into the manuscript. I'm quite the story vulture, and I keep a notebook of anecdotes people relate to me, after first asking: "can I have that?" They almost always say yes. Evelyn's weakness for stealing flowers, Eunice's story, the distribution of fancy desserts to street people, and the story of Melissa when she opened the windows to let out the spirits of the dead, were all collected this way.

Fiction is really truth with lies, because anything we make up has to, by necessity, come from *somewhere*. So while no characters in *Far from Home*, or their stories, are based on real people or events, all of them pull something from personal encounter or experience. You don't need to be an expert in something to write about it, either: if you're a living, breathing human being with empathy, it's not hard to put yourself in the shoes of a water witcher, a business tycoon on the lam, or an octogenarian with an attitude. It was great fun to research things I knew nothing about, sitting at some coffee shop while the local dowser opened up, or a truck driver waxed on.

There is plenty of my childhood in anything I write, all of it a mixture of truth with fabrication so that it's impossible to know what is, and what isn't—sometimes even for me, once the novel gets into my bones. Memories take on a different glow when you hand them to a character and let them run with it. Embellishments happen. Endings change.

That said, my siblings take pleasure in picking out the familyisms—things from our childhood that we all remember—that make their way into my novels. Perhaps it's a turn of phrase, or the long-dead family dog resurrected. Chocolate marshmallow cookies like the ones Howie loved will always be derflops in our family, thanks to a kid in an Oregon campground around 1952 who was sent by his mother over to my parents' campsite with a welcome gift of cookies. He probably said "deer-flops," because in truth they look a little like that; my mother heard "derflops," and so derflops they became.

I really did have an imaginary friend named Linda, and a real friend who died at six years old, and left me her Easy Bake Oven. When I do write about real things, it's important to me that these memories are treated with reverence, and of course, humanity. Because we've all lost people we love, I know that a point of connection will be there for the reader, and in that way memory becomes story becomes the touch of one heart to another.

Points of connection, points of departure, finding direction: these are the stuff of human experience, yearnings that find their way easily into almost any story. And so I often think I'm writing some sort of revelation, only to find it's a root of a universal theme: love, loss, joy, sadness, challenge, triumph.

And therein lies the metaphor: in the root of a theme or the seed of an idea, and from these miracles grow the story, a mountaintop pine that moves and dances in the wind.

About the Warm Fuzzy

In the winter of 1981 an event happened that changed my life. Okay, two events: one was the birth of my first child, who arrived in the world in 1982. As it is for anyone who experiences the sudden addition of a child to a previously autonomous life, this baby's arrival bisected my life story: there was Before Baby, and there was After Baby. Life would certainly never be the same. But an event that preceded his birth had a similar impact in a wholly profound way.

To set the stage: I was a single-mother-to-be, and I was twenty-one years old. I had arrived in the British Columbia town of Nelson, not quite middle-of-nowhere on a mountain pass, but certainly in the wilds of the B.C. interior. I arrived in June, shortly after which baby-to-be announced his intentions. I needed a plan, and so I decided that, since Nelson didn't have a used bookstore, I'd start one.

I've always loved books. I haunted used bookstores in the cities in which I've lived, made libraries my second home. A bookstore was a natural fit. In no time the nature of community made itself known: friends helped to build and paint bookshelves; boxes of books were dropped anonymously at my doorstep. I knew very few people, and yet the support for this pregnant hippie girl was tremendous. By November I opened a tiny used bookstore in a basement space. The baby was due in February.

At that time, I was subletting a room in my house to a fellow who, ironically, was commuting from his *truly* middle-of-nowhere mountainside community in order to teach a course at the local college on how to find a job (it was the only job he could find). The community John came from was a Quaker community—the

Society of Friends—and a friend he became. He was a kind person to have around; a good ear, non-judgmental, and very respectful. John taught me the meaning of the warm fuzzy: the small, kind things you do for somebody, just because you can.

John knew I was having a hard time. He must have told people back home, because one afternoon two young women I had never met came into the store and introduced themselves as Jeanne and Rosemary. They said they had heard I could use some help, and so they were offering to store-sit for a month when the baby was born so that I could stay home.

I don't believe that, until that moment, it had occurred to me to wonder what I was going to do at that time. I'm sure I didn't have a clue what a newborn would really mean to my life, but I knew angels when I saw them, and I accepted their offer.

These two women did exactly what they said they would do, and with tremendous grace. There would never have been enough money to feed and house myself and the baby without the store being open for business, and I could not have kept the store open in that first month while adjusting to life with a new baby. Rosemary and Jeanne descended like angels, opened the store every morning for a month, and then slipped away—quietly and without fanfare—as the very best angels do.

They knew they were helping me out at a tough time, of course, but what they might not have known is how they have affected my life. I learned about helping, when the need is there and you can fill it. I learned that good deeds need not be reciprocal; they just keep going forward, and that if everyone participates, we might all just get what we need—physically, emotionally, and spiritually.

Since then I've been married and not married, and I've worked as a home-support worker, bookstore clerk, graphic designer, illustrator, journalist, columnist, arts administrator, librarian, and can't-say-no volunteer. My children know the tale of one cold day in a used bookstore, and two women with big hearts. They've grown up to understand the meaning of the warm fuzzy.

It's not always about the grand gesture, of course. It can be the smallest thing that gives the heart hope. That's what I want my characters to experience as they move through their fictional worlds: small kindnesses.

It's a free refill on a cold day. It's the tip left on the counter, just under the edge of the saucer, when you weren't expecting it.

Anne DeGrace

Photo by Timothy Schafer

ANNE DeGRACE is a librarian, journalist, writer, illustrator, volunteer, mother and multi-tasker. *Far from Home* is her second novel. She lives in Nelson, British Columbia.